MINOR
EXPECTATIONS

GARRY THOMAS MORSE

TALONBOOKS

Talonbooks
278 East First Avenue, Vancouver, British Columbia, Canada V5T 1A6
www.talonbooks.com

First printing: 2014

Typeset in Garamond, Perpetua, Lithos, Palatino, IM Fell, Century Schoolbook, and Kaushan Script

Printed and bound in Canada on 100% post-consumer recycled paper

Interior design by Chloë Filson

Cover design by Typesmith

Cover painting: Johannes Vermeer, *The Art of Painting*, 1666, Kunsthistorisches
Painting, page 178: Johannes Vermeer, *The Little Street* (*Het Straatje*), 1657, Rijksmuseum

Talonbooks gratefully acknowledges the financial support of the Canada Council for the Arts, the Government of Canada through the Canada Book Fund, and the Province of British Columbia through the British Columbia Arts Council and the Book Publishing Tax Credit.

Library and Archives Canada Cataloguing in Publication

Morse, Garry Thomas, author
    Minor expectations / Garry Thomas Morse.

(The Chaos! Quincunx)
Issued in print and electronic formats.
ISBN 978-0-88922-891-7 (pbk.).—ISBN 978-0-88922-892-4 (epub)

    I. Title. II. Series: Morse, Garry Thomas. Chaos! Quincunx.

PS8626.O774M565 2014   C813'.6   C2014-903249-8
                                               C2014-903250-1

Minor Expectations

Also by Garry Thomas Morse

*After Jack**
*Death in Vancouver**
*Discovery Passages**
*Minor Episodes / Major Ruckus**
*Rogue Cells / Carbon Harbour**
Streams
Transversals for Orpheus

*Available from Talonbooks

"*You said it was the thing in life you desired most to arrive at, and that wherever you had found it – even where it was supposed to be most vivid and inspired – it had struck you as deplorably lacking intensity. At the intensity required, as you said, by any proper respect for itself, you proposed if possible yourself to arrive – art, research, curiosity, passion, the historic passion, as you called it, helping you. From that moment,*" she went on, "*I saw. The sense of the past is your sense.*"

— HENRY JAMES

Preface

Readers of *Minor Expectations* may wish to know the origin of the work.

It was this way – during my usual visit to Dorking to participate in a feature about William the Conqueror (who incidentally shares my namesake, as he was called William the Bastard, and often to his face!), I was taking one of my long solitary walks, with pipe in mouth, when I happened upon a very beautiful woman paging through a manuscript with a silky black cover. Being of a progressive bent, I applauded her attempts to improve her mind, but it was not very long before I had run out of chat-up lines. I switched to a few nuggets of modern philosophy and critical theory, those which usually in the company of a mug of ale do the trick nicely, but she remained unmoved. By the time I had decided to resort to the heraldic codes that very well might link me with William the Bastard, she was already on her bike, and I mean that figuratively. The literal truth is that before I could ask if she fancied a quick cuddle, she was well away.

It pains me to relate her eagerness to flee my company, but this is my only explanation for her neglect in looking after the manuscript, which I found upon the same path. I pried apart its sticky leaves as best as I could with a makeshift paper knife – and slowly discovered it to be a tale of the grossest kind, with more than one scene involving love's sweetest mystery, and yet without the pronounced moral fibre of productions like *Rent Boy's Return* or *Sinderella with Squirrel*. I sat down on the nearest mound to enjoy this surprise, and did not get far before I was bowled over, literally and not figuratively, by the beautiful woman, with her bosom heaving and her fists beating my chest, demanding the return of her book. Then she tried another tack and begged me on her knees to give her back the book. Up until that point, I had not put two and two together, and this information came as such a shock, I swooned away with the most delicious sensation I had ever experienced in my life.

It was some time before I knew where I was, or what I was about. She shook me gently to rouse me, and apologized at once for having "brained" a celebrated critic, and what is more, an estimable man by all accounts. As she rubbed and even chafed me to relax my body, I came out with a continuous stream of bawdy expressions that must have seemed quite shocking on the lips of a thoroughly upright personality, although a doctor once told me that even the best of men often uses frightfully obscene words, when recovering from a fainting fit. She blushed and admitted that in spite of my temporary difficulty, she had resolved not to take advantage of me and to behave as honourably as possible toward me.

After that, she entrusted me with her sticky manuscript, but she would not reveal to me how she came by it. She also swore that were it not for her having pledged herself to one man and one man alone, she would not have hesitated to jump my bones where I lay. Left carelessly about, this titillating account of a woman's trip through time, with many episodes, was likely the catalyst for a scandalous sequence of events at my lodgings (suffice to say they involved more bed than breakfast), which led me to believe that many of these unexpurgated pages were unfit for public consumption and could even pose a serious threat to more impressionable minds.

For this reason, I felt an overweening sense of social responsibility that prompted me to put aside all thought of William the Bastard and to focus on my own refinement and curation of these guilty pleasures and filthy delights, those handed off to me by a damsel in distress, as it were. We know that it was Shelley who once called poets the unacknowledged legislators of the world. If that is the case, then we might also concur that critics are the unacknowledged alembics of the world.

You are most welcome.
Alfred J. Bastard

The Manuscript

Prelude

The upshot of the state in which I found myself for days on end was a sudden decision to call on the Ambassador. The idea brought me ease, and offered an issue to my pressing need to communicate. I recalled one of the mystical texts attributed to my father, in which it is stated that for every thousand and three silences kept, one must spill everything on one's mind, even into a hole in the ground if need be. The Ambassador, then, was to be my hole. I was less concerned about my actions having an air of crime than I was about my reeling from the sense, to an extraordinary degree, of something done in passion, and of the unspeakable consequences that would follow. Nothing was more peculiar than what I had accepted, finding excitement in these circumstances that carried their own inordinate charm. How it beguiled me, this overwhelming compulsion to impart the best and worst of my knowledge, and to share this knowledge with a gentleman stranger.

The Ambassador was not a bosom friend, but he had been recommended to me with such fervour, and, I imagine, I to him, likewise as a person of quality, that our compact preceded any clasp of hands, at first tentative and later with increased enthusiasm. He did not balk over our mutual enjoyment of a good cigar, and that was a good sign in itself, for it did not take him long to assess how profoundly and permanently he might at last deliver himself. If there was a lapse of judgment to gloss over, it was that he claimed to know all about me, and he could not have made a more inaccurate remark, for there was so much more to know than even an Ambassador could possibly imagine. Fortunately, he found me charming, even as he wondered if these tremulous resonances between us were perhaps not, as minor instances, high refinements of that diplomacy which he had studied in dusty books and tracked through the wilderness of history. I made no attempt to mortify or shock him out of stateliness by suggesting that he met me as one confused, who studies the ground when he would do better to gaze up at the stars.

The Ambassador grew heavier in his chair and blandly smoked.

"So, what is this story you have for me? Is it very very good?"

"I cannot say, Your Excellency. I would say there are poignant notes of satisfaction within it."

"And is it very very long?"

"I will spare you my story in its most verifiable dimension and scope. I would not be able to say how long it is, were I not selective in the telling."

"If you mean that it is broad in scope, then why not put it down on paper? I have read your *Bromidic Etiquette* in full, and it was considered, by many diverse readers, to be a lovely little book, full of helpful hints for restraining one's more ... ahem ... uncontrollable urges, let us say."

"Your Excellency would not read this story to his wife or to his servants or, at the risk of sounding presumptuous, even to his mistress. I asked you here because I have no wish to be the only person living to know the exact nature of my tale, or as much as is possible to know. There is nothing else you can do for me. This is not a tale of grief or hardship or love gone wrong. It is more a bit of fluff with the promise of the eternal that only a gathering of lint can bring us."

"Then I am to keep this *bit of fluff* for my own pleasure?"

"Yes."

"Then how may we begin?"

"Does Your Excellency recall the notorious Cabinet of Calamities?"

"Naturally."

"Well, what if I were to tell you that while you waited in your chair, for the time it would take to finish that cigar, I would be able to climb into such a cabinet and re-emerge with the pages written, not only by my own hand, but also by some of the most illustrious and celebrated figures known to us?"

"This sounds like a parlour game."

"It can be whatever Your Excellency wishes it to be. I only require you to listen. You may bristle when and where you please."

"Then you will tell no one else and I will tell no one else."

"Just so."

The Ambassador stood up, and as he remained there before the fire, on the rug, we exchanged a long look, a look which, as it gave me everything I wanted, must have given him in return more than sufficient compensation for his pains. The Ambassador moved closer and laid his great hands on my bare shoulders. This was not quite what I wanted at that moment. I wriggled free and spoke into the fire, in place of his blazing eyes.

"The point is that I am not myself."

"Ah! But what are you then?"

"You see me as I am, and yet I am someone else."

"Ah yes. And this other person is you?"

"That is not for me to know. I have been travelling for such a long time, and it seems inevitable that I would have to stop somewhere. For some reason, I have stopped here. This person is like a snare for me. This body is like an animal trap for me."

"Still, not a bad way to spend an afternoon."

"Your Excellency is mocking my present situation."

"Then what you are telling me is that you are not Mrs. Delilah Minor?"

"I am here, yet I am by some considerable distance removed."

"Then what is the distance?"

"I might have said by some considerable time removed. Mrs. Delilah Minor is my ancestor. Of course, she is more like me than anyone could be. There is therefore some universal principle or quirk that took me unawares."

"And what does Mesmer have to say on the matter?"

"Mesmer Minor is otherwise engaged with his public experiments and will not return for a fortnight."

"Meanwhile, here I am with a restless maid who is rattling the delicate cage that is Mrs. Delilah Minor."

"She has more difficult adjustments to make than I do. If you knew the whole of it, you would barely be able to speak."

"Then try me."

"First Your Excellency must step into the Cabinet of Calamities."

"That looks to me more like a lady's boudoir."

"If I entrust you with my story, I have a feeling it will set me free."

"A hint of chivalry or a touch of philanthropy?"

I turned, armed with a suitable retort, but he was already stopping my mouth with his and crushing my velvet. Whatever was happening to me, I knew that something far more thrilling was happening to Mrs. Delilah Minor, wherever she had turned up, or perhaps I should say *whenever* she was.

"Your Excellency is quite the champion charger!"

"Ah, my dear, what a calamity!"

I

My father's family name being *di Minori*, and my inflexibly decreed name, or given name, being *Diminuenda*, my adoptive parents, helplessly reduced to peals of laughter at my earliest attempts to form so many vowels with my little tongue, must have grown tired of this gag eventually, and, perhaps struck by a stroke of inspiration that would tickle their funny bones for some years hence, they decided to call me by my diminutive, *Dim*. Naturally, I could pronounce the single syllable with ease, and in spite of the obvious irony, *Dim* I parroted and *Dim* I became.

Yet this hypocoristicon should scarcely concern you. O, assuredly, I could wax on and on about the environmental trauma of living with this moniker at that tender age, along with a series of resultant quips peculiar to our household. Whenever the doorbell rang, for instance, it was the duty of my adoptive father to yell, "DING DING must be somebody for DIM DIM!" My adoptive mother preferred the classic "Dim Dim, your din-din is getting cold." And of course, during my early school years, I was known inexorably to my peers as *Dim Sum*, especially by Polk Shaygitz, who pulled my pigtails while singing his personally crafted ballad "Dim Sum is some delicious dish."

I fear forcing you to stifle a yawn if I spend a moment longer on my trials in suburbia, from temper tantrum to scraped knee to sweet sixteen. Those years spent were not entirely uneventful, and all the same they have a pop-up storybook quality in my mind whenever I reflect upon them, since they were a denial of my birthright by blood and my veritable existence as I have come to be aware of it. As there were the Dark Ages, there were the Dim Years. Why, what were the names of the lascivious dwarf and the white queen who looked the other way – my elder warders in that so neatly manicured grotto? The entire situation had the makings of a movie of the week, and since it eventually became one, I have no wish to tread that dirt again, except where it feels necessary to complete the grave and enigmatic annals of my father, with which the reader is without a doubt infinitely more intimate.

No one ever spoke of my mother, and I was aware of my father only circumstantially, possibly the only way a child can receive the truth. Morty and Ester Shaygitz, my keepers, as I like to think of them, only muttered his name in the form of a curse, particularly when they ran into some financial snafu. As I came of age, it became clear to me that he was footing the bill for anything I received and that any act of theirs performed on my behalf was out of professional, unemotional interest. I look back and realize I would have been reared more affectionately by two forensic accountants. I also suspected that Morty and Ester, by their display of obedient yet resentful behaviour, were at the mercy of my father's goodwill and afraid of losing favour with him. I was their bargaining chip and they treated me accordingly. Until the time I wish to speak of.

Morty and Ester appeared to enjoy putting on a transparent pantomime about being in sales and "busting their hump" to support my lifestyle. I would agree with them and offer to work to assist them, but that only seemed to vex them further. Nevertheless, I was to be enrolled at the Blessed Mensch at the end of the summer. I recall my male provider's steps as he came into the house with his "humpbusting" case in hand. Then I heard him creaking downstairs. I have no idea what possessed me at that moment. The basement door was ajar and I had only ever seen it locked. Perhaps I thought to discover some additional record of my birth and corresponding particulars. The reader is no doubt thinking, *Forget it, do not for the life of you go down there, it cannot be good!* But there might not have been a story, or at least not the same tale, without my transgression. I was barefoot, and taking great care not to creak, down I went ...

My undoing began with a squishy sound. Morty was hunched over a luminescent counter beneath a bright lamp, and laying out metal instruments. Then, with a wry grin, he put on a pair of pink gloves. He popped open his case and pulled out a large box with warning labels all over it. When he unlocked the box and lifted out an object, I recognized it as the kind of object I had seen on a live transplant show. Strange as it might sound, I was less surprised to see Morty handling a human organ than I was to see him doing something interesting, or anything other than sitting on the couch and stuffing his gullet with beans and tortillas. The reader need not imagine the fallout from that! Morty turned his head and caught me peeping. There was a funny look on his face.

"Musta forgot to lock up."

"I won't tell, I swear."

"No one'd believe ya."

"Not even the police? About what you really do at Sensitive Plant?"

"Dim, I save lives."

He inched closer and closer, and then seized my wrists. I stood there, as if in a trance. Then he let go suddenly. I only snapped out of it when he opened up the front of his Sensitive Plant jumpsuit and a quite different organ flopped out. He moved closer.

"Gross."

"C'mon ..."

"Typical Morty!"

"Let's forget all about those parts."

"Is *that* what my father pays you for? Or *this*?"

This time, his face and body seemed to flop, visibly drop-kicked. I raced upstairs and slammed the door behind me. I was not in any way flattered by his feeble advance. In hindsight, I realize that his frustrated ambitions, however small, coupled with resentment toward my father, had warped into a desire for possession, not out of genuine interest in me, but to simulate a reversal of fortune and primitively attempt to alter the circumstances that bound the four of us together, no matter how stupidly. Without even using my Thighhilation training, I was telling him, *Do not dare try to screw me in the place of my father. Do not seek a little screw when you are after a big one.* He selectively forgot this incident, in the manner of a tradesman who understands he must not push his luck and oversample his livelihood, lest he lose it altogether.

I wish I could say the same for Polk Shaygitz, who was a blood relation of Morty and Ester, although I could never work out exactly how. If truth be told, nor did I wish to. He was a veritable ogre of a boy, and for his age, as wide as he should have been tall. I was never permitted to partake in their midnight conversations, but I had connected the periodic appearance of Polk with a windfall that would cause my surrogates to behave more pompously and erratically than usual, judging by the whips, shackles, and burn marks in the attic, which was really just one extensive floor bed. Fortunately, the movie of the week about these years did not dwell on the bloody corncob, although the middling actress playing me took a great liberty by screaming at the sight of it. As for Polk, he was something of a mule for no small amount of product, whether organs or otherwise. I dreaded his visits, since he was given carte blanche to torment me. I suppose I should be grateful that due to a number of missing chromosomes, in spite of his seventeen years, he had not yet learned what pleasure women can afford to those who show them kindness, and it brings me no small amount of glee to report that he never did have the chance to learn this lesson.

After talking shop with his in-laws, this wayward swine never failed to enter my room in the middle of the night and beat the proverbial stuffing out of me. And in the morning, Morty and Ester would say nothing about my bruises, other than to make some trite remark about the friskiness of boys at that age. I realized I had no way of fighting back, at least not while living under this roof. But then, after sporadic doses of this treatment over months, I found my opportunity. I was eavesdropping on a nightly tête-à-tête and heard enough of their muffled conversation through the basement door to gather that Polk was undertaking a new smuggling operation in the morning. I crept into the kitchen and rifled through his jacket, finding a powdery pick-me-up in one of his pockets. I then ground down whatever medication I could find in the bathroom and added it to the mix. That night, I nearly welcomed his fists, and waited without moving until dawn. I remained conspicuously underfoot, hoping for my chance. Fortunately, Ester put down Polk's Dunkachunk mug full of coffee on the kitchen counter and

I was left alone with it for a full minute. I unscrewed the lid and dumped in the powder all at once before resealing the mug and shaking it vigorously.

Polk never returned to harass me, and neither Shaygitz spoke of him again. Truly, I have no idea what became of him, but I can surmise a few plausible outcomes. My favourite fantasy was that after downing my concoction, he swerved off the highway and then over a steep cliff, and that any evidence of foul play had been obliterated in the preposterously large explosion at the bottom. Another notion was that a gang of edgy drug lords had become suspicious of his twitching and had opened fire. Or since reality is often stranger than fiction, I expect that he keeled over just as he was about to insert/receive a virgin corncob. For the faint of heart, it is possible that his wacky behaviour tipped off the authorities and that he never made it through customs. I also loved to daydream that a bag of wacky dust had suddenly burst inside his stomach cavity. He was the sort of character who did not need a hearty push to meet a miserable end. I had merely performed the service of hastening his downfall, which could only leave me and some other, unknown souls better off.

Of course, you must read on in order to understand how trivial these incidents seem now, considering what was to happen. I mark it as the time I was informed that I was going to be sent to Ecole Jeune Colibri and that it had all been arranged. I was not certain, but I sensed this was the first decision that went against the wishes of my father. Ester said nothing, but she seemed nervous about this change of plan.

I need not say more than a word about the goings-on at that atroluscious school, for the name of that celebrated retreat is no doubt already familiar to you. Every time the gates open, another femme fatale flutters out with a dozen lurid designs, aiming to rise to the top of the food chain at once. Then within months, a scandal will arise for the notorious alumna, which neatly lays her name upon the burning lips of everyone, until some priceless public ritual can be performed to cleanse her of her sin and rehabilitate her, often through a perfunctory marriage that establishes her for life. In secondary cases, she remains notorious, even in a duty-bound fashion, and although in broad daylight she is cursed, from evening until dawn she is covetously made increasingly famous until, unlike her illustrated counterpart and former schoolmate, who lives in the limelight upon her gains alone, this crafty minx finds every back door open to her and every national secret at her disposal. For having only taken an infrequent sexual gambit at her discretion, she gains what others would without hesitation give their lives for. I do not need to pore over the endless details in the story of the concrete-mixing conglob heiress Tara MacAdam, known more readily to you through constant celebrity reports as TarMac. Nevertheless, there is no eyewash station for the effects from seeing that private runway footage of her with a presidential candidate that (some say) eventually won him the election. And as for nine out of ten men and women, you only need whisper her name in their ears to see them instantly cream their khakis.

The Minori are an old and honourable family, and I would not be worthy of the name were I to tell tales about the unimaginable exploits of the frisky young creatures at that school. Nor would I wish to wipe congealed mud on the houseboat name of TarMac, so often a malediction at the dinner table and a forbidden cry in the bedroom. For argument's sake, let us imagine there was a girl a few years older than me, who bore a remarkable resemblance to the fetching 'tarlet Miss MacAdam, and since I have no desire to be found under the paving of a MacAdam road or runway, I will refer to this young lady of memory as Exstasia Vye. I cannot say how refreshing it was, at the top of that remote mountain somewhere in the Kanadas, to feel the blindfold being unknotted and to find beyond the paisley veil not the gormless faces of Morty and Ester, but instead the sharply inquisitive face of Madame Hautalon and the come-slither glare of Exstasia Vye.

"Well!"

"It would be a waste to look around for your guardians now. They drove off without a word."

"Madame ..."

"Madame Hautalon."

"Madame Hautalon, if I never see them again, aside from roasting upon a spit in the Sixth Circle, it would be three ticks too early."

"Ah, listen to this, Exstasia! This one is something of a wit."

The two women embraced me warmly.

"You arrive with excellent recommendations. For this reason, I will oversee every aspect of your instruction personally. And Exstasia, our prize pupil, will show you the ropes ..."

"And whips, and chains ..."

"Exstasia is making sport with you. Pay her no mind whenever she acts up. However, in all other things, humour her and heed her advice."

Madame Hautalon squeezed my shoulders tightly, looking me up and down scrupulously, from head to heel.

"You will certainly make a welcome addition to Ecole Jeune Colibri. Now go with Exstasia and collect your uniform. You are to room with her."

We walked in unison along the perimeter of the lofty and ornately barbed gate but we stopped when a hissing sound burst through the chokecherries. This was a nuisance, because I had wanted to ask Exstasia how those excellent specimens of *Prunus virginiana* managed to survive at this altitude. Later, I learned (in more ways than one) of Madame's green fist that made everything it seized bloom something awful. She even knew that Native people had used the bark as a tonic for strengthening their women after childbirth. She sometimes sang the Gitksan word to herself under her breath, while chewing on the bitter berries. When I asked her what the word meant in the middle of an embrace, she chuckled softly.

"It makes your mouth and throat so nothing slips on it."

But I digress. A nose of peeling skin and giant boils was prelude to a spotty face that sprang through the chokecherries. It was a gnomish boy with grey eyes dully flickering under the hood of his cassock.

"Ex! Let me in!"

"Bugger off!"

"I need to ring the bell."

"Not today. I'll do it."

"No ... that's my job!"

Exstasia turned her back and gave me a sly sidelong glance, handing me a small black device. The boy-thing clenched the bars of the gate and strained to see what was happening.

"Press this button."

I obeyed. The boy was sent reeling backward, with hands trembling. He lay prone for a long while, before letting out a pitiful groan.

"Ex ... why ..."

"Every day you come to the gate and every day I do the same thing. And neither of us can seem to get enough of this farce. Trying to electrocute you is all we have, really. It's what Madame calls a symbiotic relationship gone awry."

"I expect so, Ex. Same time tomorrow."

We made our way toward the dormitories of Ecole Jeune Colibri.

"Must you really give him a shock like that?"

"Why, you were the one who pushed the button. Today could have been his lucky day. Besides, soon enough you'll find out why."

She had three years' advantage on me and I bowed to her air of authority. In addition, I felt no small amount of admiration for her bearing and way of speaking, and at the time, there were worse things than aspiring to be like her in every way. She drew a key in the shape of a bird with an upturned bill from her pocket and unlocked a room marked #313. Then she swung the key about on its delicate chain, scrutinizing me much as Madame Hautalon had.

"You must put on your uniform for inspection."

I stared at the neatly folded pile of clothing on the queen-size bed.

"Go on, then. Madame says that a uniform is vital in revealing the personality of the individual. If you learn nothing else, then learn to rely on yourself and not spurious and garish ornaments that only clash with your inner beauty. Understand how sameness becomes difference. Learning this lesson is the key to succeeding here."

I blushed, for Exstasia was in quite a hurry, and removed my sweater and slacks for me, and then paused to roll her eyes dramatically at my discount netherwear from Scrounge.

"No, this won't do at all."

She bid me strip and try on those marvellous fripperies. I was surprised to feel the dark silk sliding over my bare skin. Next I put on the cream-coloured shirt and obsidian skirt. Silk! I was stymied as to how my guardians could pay for this school, until I remembered it was my absentee father who had so generously footed the bill. Exstasia kneeled and eased my legs into lovely boots, before draping a long matching coat around my shoulders. But I threw off the protective garment in my eagerness to make the place my new home. Then I unpacked a new mezuzah and peeled off its adhesive backing. I was standing on a chair, reaching to place it above the door frame, when a grim-looking girl, as if on cue, threw open the door and knocked over the chair, sending me flying back into the arms of Exstasia. We tumbled onto the bed, and giggled helplessly at the fixed sneer on the girl's face as she watched us from the doorway. She looked up at the mezuzah and grimaced.

"It figures. They let *them* in everywhere."

"Why, Ursule, don't you have a rally to organize?"

"The Jews ..."

"Goat's blood at twelve o'clock!"

Exstasia jumped up and slammed the door suddenly, and we both laughed to think of the girl's shock to be bumped on the nose or noggin like that, and right in the middle of making her point.

"I say, we are going to have a lot of fun together!"

"What's her problem?"

"Ursule ... she's just had a weird upbringing. Supremacist politicos ... the usual."

I said a silent prayer that sounded something like a curse. Exstasia would often excuse the girl on account of her upbringing or home environment, but as far as I was concerned, she came out of the womb stomping and screaming anti-Semitic palaver, and would eventually meet her maker with the same folderol on her flapping tongue.

There was a knock on the door.

"Well, young ladies? Are we decent?"

"As we'll ever be!"

Madame Hautalon opened the door and allowed her eyes to drink me in. She did not say anything for a long time.

"Madame, are you all right?"

"Yes, of course. But you are the spitting image of Bromide ..."

"Bromide?"

Her eyes darted about the room and fixed for a short spell upon the outer border of chokecherries.

"Now it is the hour when young ladies must take their power nap."

She hurried off, leaving me once again alone with Exstasia.

"But what, pray tell, is to be the nature of my instruction?"

"If you like, the most ladylike of libertinage."

"Hehm? No books?"

"A few, yes. One only requires a few books that one loves. Or so Madame says. They should be enough to last your entire life."

"Nonsense. That sounds positively ludicrous."

"Hah! Your father was far more open-minded."

"What, you knew my father!"

"Only by reputation. But Madame mentions him now and again. She has the highest hopes for you on account of him."

"Really? Then where do we begin?"

Exstasia pointed to a bundle of seven thick volumes on the shelf.

"All Jeune Colibri girls are expected to read Marcel Proust's masterpiece. I am on the fourth volume, myself."

"Are we then to be tested on this text?"

"No. And yes. In ways you cannot possibly imagine. Unless you are everything Madame says you are."

"Everything with you is a tall order indeed!"

She nodded and waved her hand casually toward another set of volumes bound in red morocco.

"Begin in English. Then start over in French. Many girls fail this simple task and ... ah, it's too horrible to consider!"

"What?"

"Just read the books."

"All right."

"If you get bored of that, although I have no idea why you would, alternate with some light Marquis de Sade. We have a few of his tamer early works, clearly intended for the public to puzzle over. I would recommend his juicier epics. Try *Justine*, if you get off on victimization, although Madame by far prefers the power politics in the sequel, *Juliette*. And let's see, there's some Baudelaire and Rimbaud in the Pseudo-Symbolist section, and here is some Sackville-West, Sagan, Sarraute, and the inimitable Sybil of the Rhine from the twelfth century ... listen to this ... *When a woman is making love with a man, a sense of heat in her brain, which brings with it sensual delight, communicates the taste of that delight during the act and summons forth the emission of the man's seed. And when the seed has fallen into its place, that vehement heat descending from her brain draws the seed to itself and holds it, and soon the woman's sexual organs contract* ... anyway, not too bad for a nun ... and speaking of the erotic, have you ever heard of Robert Desnos?"

"Sorry, no."

"Read his surreal erotic work *La Liberté ou l'amour!* Only for kick-ass kicks, mind you."

"How about this page-burner?"

She stifled a laugh.

"*Minor Episodes*? Yes, for some reason all the girls are supplied with that. A trashier hit biography cannot be found. Still, if you like that sort of thing, I am certain Madame would be only too happy to read it to you."

"Whatever."

But I did as she bid me do and applied my attention to the required reading, including Proust. At first, I was stuck on the first paragraph. This man's epic about how a snotty little boy used to fall asleep seemed puerile at best. And who really cared if in the darkness of his room, he felt the scales of time falling heavily upon his eyes? Yet I plodded on. It has been put to me that my real mother often used the expression "plugging away" in full harmony with her musical inclinations. For my own part, the brute mechanics of music continue to elude me. Why, I could not catch a tune out of the smog until I ran into it. At least, according to my less than savoury guardians, in their sad patois. And alas, I have no pipes! Often I imagine the moment my father first heard my tuneless tonsils screaming away thirstily, and how with a bottle of milk he decided to christen me Diminuenda. So it went. I would at every attempt drop the book after a few lengthy sentences and drift into my own realm of dream and memory, just as the author described his snotty little character to have done. It must have been after my rereading of the first volume that I began to inhabit a fictive demimonde beneath the tepid fluctuations of reality. The most horrible happening could befall me and yet I would remain unfazed. I felt aloof as a drama critic kneeling beneath the footlights of my own life. And there I was milling about the parterre, rubbing elbows with ladies of fashion and deigning to wave back at myself. Then it became apparent to me that any soul with the smallest creative spark must be subject to similar imaginings. Notwithstanding, Madame Hautalon was the first to confirm my suspicions.

"Beyond these barbed gates, lesser men will judge you without even an ounce of flexibility. They will expect you to gratify their every whim, without restitution for each crime they commit. Whether the crimes against you are physical or emotional or, worst of all, mental, each one ensures that you lose your own mode of expression and accept a predefined path of existence, as narrow as a new thong or girdle. Remember to recognize the worst crime, Diminuenda. The slow euthanasia of the imagination."

I took this lesson to heart and kept many of my most offbeat notions to myself. I understood that pleasure was permitted to exist in an illusory form but not so broadly that it openly flouted convention. In other words, Truth was a welcome ideal, but in practice a source of terror to many. For I had inherited the genetic intelligence of my parents, who possessed an unsinkable anti-social streak combined with a positive contempt for social hypocrisy. They had put on their faces and offered their gifts to the world. But they would have been just as happy, if not more so, in the most desolate isolation. Presently, where had they vanished to? Some said *Dystopia*, the undiscovered *Isles of the Unblessed*, where each thought gave birth to action and life was suffused in a layer of dream. I thought of this place every night and hoped to wake up and find myself there with my cavorting *progenitori*. If they had found personal freedom, where was my share?

However, during these formative years, it took only a single volume of prose to free me of these romantic illusions that plague so many young girls and distort their images of self. I now had a means of analyzing the framework of a solitary passion, in order to reconstruct it like a mathematical problem or to dissemble it entirely, if I so desired. I know that many would argue against such cold-heartedness but that is only the argument of a society that breeds illusion and sprouts ignorance to suit its ulterior lack of purposes. To cast off one's illusions can be painful. But in the long run, it makes the soul strong, and in tune with the goal of the mystics who invite us to beat our souls with a stick, but neither lecture nor order us to do so. To cultivate your own illusions at will makes you stronger still.

Indeed, it felt far easier to attempt a "disconnect" in terms of my life. I did not see the individuals in my life with my own eyes, but through the eyes of this author, or within the author being born out of the reader within me. I have heard so much criticism and so many expressions of fear about the authorial voice, but I have decided this is merely reactionary panic. The truth is, some do while others watch. The watchers will always outnumber the doers. Reading this book was an intimate encounter unlike anything I have experienced within the humid confines of my own life. The author spoke, and instead of blindly worshipping his ideas and memories, I adopted the lightest surface of his philosophy and observed my own life and memories with his life. This was a gift, and I have nothing but respect for the individual who dares to write, not to please a fickle faddist populace, but to please herself. The people I thought I knew in my life were no more than spectres and shadows cast upon the wall by a whirling night light. If little figurines in harlequin garb insisted I was a royal daughter in some *commedia*, how was I to contradict them? I would bide my time and wait to have my own way.

It goes without saying, I was beset by strange reflections and imaginings. I used to slip out into the alcoves and stare up at the moon, as if trying to make out signs of the energy with which she managed to move seas. Exstasia used to tease me about this fixation and suggest that I start a lunar cult at once, and without delay she would arrange some very interesting rites of worship. I put to her at once that such rites were not my scene. In response to this reply, she pulled my hair back and planted a friendly kiss upon my forehead. Strange girl!

I recall a moonlit night at the knell of the bell moving among the alcoves to see the cool clear sky better, along with star formations I held no hope of ever identifying.

"Curfew is past."

The local gnome-boy was addressing me from underneath an arch. I would say a Roman arch so you understand at once, were it not an Etruscan design appropriated by the Empire for its buildings. I certainly did not trouble this lurking creature boy with this choice nugget of information.

"You came out at the sound of the bell. You are a Romantic."

The harsh sound of the bell was no more Romantic than the arch was Romanesque. Only an exotic influence of early campanile supports.

"How did you get in?"

"I ring the bell. It's my job."

"How wonderful for you."

"Are you looking to meet someone ... a boyfriend? A ... lover?"

"Or husband? What d'you think?"

"It is not uncommon for the young ladies of Ecole Jeune Colibri to be promised to celebrated international gentlemen of great means and repute in a contractual arrangement that resembles matrimony. There have been many excellent matches ... and sometimes young ladies disappear in the middle of the night ... they are known as *filles de moi* ..."

"Are you suggesting this is some type of slave farm?"

"There is no question about that. But who in the end is the slave?"

He held his hand over his heart and smiled at me. I hesitated.

"May I be perfectly candid with you?"

"Please, miss!"

"Your looks are loathsome but your words are keen, even cunning."

"But does that matter to a woman ... of beauty?"

"It does to me."

"Then we can be friends?"

"Friends? Yes, friends. I concede."

The instant this verbal agreement was ratified, he took the opportunity to blame it on the moon and leapt upon my person. I struggled against the wall in my mandatory nightgown, which allowed him to touch me through the sheer material and give me a profound lesson in his more than able anatomy. I was repulsed of course. On the other hand, since I had never been this near a member of the opposite sex (save for my pervert of a step-parent) I experienced an alien sensation all over my flesh. This was swiftly replaced by contact between my knuckles and his slobbering countenance. He went flying across the courtyard cobbles. He rose with bloody lip to mount a second attempt but a spotted dog appeared out of the dark and sank its teeth into his ankle. The bite itself was insignificant but the dog began to drag him away across the stones, scraping his exposed skin on the stonework. The dog, although I only caught a glimpse of it, seemed very familiar to me.

Once I had retired to my room and Extasia's profound snores, I felt awash with pleasure, first in recalling each forbidden touch so alien to my senses, and second in feeling safely recovered after a short and silly misadventure. This encounter by moonlight had roused something unknown within me. Hunger? More than this. I felt drawn toward the sleeping form of Exstasia. I wanted her view on the matter. Now, not in the morning. But she looked so peaceful in her sonic disruption of the room. That night and into the early hours, I watched her sleep.

The next night (I can hardly wait to relate it) I sat at her side for over an hour. When not snoring, she made other funny breathing noises while she slept and often I wanted to laugh outright. But I had no wish to disturb the way she looked, like a watercolour. I leaned over in a decisive moment, and pressed my lips to hers. The sensation was welcome and for a long time she responded to what I presume was a figure in a dream. But it was me! Her eyelids stopped fluttering and she awoke, slightly startled.

"It's you."

"Sorry."

"You would not be sorry if you knew the warp and woof of my dream just now."

"You are ... lovely."

She did not answer. She reciprocated with a warm kiss and I confess I did not wish to return to my own bed. But she bid me do so, and feigned fatigue with her hand over her forehead, although I suspect she did not sleep the remainder of the night. My head fell back into my pillow, filled with a sense of accomplishment, and I began to reflect upon the material I had been reading only an hour ago. For a negotiable fistful of francs, the young ladies got up to such mischief. And I felt haunted by the lightning of the fictional *bois* and the invitation to meet behind a seaside restaurant by the swell of a moonlit tide. For ... what, precisely?

The next morning, Madame Hautalon roused me out of bed with a spanking ruler.

"Looks like someone had a late night ..."

"Ooooh, show mercy, Madame! I must have slept in."

"While you were in the Land of Nod, Exstasia informed me of your ... nocturnal habits."

I reddened.

"Madame! I ... sorry."

"Now then, have you also been taking out your frustrations on our bell boy?"

"*Oui, Madame.*"

She tapped the hummingbird insignia on the back of my nightgown with her ruler.

"*Tac tac tac!* Very well. Tonight at midnight I will collect you. Meanwhile, mind your studies. I will be testing your comprehension before you know it!"

All day I flipped through those onerous tomes and performed my assigned chores, without so much as a word from anyone. I even kept an eye out for my gnomish admirer, but he did not appear at the gate once, and the bell did not ring once. Exstasia did not return to our room in the evening and I was left quite alone to stare down the clock on the wall, whose normally silent strokes ticked slowly and mercilessly toward midnight. Then as I tried to concentrate on my assigned reading and comprehension exercises, I noticed passages that had been underlined in red ink, and these only ignited the delicate tinder of my imagination.

Les doigts de notre charmante supérieure chatouillaient les fraises de mon sein, et sa langue frétillait dans ma bouche ...

The beauty of the marked phrases reached me with a power all its own, even devoid of meaning.

Les empreintes de doigts disparaissaient peu à peu, remplacée par les zébrures rouges du martinet de cuir de la correctrice ...

I lay back on my bed, unable to sleep for my excitement, and yet closing my eyes to picture these torrid scenes, supplanting the names and faces of the characters with those I knew more intimately. Ecole Jeune Colibri was for the most part publicly funded as an alternative religious school, and for this reason, I knew nothing in these books could ever happen here. However, our lessons created much confusion, since they were the most obvious source of temptation. After watching instructive curriculum flicks like *The Raw Transfiguration of Sister Trinity*, *Cheap Indulgences*, and *Burka Ban 4*, my views about the correct mode of devotion and rites were rather distorted. Also, we were never told to praise a higher power of any kind. We were only told to respect those in authority over us, and for my part, it was easy to respect and admire Madame Hautalon. Even now, I was imagining her calm, confident face, questioning me about my slight transgression upon school grounds, and then administering my punishment without a flicker of regret. Perhaps Exstasia and the other girls would be there, staring intently at the scarlet zebra stripes decorating my exposed flesh ...

There was a knock at the closed door that disturbed my reverie. It was Exstasia, who smiled at my pose and the state of disarray of my skirt. She tossed me a new outfit and told me to change clothes and to be ready in five minutes. She closed the door again and I looked at the tag. It was a dark, slinky jumpsuit made of some type of new synthetic called BreatheX. I stripped down to my smalls before putting on the outfit, which sent currents of warm air up and down my body, stimulating every nanometre of my bare skin.

It was midnight. That was the last thing I observed before Exstasia covered my face with a veil and tied a band of thick black cloth about my head, so that I saw nothing but darkness. She put her arm around my waist and led me carefully through long corridors and down cold flights of stairs. I felt rather disoriented, although my sense of anticipation far outweighed my sense of dread. Then, through the stillness, I could hear murmurs of excitement and a cry of anguish. When the band of cloth was briskly unknotted and the veil was removed, the first thing I saw was the bell boy. At the sight of me, his face took on an expression of hope mingled with bittersweet despair. If he had been afraid a second earlier, he now appeared stoic and stalwart, which was admirable, considering his condition. He was clad in nothing but a tattered loincloth, which betrayed his less than admirable bulk from the side and rear. He turned his head to look at me, as if I had the authority to release him from his coarse restraints.

"*Oui, regardez ce que vous adorez!*"

Madame Hautalon was clad in a jumpsuit similar to mine, except with rather provocative hooks struggling to hold the front together. She struck a delicious pose, leaning back in her thigh-highs before flicking a long switch at the spotty buttocks of the bell boy.

"*Imaginez que nous vous punissons!*"

"Ohwww ..."

I had not noticed that Exstasia had slipped away for a few minutes, only to return in a sheer gown through which her bare body was translucently visible. Madame Hautalon nodded her approval before asking her to stand in the corner of what I would call the dungeon, although I began to discern that the old bricks were actually excellent fabrications made from an unknown material. When I observed the two women standing apart, I thought of my readings and imagined the lovely hands of our mistress fondling the warming figure of Exstasia. I imagined a hearty slap upon her buttocks and a spasmodic reaction between her thighs. At this point, about thirty girls began to file in. All of them were dressed exactly like Exstasia and all of their faces were intense with interest. I only recognized one of the girls as Ursule, whose hard beautiful face showed the most enjoyment at the predicament of the bell boy. Then to the right of the girls, I saw a silhouette moving behind ornate columns of faux stone.

"Who's that?"

"One of the more regular patrons of Ecole Jeune Colibri. Don't mind him. He won't interfere in our business."

Madame Hautalon resumed flicking the switch at the bell boy's back and buttocks and thighs. Ursule stared intently, her face becoming more and more monstrous. But with each flick of her wrist, Madame Hautalon looked younger and fresher. Was it true? Did cruelty really rejuvenate? One day, this theory would lead to my launching an age-defying unction called Minor Revamp, but I digress. At last, she mopped her forehead and held out the switch for me to administer.

"*Prenez le martinet.*"

"*Madame, vous êtes sûre?*"

"*Oui, c'est notre sort.*"

I accepted the switch from Madame Hautalon and lifted it with a hint of apprehension, in consideration of the bell boy's raw red backside.

"*Madame ...*"

"*Fouettez-le.*"

I stood forward and gave the bell boy a feeble lick of the switch. Nonetheless, due to his sore flesh, he emitted a short gasp.

"*Punissez ... plus fort.*"

I struck him again with the switch, this time throwing my arm into the action. This time his body stung with a flash of pain. He let out a low moan, although I could not discern whether this indicated pain or pleasure or both. He appeared to welcome any form of attention from me, no matter how severe.

"*Diminuenda ... je t'adore ...*"

I struck him harder, increasing the frequency of my strokes.

"*Je t'aime!*"

I did not hate the bell boy. On the contrary, I was quite indifferent to his plight. All the same, out of this diffidence came an instinct for savage cruelty, one I attribute to no species but our own. I relished the intense suffering I was causing him. It was in fact the only intimate contact that could ever exist between us. Clearly, he understood this, and for this reason he welcomed the assault with fervent ardour. In that instant, noting the zeal that lit up Ursule's rapt face, I realized that in spite of our differences, there were only a few imperceptible degrees between us, when it came down to it. This was an early lesson I would never forget; namely, that in extreme circumstances, the most rigid of personalities could collapse, and the most frail could rise to the occasion. If Exstasia and Ursule and I were ever stranded at sea in the same lifeboat, I could not say with any certainty who would make the first move to eat the others. Or would that charming miscreant be none other than myself?

"*Tac tac tac ... oui.*"

Madame Hautalon smiled with satisfaction.

"*Maintenant, embrassez votre amie.*"

I turned at once to Exstasia and tentatively held her waist.

"Baisez-la."

I turned many shades of red at this command, since it was a wicked double entendre that would one day prove true in every form of the word. But I responded eagerly and pressed my lips to hers. She did not resist. She even permitted me to taste the tip of her tongue in my mouth, which left me giddy. Even the bell boy forgot his fresh pain while craning his neck to observe our kiss in avid wonder, an act that would one night prove fatal to him. The other girls watched with interest, save for Ursule, who regressed to her usual look of disdain.

"Elle n'a plus besoin de bandeau."

I have sworn to keep secret the subsequent events of that evening and innumerable others. However, I have betrayed my sacred oath in order to give you the tiniest glimpse into my upbringing. Suffice it to say there were countless nights like this one, involving strangers in the shadows and victims prime for punishment. Admittedly I had my helping of all these things, and with impunity. Thus, my early years at Ecole Jeune Colibri seemed to flit by in the bat of an eye and the beat of a hummingbird's wing.

II

I should like to say those years in the interim were completely happy ones, but at every turn I was thwarted from my heart's frivolous desire. Is it so vainglorious that I wished to be known by multitudes for my own unique qualities? After all, I was a Minor, and for us, this empty-headed dream is second nature, and as natural as breathing. A Minor's first word is likely to be a brand name in a product spot. Perhaps it was only an inferiority complex that sprang from being called Dim for so many years. In any case, I wished to be famous, to have my name in lights and my hands in starry concrete. I liken myself at this moment to Herakles in his early years, pausing at a crossroads between the tempting lure of the goddess Vice and the stingy guarantees of the goddess Virtue. My earlier years of an interior life marked by industry suddenly evaporated. Those truly happy hours were warped by my new fantasies to seem stifling and unbearable, although their primal sympathy always remained nearby, like some wily projectionist hiding behind the screen of my newfound illusions.

Thus, the labour that had enriched my mind had been an utter waste of time. It brought few friends into my sphere, and if anything, made me feel odd, especially if I were to speak a single thought that crossed my mind. In addition, I had acquired no talent to talk of, and my stark braininess intimidated and terrified girlfriends and suitors alike. I learned what it was to live in the world as an ordinary soul, but what is more, what it is like to be alone. I cursed my tomes and their confusing teaching and instead focused on vocal tricks and performance art, or anything that would get me through an audition. I gave up my junior librarian liaison apprenticeship and waited tables in restaurants and bars, building up a vast network of aspirant singers and models, puffed-up hacks doing extra work in horrible productions, and unscrupulous agents and talent scouts who never failed to leave behind a Mephistophelian bargain with the bill.

What is worse, I only encouraged such attentions and relationships. I was mercilessly flirtatious with influential people of either gender, any of those I deemed part of the "influenza," since they seemed for the most part "sick" to my refined sensibilities. I thought I could wag the dog without shedding any fur. But my family name had fallen into ignominy, and I was forever associated with the trashy movie of the week about my wretched foster guardians, the one you have no doubt watched some dreary twilight to pass an unenjoyable hour or two. Though I could not sing a single note to jump-start my career, I nonetheless attempted to cash in on my mother's dear departed name, and tried to release a tribute album to the inimitable F Sharp. Each of her songs, even "Stalking after Midnight," died in my throat, and the murky but scarcely dark rock-a-hilly folk album, *Twang of Deliverance*, faded into oblivion.

I was at a critical juncture, short on cash and keen for speed, when my landlord, Luther, approached me with an intriguing proposition. First, I feel I must point out that Luther had many male callers and the majority of them called him a slut, sometimes as a jibe and sometimes as a recrimination. I will not repeat the hundred other slurs I heard. Nonetheless, I was desensitized by each startling word I heard. He was a curiosity to me and his offer was even more curious to me. I guessed that I would be of little use to him, given his driving interests, but I was surprised by the sudden emergence of an enterprising spirit within him. He assured me that I didn't have to change a thing with regard to my living arrangements, aside from installing a fishhole in a corner of the room. This would provide not only my rent, free of charge, but also a respectable income for the pair of us that would suffice until we were famous "4eva."

I am by no means advocating this as a feasible business plan. I had intended to rise above the tawdry mores of my fellow alumni. But the next thing I knew, I had a Fishhole 5020 installed in my bedroom. *So it has come to this, Diminuenda*, that is what I thought at the time. Bottomfloor Unlimited picked up the feed at once, and the routine was simple. When it was time for bed, I would change into my night attire directly in front of the bulbous lens. Luther would pick out dozens of new items for me to try for the sake of variety. He had many theories about which scenarios called for quality and which non-allergenic fabrics would provide the beauty rest I required to continue in this business. I knew I was at a loss without his constant coaching. At first I was nervous in front of the fishhole, but after a few nights, I began to experiment with the routine. After all, I wanted any prospective talent agents to see that I had a knack for kookiness, which would at least propel me into the romantic drivel genre, if not at once into stirring dramas.

I began with simple, plain nightgowns flowing from shoulders to feet and gradually, over a few weeks, progressed to two-pieces, which grew racier and more shimmery each day. But I did not doubt Luther in his instruction, since he had an eye for colour. I suppose my descent into madness began with the butter. It was based on an old Minor hand-me-down theory that if you performed a single nonsensical act, there were hundreds of people in the world, if not thrillions, who would call this act a glowing work of art. So I thought nothing of it when Luther suggested I play about with a hunk of butter. He said the folded arms and flirty scenes of rapidly approaching self-love were fine. Fine! They were fantastic! But he hypothesized that an added ingredient that would undoubtedly attract additional observers would be a sizable stick of butter. I inquired what I was to do with it, and he said it would be fine just to taste some with my finger. I must have become addicted to this bedtime snack because I used the butter almost every night. This, incidentally, is a craving that has never left me to this day.

Perhaps my tale would have taken a different bifurcation entirely had I not made even this one small concession, for the butter seemed intensely real in a world of artificial toppings, and many a pair of red-rimmed eyes were glued to their personal interfaces for the sole purpose of watching me taste a solid brick of the stuff and express some modicum of enjoyment. As the male of any species is likely to argue, once one concession is made, another falls hard upon its pointed heels. Luther suggested that if I were to entertain any of my gentlemen callers, it would be a small matter to convince them to come back to my room and, as he put it, taste fifteen minutes of limelight. Of course, the pecuniary aspect of this arrangement would have nothing to do with either my pleasures or pains. The fishhole in a corner of the room was after all, incidental, and relatively harmless. Do not judge, but I jumped at this chance, unable to resist additional opportunities to display my theatrics to hidden hordes of spectators.

So it went, in ways I dare not describe. I had not been quite so beside myself since my formative years at Ecole Jeune Colibri, and could not be quite stimulated without the constant attentions of that fishhole in the corner of the room, observing my every kiss and caress and at the same time capturing artless instances of my sincere lovemaking. The men I met were most agreeable to this situation and some of them welcomed the chance to return more than once for only a small percentage of our monthly take. I thanked my stars that I lived in this epoch of such unprincipled souls, and then laughed and reminded myself that each age was more or less the same, a suspicion I was about to verify with my very own eyes and ears. I corrected myself and rejoiced with Luther, since we lived in a time when breathless synthetics and low-quality entertainment were a winning formula for obtaining success and sustenance.

This rental experiment gone awry had roused the Colibri girl in me. With Luther, I ordered the accessories necessary to put on a more than decent show. The excitement and the cosplay and the keen sensations were all factors in causing me to become more and more daring, although some might say debauched or even dissipated. I would challenge them to insert a fishhole in the corner of their very own bedrooms before casting aspersions on me. For I have never been one to shy away from my earnest passions, and it was only another small step to exhibit them and make them public domain, for a nominal fee, naturally. *Quant à moi*, it was like lying naked in a dewy sodden field and staring up at a cool night sky of stars and knowing that from a great distance, each of them was burning bright with desire and only wanted to watch me.

It might be said that everything was going swimmingly until a day I recall distinctly. I was writhing on the weathered mattress (a special effect) and alternating the attentions I was lavishing upon two charming boys, Lars and Toby, who had returned innumerable times to earn a bit of easy cash to put toward their otherwise insurmountable student loans. I was pretending to smother Lars into a classical knee-jerk orgasm while navigating Toby to the aft of me for acts of love's sweet administration I dare not name. We had done a number of these snuff mock-ups, or *snuffies*, for which we became notorious, and this was one of the more stimulating ones. In fact, I was asking them to form the soft white breading of a fatal manwich when the peculiar little man burst in on us, and brandished an official correspondence bearing the corporate seal of the parent of countless bastard companies and subsidiaries, Minoris Megaglobular Massive Golf Umbrellas (MMMGU).

This hunched, hobbling, and wizened creature asked for a moment of my time. I bid Lars and Toby retire and they left in a foul mood, leaving only a barrage of uncharacteristic ejaculations in their wake, having never been left so unsatisfied before. I donned a plush blue robe and covered the fishhole.

"Well, what is it?"

"Allow me to present myself. I am Timothy Gimmick, something of a hatchet man and suspicious delivery boy all rolled into one. I did your father dishonourable service for the best and most decadent decades of my life."

"The pleasure is mine, good sir. But what is this about?"

"Ms. Diminuenda Minor, I was one of the few surviving emissaries selected to carry out this special task the second you turned twenty-one years of age. This is more than the execution of your father's will. He didn't wish to leave this job to bunglers and middlemen, as he put it, only the trusted family serfs each scion of Minors had relied upon for generations, and I, serving faithfully as the Gimmicks have always done for the Minors ..."

"Dear Mr. Gimmick, could you kindly come to the matter in question?"

"Indubitably, Ms. Minor. I am here about the matter of your inheritance."

"You must know I inherited nothing."

"Yes, Ms. Minor; this is regarding your real inheritance."

"This must be a joke. Everything went to extraneous shareholders and synagogues and tattoo parlours."

"On the contrary. A sizable portion of the Minor means and estates, and what is more, the very legacy, is put aside for you."

"Really!!!"

"However, there is a small catch, a *minor clause*, if I may be so bold as to repeat your father's precise play on words."

"But what is this catch or clause you speak of?"

"To learn that, you must return with me at once to Mansion di Minore."

"But I am not ready. My things! To be perfectly candid, I need a good scrubbing."

Timothy Gimmick waved his hand about the room with an air of indifference.

"Your new life awaits you, Ms. Minor. Yet, to discover it, you must be prepared to leave all of this behind ..."

Luther did not take the news well at first. He had been scrambling to prepare the necessary paperwork for our clincher deal with Spurt Entertainment Extensions (SEE) and now it appeared his labour had indeed been in vain. Also, in his perverted, avuncular way, he was worried about my going off alone into the world, without him being around to secretly record the footage. But his caring side gave way to the backdoor-dealing part of him, since he knew that it was better to be a sympathetic ear for an heiress than to be the tenement manager of a libidinous tart. He patted my bottom fondly and Frenched me farewell. I stepped into the floating limuck sporting only my blue robe, with Lars and Toby clinging to me tightly on either side, their eyes and bodies moist with emotion. I bid them tender entreaties and we made wonderful mendacious speeches about never parting in this world and beyond. Then the door closed and I vroomed closer and closer to my outlandish destiny.

As we rode through falling darkness, Timothy Gimmick explained to me that the mansion functioned centrifugally in tune with shifting plates beneath the earth and would surface in a new place every day. Sometimes on an island, sometimes under a sea, sometimes in the side of a mountain. This preamble lingered in my ears as we sped directly into the yawning side of a cliff face. We were roaring down one of the tunnels that led to the heart of the family structure. After leaving the parked limuck and disrobing, I was led into a cleansing stall by a series of automatic handlers that sprayed me at once with an entire line of immediately recognizable fleshplash products in the Minor line. I emerged, spanking clean, and found a dark flowing gown, as well as ancillary unmentionables waiting for me, all of them marked with the MMMGU logo.

I waited in the vast library, perusing the most arcane of volumes. In fact, I laughed heartily to recognize the original *Minor Episodes*, the autobiography that Minor himself had insisted be made into an extravagant coaster for three mugs. I flipped through and noted the graphic detail in the erotic dream sequences about my mother, the incomparable Miss Sharp, and that interfering ogress of an *aunt* of mine, Bébé Lala, who was responsible for filling my head with filmy thoughts at an impressionable age. I have neglected to mention the years of her feeble tutelage, due to the pain it would cause me to recount such a drossy and even frothy tale. Then there was the enigma himself, the mystery man who had torridly sundered his way around the world and farther, leaving gifted progeny everywhere. So why was he in death taking an interest in me that he had never shown in life? Me, Diminuenda, cute but cunning, wayward but wily, and what is more, a wilful woman on a muddy slide toward infamy. Now ... the heir apparent of my father's worldly possessions?

Timothy Gimmick opened the library doors and gave a slight bow. "Allow me to present Master Vermicello Fuddlemuck ..."

"Hi."

A man in a chair hovered into the room. He lit a cigar and adjusted his monocle, before floating down to a writing desk and pulling out an assortment of documents and a purple box.

"It's the damnedest thing. One afternoon I got up from a nap and I couldn't feel my legs. They laughed, they did, said I wore myself out chasing ambulances. Maybe there's something to it. It takes quite an important cock of the walk to get smitten by the Almighty. Whereas you, on the other hand, my dear, have just been doled out more than a dollop of luck. But not more than is your fair share, granted."

"Mr. Fuddlemuck ..."

"Master Fuddlemuck! That's a non-conditional clause."

"Sorry. Also, not to sound graspy, but what's my slice of the cooked goose pie?"

"You must become a proper lady by the stroke of midnight."

"What!?"

"I must apologize. I am joking of course. But that's just the sort of thing they would make a movie about. And they say solicitors pick your pocket."

Fuddlemuck puffed thoughtfully.

"No ... your father's intention is to give you everything, more or less. But he has a few ... errands ... left for you to carry out. Standard stuff, really."

"Such as?"

"Well, walk the dogs and feed the piranha ... the usual things."

"And ...?"

"Ah, yes ... this is a bit trickier. You see, Diminuenda – I may call you Diminuenda, mayn't I? Well, Diminuenda, your father's last wishes were to recover a few items of artwork. He felt it was imperative to do so, even with his dying breath."

"This doesn't involve anything illegal, does it?"

"Comes from a fishhole romper room full of swingers and asks if anything illegal is involved! No no no, it's not like that at all."

"Go on."

"You see, your father wants you to take a few trips to recover these pieces of art. Or sometimes just to mark them up. A few squiggles here and there. It's a day's work, really."

"Where do I need to go?"

"I think you've hit it on the nail, my dear Diminuenda. It's not so much where as *when*."

"What, when?"

"In this box, or so I am told, there is a device with corresponding instructions that will enable you to travel both spatially and temporally. You must learn its functions and travel through time to your father's target sites and follow his instructions to the letter."

"What are you on about?"

"Don't be so naive, my dear. You're not fooling either of us. Time travel has always been possible. Only not everyone can afford it. Yet. Did you think that Minor Time Unlimited was just twiddling its thumbs and putting on puppet shows for the masses to rot their brains with? They've had more than a prototype since before you were born, missy."

"_?"

"So, my dear. You open the box and figure out the device and follow the instructions. Once you have completed each task, you will be notified of what is to happen next. The rest is out of my hands. I do not even have access to this box. Only you can open it."

With that, he blasted off in his blasted chair.

Timothy Gimmick appeared and made a few solemn noises about leaving me alone with my father's things before bowing and falling backward into a darker part of the mansion.

I broke the official Minor seal, to much yelping, and opened the contents. There was a letter for me.

Dearest Diminuenda,

You have no doubt wondered, perhaps your entire life, why I chose to abandon you to the vicious mercies of the world. Naturally, the first assumption is a motivation of self-interest, since children in their earliest years are seldom interesting, and sometimes even less so the older they are. I cannot argue that I wanted to be any different than the ancient monarchs of myth, to have my fun and then leave you exposed upon a mountaintop or craggy hillock somewhere out of reach.

But this is not entirely true, either. Your mother was very dear to me, more dear than I would have ever let her know. Of course, it was mere quantum accident that brought us together, time and time again, since to paraphrase Heraclitus in a long-ago-torched text, irony is nature's sense of humour. Keep in mind, ironically, she was the only woman I would deign to bend and warp the boundaries of space and time for. Now, having done so and having experienced diverse and multiple realms of such sublimity, it is only natural that in my altercosm-hopping weariness, I should want to share a taste of these pleasures with my favourite daughter. And yes, you did not misread my words. *My favourite daughter.*

For this reason, I was forced to reflect (something I simply cannot stand) upon my own excesses and the extent of my will to power. I have known and produced a veritable vomit of largesse. Even in multiple dimensions, the past had somehow dogged my steps and caught up with me. How could I raise a daughter without spoiling her and moulding her into seventy-seven times the monster I had been? I could not like a vengeful god try to swallow you to save you from yourself, as Gaius Julius Caesar Augustus Germanicus tried to do. Nor could I trust myself not to make you a creature of my own, without knowing anything of your own person or individuality. This is the very spirit that society so often quashes in the young, while in the same breath pretending to help the young to a better future.

In other words, I would not sort you with my servants, nor consider you one of my retinue of frigiot savants and club-footed artisans and rhetorical liquidators, the kind of stock my overproductive loins have engendered and fostered and maintained throughout all of history. No, you have already likened yourself to Herakles, because you know your upbringing was meant to be mythical and the trademark of the origin of heroes. This is why you will forgive me for not helping you and for making you take a route that was steeper and thornier than that of all your half-siblings. This is a token of my favouritism, because I had faith in you to carve your own path in the world, no matter the odds. You are a Minor, dear, and perhaps it is time you were permitted to enjoy the fruits borne of such an ancient and bountiful tree.

So far as being dead goes, you might call it a cakewalk. In fact, my present situation is far too complex to describe in the context of a postage-stamp obituary. Let us say I am in a bit of a pickle (more of a gherkin, really) and I could use your help. So, *dead* is not really the word. *Indisposed* would be more appropriate, at least for this planet. I have absolute faith in you, but I did not want to leave it to mere chance that you would take all this trouble to help out your dear old dad, so I added the incentive of my worldly estates and subsidiary congloms, just to keep you interested. And if you are successful in accomplishing these small tasks for me, you will undoubtedly become my sole inheritrix.

You will find everything you need, including my precise instructions, in the purple box. Of course, I have additional resources at your disposal, suitable clothing and equipment and the like. But what you need most has been prepared and tailored to your physiognomy and neural pathways. The box contains the latest release of a time-travel device built by one of my companies. I am certain you would be amused by the events that led up to the theft and recovery and theft of its chief component, the tachyonometer, but that is a story for another time. I had it fashioned in the shape of an amulet, which you must wear at all times. It also contains a Venusian translation module for all known Terran tongues, which has a reliable level of accuracy. Most things should be apparent to you, but if there is any confusion, just fondle your amulet and it should readjust to give you a fresh translation.

As for the purple box, it will open for you, provided you utter the secret decoder phrase and play the little ditty you were compelled to learn as a child. It will only open when it detects your voice and brain activity while you are doing these precise things. Inside, you will find a neurochemical infusion, an NGF (Neuron Growth Factorizer). You are free to read the thousands of pages about controlling and repairing the device or you can just pop the NGF and absorb the information instantaneously. I'd recommend this option. It's quite the wild ride!

Well then, good luck and take care, Chestnut. Also, try not to be too hard on your aunt Bébé. I know she has her low-cut plunging drawbacks, but after all, she loved you from the start. You have no idea what risks she took for you and for your right to win your inheritance. She wanted me to keep you, in spite of my cool brilliant reasoning. I know she's not your mother, but she always thought of herself as such, in some weird needy way. So cut her some slack and maybe buy her an island when all this is over.

See you when I see you,
Marcel

I put down the letter, too overcome with emotion to know how to react. Instead, I went directly to the purple box and recited the phrase I had been taught as a child. "In my father's mansion are many mansions ..."
The purple box hummed and purred as if it were being stroked and petted.

Then I sat down at the piano in the library and began to play. I got the positioning wrong at first, and it took a few attempts, but eventually, I was recalling the fingering for the second movement of Beethoven's Piano Sonata no. 24, the one in F-sharp major. I realized only now that this was his rather gauche homage to the memory of my mother, Ms. F. Sharp. When I reached the wacky conclusion of this short piece of music, the box turned colour as if having just been fed a hearty and most satisfying meal and virtually burped itself open.

I found the amulet and immediately fastened it about my neck. I could feel it stirring and fidgeting with activated circuitry, attuning itself to my own erratic biorhythms and zany afterthoughts. Then I opened the box labelled NGFs and found a legend that provided more detail for each of the pills, based on the respective pill-stamp.

"Gimmick! Glass of water."

It arrived at once and I downed the time-travel instruction and repair manual, followed by the list of tasks to undertake. Then I drank the glass half-empty.

My head felt like it was shaking for a second, and then it felt like my mind was flowering open. I must say, this sudden awareness was completely startling and delicious. I was tempted to take all the other pills at once but that would have been a mistake. Already I knew that NGF addiction was to become a mounting problem in the future, and the learning drug went hand in hand with the touristy needs of time travel. Straight away, I could feel a little Minor reclining in a dark corner of my mind, advising me to have an early dinner and a decent rest before using the device. There would be more than enough time even if I didn't leave for a week or a month or years. But tomorrow morning would suffice. I picked up one of the makeshift Venusian brochures for Ancient Greece and instructed Gimmick to prepare us some supper.

After throwing caution to the wind and pouring half a bottle of wine for myself in one of the family goblets, I sat down in the kitchen and offered the rest to Mr. Gimmick. He begged a moment longer to check on the grilled ostrich and saucy duck positively stuffed with foie gras, before downing his glass with gusto. He sat beside me and poured himself another glass.

"This is the life."

"None too shabby, no."

"Of course ... it might get lonely."

"Lonely?"

"Kicking around this long and thick old mansion, all by oneself."

"Mr. Gimmick, what can you mean?"

His eyes grew misty.

"That may you never wrench from my lips, no matter how many kisses you may proffer!"

"Now you have me curious."

"Have you? Yes, to be sure. Your foster people were not the only ones, you know. There were visits! We used to sit in this kitchen and play and laugh. You were a little charmer, even then."

"And now?"

"Now I am an old fool, drinking wine and about to pour himself some more."

"And I am more than grown up."

"Yes, indeed."

He seized a plate and smashed it against a wall.

"To the devil with your beauty!"

After that, the tension between us simply melted away. We enjoyed more wine and tucked into our ostrich, pausing only to feed one another hunks of foie gras. I commented on the excellent quality of the wine and he nodded, reaching for the bottle and pointing to the label, a thorny M & G spelled out with vine leaves.

"This stands for Minor & Gimmick, a union of two old families, since my family has worked for your family collecting and crushing grapes and making the wine for many generations. Originally, we were simply going to call it Gimmick Wine but one of the lawyers from the Minor Joy Division objected to that."

"Ah … what a history we share."

"Of course, the Gimmicks have always been ready to lay down their lives for the Minors. Why, I'd die for you if I had to."

"I'd have to pay you to do it."

"You know, it is often said, many a time a Minor character has gotten out of a real fix through the use of some Gimmick."

"Hear, hear."

I drank another goblet of wine and found that Mr. Gimmick had begun to look more distinguished and even borderline handsome.

"Also, it is common knowledge that whenever there was a service to be performed, a Gimmick would scramble to do whatever was necessary to please his or her Minor."

"Why, what can you mean, Mr. Gimmick?"

"Timothy, please."

"I am beginning to suspect you of having imbibed more than your usual share … Timothy."

"No, not at all. I come from a long line of sturdy pisstanks. Have no fear. I could do you, goblet for goblet, were I not itching for another type of amiable antagonism …"

"I must retire to bed, Timothy. I have a long day tomorrow."

"Ah, yes, of course. We do live in interesting times. I'll show you up to your room. I suppose you could take any room, really …"

We made it as far as the sofa. We were fumbling about in the dark when Timothy seized hold of me and we fell upon the loveseat in the shape of a massive *M*.

"O forgive me, Ms. Minor! It's not me, it's the wine!"

But while he protested and castigated himself, his hands worked quickly to remove my MMMGU monogrammed housecoat and to make love to my most sensitive parts with his lips and tongue. I appreciated his attentions, being in a celebratory mood, but the reader will be shocked to discover that I was so used to gratifying my desires in front of the fishhole that the mere activity of sex itself now seemed to lack the flavourful germ it had once harboured for me. Or I needed some stimuli, and something stronger than wine to feel swept away by the faint transports a Timothy Gimmick could offer me.

Fortunately, at that moment, Master Fuddlemuck floated silently into a corner of the room and parked his chair mid-air, where he had the best vantage point. My eyes caught his and we shared the delectable secret of his zeal for voyeurism. For all artistic natures have a secret passion for watching and listening to the lives of others. Judging by the steely glint in his eyes, I gathered that Master Fuddlemuck had indeed been the master of his days, and the thought of his pre- and post-handicapable escapades, combined with the clumsy advances of Timothy Gimmick, was enough to send me into the type of amorous raptures only my imagination could reach. Before I conked out, the last thing I remember is the diverse smiles of these two very different characters.

But my dreams had already progressed to my first destination, in Ancient Greece.

III

Concerning my investigation of the artists and philosophers of Greece, there was one night worthy of reporting upon, in my estimation. Now like a tourist bearing nothing but a cheesy slogan on the front of her shirt, I struggle to find the words to describe what I took in on my trip. Thankfully, there were more than a few scribes present, although among themselves they remembered their own speeches most differently, so the challenge for me was to sift through their respective accounts and convey the meat of the matter. Before I present my own adulterated record, allow me to paraphrase Socrates himself, and agree that truth is a many-headed monster, especially when you are most in the mood to capture it.

SOCRATES
You there, Epiktetos, why linger about our doors like a stranger or god, unsure whether to reveal even your smallest toe to our hospitality?

EPIKTETOS
What? Do I linger? You have me at a fault, Socrates. I must have been daydreaming or lost in some leftover thought from your thinking shack.

SOCRATES
Why not enter at once, and cast off your cloak and lay your thought out on the table, where all of us may admire it?

EPIKTETOS
Am I certain it is only my thought you wish to examine?

ARISTOPHANES
A thought of Socrates has the same size and shape as a *plagiaulos*.

SOCRATES
It is the custom here to go like a god – naked.

ARISTOPHANES
Yes, do come in, Epiktetos. Do not twist in knots like one of your red figures shooting his seed into a pot! But beware of this man and the customs he is accustomed to. Or a customer of. He only believes in the gods when it suits his fancy to do so.

SOCRATES
I do not understand your inference so instead I will treat it as a compliment. Yet, I wonder how it is that you never appear to miss an opportunity to deride me or toss those words at me that taste like the bitter dregs of a

drained *kylix*. Whenever I am invited to hear a new work of yours, I am obliged to stand among sitters who pelt me with sheep stomach, since I am portrayed as three times the fool I already am.

ARISTOPHANES

Surely this is because you are so wise, and because I am only a mean maker of lowbrow comedies that frighten common folk, not to talk of tyrants, and will never be bright enough to merit those kind of attentions.

SOCRATES

I will let the matter rest, since your words are like poisoned honey that will bring me ill much later, but at the present seem sublime and sweet. Speaking of which, I could bear a dozen such ills, were only Epiktetos to find a comfortable place at the foot of my couch. Ah, and who is your little friend with you? Do invite him inside.

ARISTOPHANES

Goodness, Socrates, that looks like the *eromenos* we were quibbling over in the street. If I were still able to turn colour, I would be a shade of Phaethon's excited instrument at present.

SOCRATES

Must you always turn beauty aftwards and be little more than a crude version of Kallipygos admiring her own brilliant rump?

ARISTOPHANES

I was speaking of the god's whip to drive the steeds of Helios onward. You are naturally the first to mention an ass.

EPIKTETOS

This is my new friend Hilarion.

SOCRATES

Indeed, partake of some wine and sit by me. I say, why do they call you Hilarion? Are you another maker of farces like Aristophanes here?

EPIKTETOS

It is his misfortune to have a comical name and a tragic face. I can only suppose his parents heard him screaming when he was born and thought he was going to be a merry boy. Not so, for I have never met someone so gloomy or grave.

HILARION

Is there going to be a dinner? I will stay if there's going to be a dinner.

EPIKTETOS

Ha, what did I say! This one is straighter than an arrow to the mark.

SOCRATES

To be brief in speech says nothing of a young man's stamina. But wherever is Parrhasius? I should like to continue our discussion about painting.

AGATHANGELOS

He spoke of some new inspiration. Could he be in love again?

SOCRATES

Perhaps another flute girl has caught his painter's eye, if that is what you mean by love.

ARISTOPHANES

So long as she can blow and play him a tune and lead him a dance, that is his maxim, no?

AGATHANGELOS

No, I heard it was an incomparable beauty. A Helen!

ARISTOPHANES

Nothing but trouble and strife, you mean.

SOCRATES

Forgive me, for my mind is slower than an old tortoise before Hermes suggested making use of it. Even then, he only found the shell to make music, and not the creaky, tired creature inside. But tell me more of this comparison I do not understand. Why is any woman a Helen, or why is Helen any woman?

EPIKTETOS

Socrates, why do you always speak of the gods, when you are doubtful to the quick of their existence? You say you know nothing of them, and yet talk about nothing else.

ARISTOPHANES

He is like one of the hypokrites who bellow their belief on the stage and then retire home to mumble blasphemies.

SOCRATES

I swear, by the pithiest bolt of Zeus, this man will be the end of me.

AGATHANGELOS

But your pupil caused you to digress from your original question, Socrates.

EPIKTETOS

My apologies, but Socrates himself has taught me to question everything, which in itself is a wearying profession. He was speaking of love, and Helen.

SOCRATES

I was speaking of Helen. Of the other matter, I am too foolish to comment. And perhaps that goes for the world. But in terms of Helen and only Helen and only such things that concern Helen, do you find Helen beautiful, Agathangelos?

AGATHANGELOS

Indeed I do, Socrates. This is common knowledge across our fair country and elsewhere.

SOCRATES

Now, do the rest of you agree that Helen is beautiful?

EPIKTETOS

Yes, certainly, Socrates.

HILARION

Everyone knows this.

ARISTOPHANES

I will tether my tongue and await the unloosening of yours.

SOCRATES

Not that I have spent much time on the subject, but I sometimes wonder whether Helen is beautiful or if instead it is beautiful to be Helen.

EPIKTETOS

He will talk like this for a long while until we all become dizzy.

SOCRATES

Still you come to me to clarify your thoughts, Epiktetos, which never ceases to amaze me. But once again, you have sought to confuse me and make me forget my thought.

EPIKTETOS

Helen is beautiful?

SOCRATES

It is very much like a line from a play. Let me say that for my part, I do not know that Helen is beautiful. I only have heard she is beautiful by report. This is a much easier statement to make in a play without getting pelted with sheep stomach, is that not correct, Aristophanes?

ARISTOPHANES

I do not know that, Socrates. For those who make a cult of Helen, her celebrity is worth precisely eleven hundred peltings of sheep stomach. Not to mention the dregs of my bitter cup.

SOCRATES

How you twist the meaning of clear expression and draw it to your knees as one draws comely boys to oneself from the marketplace or doorway! I am stunned in mid-thought to consider the potency of your honed wit and dare not speak another word, for fear of appearing even more foolish than I am.

HILARION

Is he always like this?

ARISTOPHANES

O pour some wine and let us have it, Socrates! Then while we are struggling to untangle the Gordian knot of our minds in the morning, we will have a new riddle with which to pass the time.

SOCRATES

I will continue, so long as I am not pelted with another bowl of sheep stomach.

AGATHANGELOS

Indeed, please do so. These boys will be bitter old men by the time you finish.

SOCRATES

To review, I asked you if you agreed that Helen is beautiful. I then went on to consider whether she is beautiful in her own right or whether she is beautiful in the mouths of others.

ARISTOPHANES

I am certain she is delicious in the mouths of others. But carry on.

SOCRATES

I am like an offering, carved into parts by your wits, one at a time.

EPIKTETOS

O do not give him opportunity to make excuses. I know the man. He will talk for five nights to avoid saying another word.

SOCRATES

My, Epiktetos, how the wine moistens your tongue and emboldens your fey nature! As the sandal seller Mnason is often heard to say, come and see me tomorrow when you are sober.

AGATHANGELOS

Many apologies, Socrates. Tell us more of Helen's beauty.

SOCRATES

You are a most gracious soul, Agathangelos. I am keen to be convinced that your refinery was lacking from our dinners previous to this one. Indeed, the subject of manners in the social sphere is a lofty one, and although I am a plain-speaking man, unschooled in such matters ...

ARISTOPHANES

On the contrary, we need a tamer of horses to rein in Socrates the second he wanders from his point. I swear, if you do not talk of Helen at once, my next play will be about how you are a mere zephyr blowing words through our oft-blasted company.

SOCRATES

Now I must be expedient and at the same time cover my mouth, so as not to breathe in the pestilent air originating from that end of the table. Am I not a fool in the audience to applaud his barbs? Is this not *ob skene*, behind the scene where a man's character is killed, when that is what everyone gathered to observe?

EPIKTETOS

You have the floor, Socrates.

SOCRATES

My line of inquiry concerned the nature of Helen's beauty. Is it not true that every soldier went to war against Persia for her sake, with that ideal seated in their hearts to give them strength and courage?

HILARION

This is what I was taught. But this meat is truly excellent.

SOCRATES

And if any one of those soldiers were asked, "What do you fight for," is it not true they would answer that they fought for Helen's sake, if not some variation on this reply?

HILARION

Of course. Everyone knows this.

SOCRATES

Then if each soldier were asked to explain the meaning of this phrase, that he fought for Helen's sake, what would he then reply?

HILARION
There needs no further explanation. It is what it is.

SOCRATES
"It is what it is." What a curious statement.

EPIKTETOS
Perhaps Hilarion means he would only fight for a choice helping of supper.

SOCRATES
Praise his digestion for its own discreet skirmishes. But if it were a battle for Helen, what part of her would he fight for, specifically? I have heard her eyes harbour all the colours of the coat of an ibis. And I have heard of the allure of her swanny neck, which seems to be a strange attribute in a woman to consider comely. And I have heard of her bosom being more than equipped to suckle six times the brood of Priam. Yet among these charms I cannot uncover a solitary source of this beauty that makes her Helen, or the quality of Helen that makes her beautiful, so that I as a common man, may say, "This is Helen and she is beautiful."

HILARION
Are you questioning the beauty of Helen?

SOCRATES
Not at all. I am challenging my intellect and sensibility to fully understand such a beauty, along with every soldier who warred on Troy.

EPIKTETOS
I would say that we as a people value simplicity in beauty. Her simplicity makes her beautiful.

SOCRATES
Excuse me if I do not understand, but are you suggesting she is simple in any way? When I consider her sympathy with Odysseus and her temporary life with Paris and the ruse with Athene's horse, I think she must be, on the contrary, more complex than we imagine. Is she then beautiful because she is complicated?

ARISTOPHANES
I am told my silence is a rare gift even more rarely proffered. But I feel a necessity to point out that the war against Persia was about trading routes and territories and not about Helen. At the time, when our country was hot to defend its honour, her abduction seemed like a fine excuse to attack one of our rivals whose control over each passing ship had become unbearable.

She might be beautiful, but the swan in her was tempted by the parsley in the palm of a visiting stranger.

SOCRATES

Spoken like a statesman, Aristophanes, but not like the men in shining greaves whose eyes went dark under their helmets as their heads were crushed, for Helen's sake. Then what was the examinable nature of this Helen, who is openly charged with the deaths of so many? And if there is a woman named Helen, is she not different in aspect and form and action than the idealized Helen in the heads and hearts of every man speared and gored?

AGATHANGELOS

Are you indicating there were two Helens? I was just thinking of that work by Euripides, what is it called again?

HILARION

Helen?

AGATHANGELOS

Helen, yes, that is the one.

ARISTOPHANES

Euripides! Ha, he would only invent two women to flog a pair of them.

SOCRATES

I am not surprised to note your lack of praise for Euripides, or any man.

ARISTOPHANES

Lack of praise? Euripides can talk up himself! If you're autochthonous, and as gorgeous as Helen with a golden cicada in your hair, you get to hear the talk of a foreign love child who comes out on top! Yes, Euripides can cure all of our ills! If I am short on sleep, I humbly ask to sit in the front row at his latest production.

SOCRATES

I am drowsy myself, since I weary of sparring with you over the cups like a Scythian. I would drift to sleep right here, were it not that I feel possessed by a peculiar *daimon*, which restores my confidence that I have something to impart. Treat me like a jug of wine and pour me directly into your ears, without even stopping to taste what nonsense you are imbibing.

EPIKTETOS

I will rub your knees to keep you alert.

SOCRATES

Indeed, and I suppose there is much you might do to keep me on my guard.

ARISTOPHANES
Observe that Socrates is not sulking enough not to grin at the ardent fondling of Epiktetos.

SOCRATES
Retorts crumble and fall from my lips, and Epiktetos most kindly brushes them away with his touch. What is more, I am entranced by the words of Diotima of Mantinea, who gave me many discourses and much instruction on the nature of love.

ARISTOPHANES
How so? Was she one of the *pornai*?

SOCRATES
I will not give that remark the satisfaction of an answer. I knew very little of her origins. By report, she was wise and generous in all matters of love. Then I, being a young man about your age, Epiktetos, sought her out to further my knowledge in this regard.

AGATHANGELOS
But was she beautiful, Socrates?

SOCRATES
A fair question, although I have no answer for you. She was not a Helen, and yet I found her beautiful enough.

AGATHANGELOS
What do you mean, she was not a Helen?

SOCRATES
She lacked the reported traits of a Helen, and those of many women in Greece who no doubt seek to emulate Helen, and therefore become another Helen. To try to elaborate, she was small and dark, as the poet of Lesbos was reputed to be. Some would add the epithet *ugly*, but I do not agree.

AGATHANGELOS
Was she ugly, Socrates?

SOCRATES
Once again, I have no answer for you. But she was not a Helen.

HILARION
But what did she tell you, this Diotima of Mantinea?

SOCRATES
She said that the ideal of our love, however subject to mysterious properties, becomes love by virtue of that very ideal. There is no inception of this love.

It is, and continues to be so by degrees. Whether it grows or withers, or does both at once, this love is always alive. There is no beginning or end to it, which suggests that it does not belong to the realm of mortals. Also, the properties of the beloved are instantaneously subjects of this love and its strange alterations. This love instructs us in what is beautiful, and yet outside of such a love there is no objectivity, because outside of it nothing is independently beautiful.

EPIKTETOS

I am enraptured by your talk. Say on, Socrates.

SOCRATES

Then I asked her, what of Helen of Argos, who is deemed to be the most beautiful woman in the world? How may she exist in a world of divisive ideals of respective beauty that are inspired by love? For many men have ventured their lives, perhaps for one glance from her before a spear from her captors could find its mark. Is that not evidence of her singular beauty and its power working within the world?

ARISTOPHANES

Do these noble Greeks of whom you speak even exist, Socrates? I should like to meet just one of them.

SOCRATES

You are one of them, since in spite of the foolishness you fill your plays with, there is much matter there, too, especially with the intention of bringing peace and respite to those noble souls forever at the brink of death.

ARISTOPHANES

Socrates, you may have just performed the thirteenth labour of Herakles, by muzzling the bite of the three-headed dog of my speech before it could even bark.

SOCRATES

Yes, I see how easily the tongue of a flatterer oils the charioteer of your wit for action.

ARISTOPHANES

Nay, not the flattery of any man. But you, dear Socrates, may spit in your hands and rub down the smooth back and rough backside of my wit.

SOCRATES

Were it a fair contest, and were I not thus occupied with the busy hands of Epiktetos, I would take you up on that offer. But, I digress …

ARISTOPHANES
All right, say on, Socrates.

SOCRATES
She answered me in this fashion. She directed me to consider the apple of discord and the man who could not decide who was the most beautiful of three goddesses. In his inability to decide lay the conflict within the breast of every mortal to decide upon what the nature of love is, within, as Sappho says, *their own eyes*. He was shown incredible beauty, and then asked to accept alternatives, such as wealth, power, and military might. But he was won over by an ideal form made manifest among mortals. He had heard of Helen by her reputation alone and for this reason alone considered her to be the most beautiful woman in the world. Then he was offered the opportunity to see that ideal made into a common reality. In this act, there is the illumination and darkness that arrives in the eyes and minds and hearts of lovers. This is deceptive and involves even the most mild hint of degradation. That is why he was given the chance to steal away with her and deceive everyone in doing so. Because Menelaus loved her only in terms of the honour she could bring to his house. But did he really know anything of the joys and torments felt by the man who snuck into his palace as a thief sneaks onto the land of a sleeping shepherd? Is not their shared shame a stronger bond than those of cold matrimony? Are they not made absolutely unique when confronted with the torch of watchfulness? For they acted dishonourably, as lover and beloved, but they also acted out of love.

HILARION
Now we share in the shame of this lecture, Socrates.

SOCRATES
To hear is not to believe, and please recall that I heard these words from Diotima of Mantinea when you tell tales of my beliefs. Do not go around like Aristophanes, telling everyone I worship the clouds.

ARISTOPHANES
Or a vortex.

SOCRATES
You cast shame upon me.

ARISTOPHANES
Or a hole in the ground.

EPIKTETOS
Let us hear him out.

ARISTOPHANES

Indeed, Hilarion. Do not be like one of the Judges of Areopagus, who condemn thought itself of being guilty before it can be brought to light.

HILARION

Forgive me. I shall focus on my food instead.

SOCRATES

But have I not discussed the dual nature of Eros before, and without being interrupted once?

AGATHANGELOS

Indeed you have, Socrates. The wine has made us too ripe tonight to take much heed.

EPIKTETOS

I too am familiar with your thoughts on that matter. But how does that relate to Helen and the ideas of Diotima of Mantinea?

SOCRATES

She said to me on the subject that the representation of a Helen, or the beloved for that matter, was akin to one form of Eros. She did not say whether this was the heavenly or the mortal form of Eros. In her opinion, it was possible for these forms to melt into one another, since they have malleable properties where the force of love is concerned. Thus, there is the ideal Helen, whose representative good is ineffable and beyond the reach of mortals. This applies to herself, as the mortal Helen, who cannot live up to her own legend. She has no flaw that can be discerned, and yet her flaw is not living up to the glowing terms of her own myth, a myth that fires the hearts of men with love and floods their limbs with overwhelming desire. Therefore, love was on the Trojan's side as a lover, since he was the only one who could meet her mortal terms and attempt to possess her qualities and properties in full. In all probability, the strength of his desire ignited hers, since as Herodotus indicates, few royal daughters were abducted by seafarers who did not provide ample opportunity for sailing off.

ARISTOPHANES

Now you sound like a member of the school of Cynics, Socrates.

SOCRATES

I am only repeating what I have heard. But is Parrhasius going to make an appearance this evening? I am thinking of a few conversations we have had, and I would like to hear him elaborate upon the subject of painting in terms of what we are discussing.

AGATHANGELOS

He may pay us a visit. However, I was under the impression he was more than occupied with his most recent muse.

SOCRATES

Then tell us, Agathangelos, what do you know of her?

AGATHANGELOS

Parrhasius, with a mad look about him, compares her to a goddess.

SOCRATES

Then I should like to hear about his erratic state of being that much more, if he is at present possessed by Eros, who is working through the beauty of this woman.

EPIKTETOS

Really? I find he's hopeless at pithy discourse whenever he's in love.

SOCRATES

That is because you no doubt speak to him of things that cannot possibly interest him. It would be another matter to talk to him of his love, which is his favourite subject.

HILARION

But what did he say to you about painting?

SOCRATES

I am not sure enough of my eloquence to convey his artistic opinion.

ARISTOPHANES

Socrates, at times you are like a large ship with bright, flapping sails, empty of goods or passengers. Surely you can give us an idea of what you discussed.

SOCRATES

I will try, Aristophanes, to do more than let my sails blow in the breeze. We had agreed that in portraying ideal beauty, a single model was not sufficent. Parrhasius required the attributes of many models in order to paint even one of our beautiful heroes. In this case, a Helen might not be a painting of a woman but instead a painting of individual parts of many women, with the parts selected for their merits in the eye of the painter. We then sparred over whether the characteristic moods of the soul could be rendered or not. Parrhasius thought they were intransient and elusive qualities, and therefore inimitable. Do you agree with this assessment?

EPIKTETOS

This sounds reasonable to me, Socrates.

SOCRATES

But I put it to him whether it was possible to represent the physical traits associated with a given mood or state of being. At once, he agreed it was possible to imitate outward expressions of love and anger and sorrow that visit a human countenance. He agreed that through the outward posture and stance of a person, an inner revelation could be communicated to the viewer.

ARISTOPHANES

Then Hilarion is the painting of a stuffed guest.

AGATHANGELOS

Socrates, what else did Parrhasius say?

SOCRATES

I asked him what he found more pleasing, the painting of an idealized beauty or the painting of an idealized horror. That is, an ugly mood or disposition given the same treatment as with an idealized beauty, except using the worst elements rather than the best elements. For is not sorrow, even upon a beautiful face, an ugly thing to behold? Is not a mighty handsome hero made ugly when he is possessed by rage? Was not Achilles made unsavoury by his incessant sulking? I should like to ask Parrhasius how he would paint the man moments before he was glorified by his mourning for his dead comrade, when instead of being hideous, he would no doubt be made beautiful by an inner light of restrained anger and grief. Of course, I am no expert, and desire his opinion on such matters.

EPIKTETOS

But how do painting techniques relate to your other speech about love and the dual nature of Eros?

SOCRATES

Parrhasius himself could agree there was a distinction between beautiful and ugly forms in painting, but could not decide upon which was better or more pleasant to observe. I think it is the same with love, since love has the power to subdue our judgment and make what we perceive to be flaws the most valuable of qualities.

HILARION

And what of Helen?

SOCRATES

She is the ideal of beauty, but we cannot deny her mortal existence either. She exhibits the dual nature of Eros, to be both distant and near, to be both lovely and unseemly. Might we not consider that our fascination with her, instead of, say, with this flute girl here, who is passing beautiful, derives from the dual nature we perceive within her and the discrepancies between one Helen and another?

EPIKTETOS

I am not certain I agree. At least with this notion of love being ugly. Is love not good and beautiful?

SOCRATES

In one sense, yes. In another sense, not so much. Do you remember, Epiktetos, when we first met, and you ran up and down to every house, declaring your love for me at every table? Do you consider this discreet behaviour worthy of an honourable man?

EPIKTETOS

Well, no, Socrates. In fact, I redden now to hear you remind me.

SOCRATES

And did you not wait for me until all hours, calling in the streets for Socrates? Did you not raise the entire town screaming for Socrates?

EPIKTETOS

Surely you exaggerate.

SOCRATES

Then did you not conceive a foul suspicion in your breast that I was not exclusive in my granting of love and its splendid favours? Then did you not torment my other friends who came to me only for instruction in matters of discourse and what we call philosophy?

EPIKTETOS

I did harbour such suspicions, at the time, yes. Rumour led me astray.

SOCRATES

You must agree that you were more than unbearable, but would you say that you were an evil man with malicious intentions, at least at the peak of your passion?

EPIKTETOS

I must protest, Socrates. I did not realize the extent of my behaviour, nor the madness of my transgressions.

SOCRATES

But were you indeed mad, Epiktetos?

EPIKTETOS

I cannot say, Socrates. I only know that at that time, everything I did seemed a small fault in comparison with the amount of love I felt for you.

SOCRATES

Now, might I not argue the other side in your blessed defence?

EPIKTETOS

Please do.

SOCRATES

I put it to you that however misguided or unbecoming you were in your behaviour, you were regardless not as ugly as everyone might think, since you were cloaked in the habit of a lover, and through love, all your faults became a fistful of small charms. I want Parrhasius here just now, to speak of how he would paint you, were he to paint you, in the pose of the lover turned away from the door of the beloved.

EPIKTETOS

I should hope he would paint me in a more dignified pose.

ARISTOPHANES

It sounds like you have become a bore in the interim, Epiktetos. The picture that Socrates paints of you maintains the whole of my attention.

EPIKTETOS

I was young. In youth, we may be forgiven the follies of love.

ARISTOPHANES

Really? It seems to me you are past one side of pederasty and not past it enough for the other side waiting. Socrates, on the other hand, may have his pick of fresh lads.

SOCRATES

Nay, I think a painting of Epiktetos in love would be most becoming. In spite of my complaints, he was after all quite endearing.

IV

I made the necessary adjustments to the tiny console panel inside the amulet around my neck and activated it for transfer. The moaning and groaning sound seemed very loud this time as my particles were discombobulated and then reconstructed in appropriate attire just outside the suburban bathhouses of Rome.

The year was AD 30 and I felt rather dismayed. It had been easy enough to make the acquaintance of the Ancient Greek painter Parrhasius, and it had been charming enough a task to cajole him into immortalizing me in that mythical painting of Atalanta, obviously pleasuring him as Meleager. This had enraged the painter's rival, Zeuxis, and the pair had engaged in a series of lavish and outlandish portraits, vying for my attentions. As a lover, Zeuxis had displayed a natural expediency and vigour akin to the exercise of his craft. Yet Parrhasius, slower to emotion and action based solely upon his passions, demonstrated a certain perspicacity that left me pliant and most willing to please him. While Zeuxis would leap all over me like an excited water flea, Parrhasius would stand there and give me the one word or look or caress that would bend me to his sensuous will, and this was not without its wanton enjoyments. In short, I was sorry to have to leave them behind.

My new task was more daunting and worrisome. I had to make the acquaintance of the Emperor Tiberius and locate the same painting by my friend Parrhasius, now in his possession. What is more, my instructions were to steal it without anyone finding out. However, my father had already provided me with a plan for accomplishing this peculiar caper. He had instructed me to plot my coordinates for these bathhouses in the hope of getting in touch with a man named Mentulus, who was to be my veritable ticket to the Emperor's feast, or *meal ticket*. In addition, my instructions were to look for a woman named Arachnilla, who loitered about the *thermae* offering visitors a variety of services. And I was surprised to find her lingering just inside the gated entrance, poised like a tiny spider waiting to spring. I could see at once why she was known by this unseemly name. She smiled with a foul but winsome grin.

"Looking for a hot dinner, my dear ... or a smidgen of mixed bathing? Arachnilla can arrange this and so much more, for less than a few *sesterces* ..."

"Greetings. My name is Diminuenda Anodyne Minoris ... the daughter of Marcellus Domesticus Minoris."

"Minoris!"

Arachnilla curled up smaller than ever and performed a sort of bow.

"Ah, blessed be the gods who poured down the liquidy limbs of that clan! May the stock of Minoris always have a gleaming bit of *aureus* or silver to bestow upon poor Arachnilla!"

"I don't have anything right now. But I am willing to work."

Arachnilla smiled even wider, and it was hideous.

"I wouldn't dream of this. You are not some freedwoman to be bandied about and lent to the rutting lap of bather after bather! You are quality, after all. I thought for some time that Minoris would save us from a detestable Republic where a poor old woman can no longer ply her trade and make even a piece of bronze. But these are my own worries. What is it that Arachnilla can do for you? I beg you, do not hesitate to say, since the name Minoris means more than a few coins to me."

"My father …"

"Praise speed its wings to the hindmost part of Minoris!"

"My father wishes for me to be introduced to a man named Mentulus."

"Mentulus! No, not that scurrilous rogue. You don't want to get mixed up with his affairs. He has, as you will often hear or see written in the *thermae*, a terrible case of the runs, and his sore well-buggered bottom cannot keep up with the foul things that run without warning out of his mouth. No, you don't want to get mixed up with Mentulus."

"This is my father's wish."

"But why worry over an old goat like Mentulus? He's not worth one of my lusty boys, and I have three who will keep you in ecstasy afternoon and evening, and without needing to bore you with poetry while attending to you … why, out of their giant cocks flows the very milk of the gods …"

"Please, Mentulus."

"All right, Mentulus. He's due here quite soon, and believe me, I know. He's always here!"

A swarthy boy with a demented look about him appeared from behind a column.

"This is Connivus. He will assist you with preparing for your bath."

Connivus slobbered merrily over me as he removed my tunic. I handed him my underwear and bra, which were in fact from a novelty store and nowhere near enough to authentic dress. Both of them were visibly amazed at the disgrace-age material, which I tried to downplay as being from a country unknown to them. He folded these things under his arm, and then took the *calcei* from my feet with his free hand. He put my things in a dank cubbyhole and showed me a tablet with some writing on it.

"What is this?"

Arachnilla smiled.

"You must be from far away indeed, daughter of Minoris. This is a curse tablet, intended for anyone who would be so foolish as to steal your clothes. This guarantees your clothes will not be stolen. Even if they are, the gods will bring swift revenge down on the heads of the thieves in question."

I stared at the writing, and fiddled with my amulet, which had caught the attention of Connivus. The writing was instantly translated (however crudely) into English.

IUPPITER, TO THE SOUL WHO PRESUMES TO STEAL MY CLOTHING, MAY HE SIT DOWN TO DINNER LIKE TANTALUS, AND DINE UPON THE MEAT AND DRINK THE BLOOD OF HIS CLOSEST FRIENDS AND FAMILY MADE INTO A FORTIFYING PASTE, AND MERCURY, AS YOU STOLE THE HONEYED BEES OF THE GODS AND LAUGHED ABOUT IT, MAY YOU STEAL EVERYTHING FROM THIS THIEF AND THEN BUGGER HIM TO DEATH WITH A HEARTY LAUGH, AND VENUS, SHOULD YOU BRING ANY IDEA OF LOVE TO THIS THIEF, ASK YOUR WANTON BOY WITH HIS SWORD OF FREQUENT AFFECTION TO ALSO REMOVE THE SCOUNDREL'S HANDS AND PRICK, SO HE CAN NO LONGER STEAL OR EXPERIENCE ANY NEW JOY WHATSOEVER.

"That is quite the curse."

She bid me follow the boy and I was led down a long corridor to a type of dressing room they referred to as the *apodyterium*. Upon the wall were several examples of erotic artwork unique to the age. The boy Connivus scampered up and down so often that I wondered if he was not rather ill. He scrutinized one picture after another, lingering in front of a pretty fresco of a man pleasuring a woman from behind while a male acquaintance did likewise to him. He moved on to the next one of two women, depicting one fervently applying her tongue to the proffered sex of the other. There were many other positions and acts represented, and Connivus took his time slobbering in front of each of them to such a degree that any second I expected Arachnilla to appear and shake him out of his sensual reverie. At long last, he pointed to one of the numbered boxes where presumably my clothes were to go. Then, as I began to disrobe, he pointed at the picture overhead of a woman straddling the face of a little man, so I would remember where I had left my clothes. He loitered in front of my bare body for quite a long time and I felt like giving him a proper slap, but instead I shot him a withering glare, and he shrivelled up on the spot.

I was given a primitive type of thong to wear, with a matching brassiere no less, and while fastening the taut and uncomfortable material about my shivering skin, I could not help but wonder where these items had last been. It dawned on me that I might need a good bath to clean up after being in this bathhouse. Connivus bowed his head and handed me the curse tablet without raising his eyes, pointing to a small pool where I was to place this item. My father's tablet of knowledge for this time and place informed me that thieves were often frightened of these tablets and felt compelled to purchase them to ward off retribution. Then Connivus handed me a pair of sandals to wear in the bathhouse, and I guessed already from the stray currents of heat along the floor that I would probably need them.

Connivus beckoned, and I followed his hunched figure into a warmer room, known as the *tepidarium*. I sat against the walls and at once felt my body warming up. Across from me, there was a lone woman, with harsh but rather striking features. She sat down beside me, smiling broadly, and began to talk at once, making me feel we had been friends for ages. I claimed to be a stranger from a remote locale and she nodded with enthusiasm, offering to answer any questions or to help me in every way possible. She introduced herself as Pulexa and when I told her I was of the Minoris stock, she redoubled her efforts to be amiable to a member of such an illustrious family. I asked about Mentulus, and she laughed, saying that usually he was looking for a woman in the baths at this hour, and it was amusing to find a woman looking for him during the appointed time for female bathing. On that day, I was in luck, because he was on his way, intending to relax and entertain himself before a long journey.

She was sitting quite close as she spoke to me, almost in whispers, and because of her abrupt and quick movements, I scarcely noticed how her knuckles were brushing my thighs at every turn and how her lips were coming closer and closer to mine. At some point, she was in the middle of a sentence about the excitement of the circuses when she clutched my knee and started kissing my lips. Before I quite knew what was happening, she was pressing me against the warm wall and touching me passionately all over. But she stopped, withdrawing her tongue as a man in a shiny loincloth walked in on us.

"Who is your friend, little flea?"

"Ah, Mentulus, would you believe this young lady is looking for you?"

"You don't say. Yet I have no salve for this rampant epidemic. What is this pretty admirer of mine called?"

"Diminuenda Anodyne Minoris."

"Minoris! My word. This is a pleasure. Why, the name is positively dripping with pleasure, if a name may be said to be dripping with pleasure."

"Don't worry. He is a lecher in his poetry but a eunuch in the twilight."

"Ha! Ha ha! That is not bad, little flea. I might have to put that in pumice."

"Ooooh, you say hard pumice when you mean floppy *papyri*. I could go further with this comparison ..."

"Pulexa, your wit will be the end of me. But before I perish from your breath alone, might we not retire to the *caldarium*? I find the hot baths inspire heated verse, and these rooms only lukewarm elegies."

"The day you write an elegy, you will no doubt be dead."

"Ha ha ha. Then save me from myself, little flea."

Mentulus led us into the *caldarium* and immediately climbed into the hot water, leaning back as if he owned the place. Then we climbed in close to him.

"So, where is your *papyri*, then?"

"I do not need them. I have everything up here."

"I think you are pointing to the wrong end of you."

"Are you quite finished, or shall I begin?"

Pulexa splashed his face in reply.

"Bear with me. This is in imitation of one of our great defamers."

> Dear Domitilla, do not tell me your love
> is strong and lovely as sardonyx.
> I just saw you with the sweating sons
> of Simplex, my lapidary in their laps
> and what is more, eagerly lapping
> the stony boners of stonier faces
> and when you saw me smirking
> your face and body turned colour
> and resembled that raw red gem.
> I would toss you out in the street
> were I able to curse any finger
> with what grows hard and wild
> and belongs to every freedman.

"Not bad, Mentulus. This time, the idea of the quartz kept my attention."

I agreed, marvelling at the translation of my amulet, and asked if we might hear another. Mentulus now looked down and spoke more nervously and pretended to brush off his verses as those of a dilettante, although his face betrayed his delight as the loosening of his loincloth betrayed his more subtle excitement.

"Lady, if you insist …"

> Spurius, you of all my detractors
> leave me bemused and tittering,
> preparing poisonous salivations

with a tired and distracted air.
No wonder. Your mother keeps
you limp with peculiar passions
and since your uncle is also your
brother, you are without a doubt
preoccupied. Then regarding my
poetry, you parrot whatever your
precious first-born tells you in bed
while doing your rump filial duty.
For I forgive your feeble critique
but some things I cannot forgive.

"O, poor Spurius!"
"This shows that no man short on wits should dare flick his tongue in my direction."
"True, Mentulus. I should not like to be on the wrong side of your tongue."
"Ha, Pulexa, you are always on the right side of my tongue."

Arythmia, you are forever out of step
with the clashing cymbals of passion
and hear only the tympany of your
own temperament, clenching your
teeth at the slightest whisper of a
woman's name. Then you swear
at Spintria for being too sensual
and swear Cardea is far too easy
and swear Idonea loves too often
and swear Jacquetta has taken
your place, when I am like the
poetic exile by the Pontic Sea
shivering over each anxiety
and shaking off each worry.
If you want me to answer
this strange enigma without
castigating your brain with
three guesses, none of these
beauties has breath to rival

> your foul pitiless gusts, not
>   even frigid cruel Marmora.

"Ah, Mentulus, you go too far. How can you say such things about poor Arythmia?"

But I was held rapt by this poem, and said so, and elaborated upon its merits.

"Yes, but she is like a heart that is out of time, and the other women all have names that reveal their respective natures. Then he is, I believe, alluding to Ovid's exile, and equating the attributes of this woman with those of the climate and geography. It's quite clever, really."

"I say, Pulexa, you must introduce me to your friends more often. This friend must be a lover of poetry, and that is an uncommon find."

"I thought you had ladies begging for you to show them in bed what you only bellowed in verse."

"Ah yes, I have my admirers who wish to pass the time in the company of a poet, without even caring for poetry. But it is so unusual to have a ... salient ... discussion."

I smiled, thinking that perhaps Mentulus was not so bad as he was made out to be. When Pulexa strayed out to cool herself off, Mentulus leaned closer to me and began to speak in a whisper.

"I am going on a journey soon, and I was wondering, Diminuenda, if you would mind accompanying me."

"Why are you whispering?"

"It's Pulexa. She will be furious if she knows where I am going and that I didn't invite her."

"I see. But where are you going?"

"To dine with Emperor Tiberius. Just don't call him Emperor. It enrages him. Or maybe it secretly pleases him. I can never tell. Nothing formal, you understand. Just us poets and enthusiasts, alone on his little island."

"Sounds interesting."

"You will be very welcome. He loves to discuss poetry, and especially with someone so lovely. What is more, the name Minoris will mean something to him, believe me!"

I wanted to ask him what it meant, but the heat of the water and room, which was closest to the furnace, was making me drowsy. I was drifting ... and leaning upon the shoulder of Mentulus ...

I need not pepper this tale with the rare extravagances that happened in that bathhouse. Pulexa returned and for quite some time, we found ways to burn away the hours in that water. Afterward, we plunged into the cold water in the *frigidarium* and laughed with our teeth chattering, before lying down beneath new panoplies of erotic artwork to have our bodies massaged with enchanting oils and then scraped clean with curved metal strips known as strigils. After the slaves had left, Mentulus called for Arachnilla and dropped a number of *spintriae* in her palm and pressed it closed so that she could not enumerate the sexual positions on the coins until she was out of the room. We were about to say our farewells when I noticed that my clothes were missing from their numbered box.

Arachnilla looked around sheepishly for Connivus and clapped her hands together.

"Connivus! I am sorry about this, my dear. Connivus! I should have made him understand you were not like the usual filthy riff-raff we get in here. Sometimes he swipes their worthless rags to sell for a bite to eat. You can hardly blame the little imp. Connivus!"

I thought of the loss of the disgrace-age polymers and the potential effect on the course of history and shrugged. Maybe the ukini would arrive earlier than expected.

"I suppose it is all right. But what am I to wear?"

Pulexa offered to lend me a lovely cloak, and Mentulus promised to buy me a new peplos or tunic on the way. I was rather embarrassed by this situation and thanked them immensely for their kindness and generosity.

I wrapped my bare body tightly in the cloak and left with Mentulus. Then, on our way, we passed a grinning Connivus, who was biting greedily into an emmer loaf. He waved goodbye rather cheekily.

Once I had been correctly dressed, Mentulus purchased the use of a sedan, and we were carried to the city limits by a team of grunting, sweating slaves. Along the way, Mentulus made many witty remarks, and also exchanged them with passersby who appeared to know him. As promised, there was a covered wagon waiting for us. I felt sorry for the slaves, but in the same breath, I admired their display of strength. One of them seemed proud to have carried me this far and gave me an impudent wink. Mentulus rebuked him at once, and he answered only that he had some dust in his eye. I boarded the coach with four wheels, which Mentulus called a *carpentum*, and listened to him impress upon the horsemen that he was a guest of Tiberius and deserved the transportation status of an imperial messenger. The horsemen took exception to this, but in the end promised to do their best to speed us along.

However, about halfway to Naples, the horsemen stopped and made all sorts of noises about replenishing their royal guests and finding fresh horses. They pointed to an inn, as if by chance, and assured us this was as good a place as any along the roads. Mentulus at once suspected them of collusion with the owner, but he appeared to cave in and agree to their suggestion. After arranging for an evening's stay, we entered the adjacent tavern and shared some wine. Mentulus had one of the simpler patrons taste it for him, and after waiting a minute or two, waving his hands in front of the fellow's eyes, he took a long drink. We had not ordered anything, but a mysterious warm meat arrived, and neither of us felt like trying it, although we were quite hungry. Mentulus told me to follow his lead until we were out of this place, and not to trust a soul.

The owner did not hide his familiarity with the two horsemen, and many a time patted their shoulders and behinds and laughed outright, grateful for the extra income. However, when asked about their own compensation for being helpful guides, the horsemen snorted and brushed us off, seeming to be appalled by the very suggestion of such an agreement. Also, the innkeeper had a boat stationed nearby and said that if we didn't wake up (Mentulus gasped at this turn of phrase), the boat would get us to Capri with plenty of time to spare. Mentulus asked instead if we could be roused after a brief nap, since it would be faster to travel at night in the wagon, and then we could keep going through Naples, since the laws forbade these *carpentum* by day. The innkeeper swore by Janus (the god of doors that swing both ways) to wake us in time for our night journey. But neither Mentulus nor I missed the meaningful look he gave the horsemen, and we both expected them to ride off at any moment.

Once upstairs, Mentulus explained that the owner was a scoundrel and he was as likely to put us on a slave or pirate ship as find us a boat to Capri, depending on the price. In any case, we could not remain under his power a moment longer. He held up his hands and begged Mercury to help us. He also swore to Jove that if we came through this misadventure, he would cease to lay an amorous hand upon me, however mighty his appetite to do so. I was taken aback by this revelation, and almost reluctant to let him swear such a thing. But at the moment, also worried about our safety, I said a few words to Mercury. I would have stroked my amulet but I was afraid of activating the time-travel mechanism, however tempting it was to do so. After all, my goal was to get to Tiberius.

We crept downstairs and looked for a way past our dubious hosts. The innkeeper was busy and the two horsemen were gnawing at bones from whatever beast was not on the inn menu, and slurping their wine with gusto. They were slow to move and looking sleepy, and it was rather easy to slip outside without being seen. Mentulus asked if I had ever mounted a horse before and I shook my head, avoiding anachronistic revelations about mechanical beasts and offering some titillating remark about riding bareback, which he almost caught in terms of a Latin idiom. I have omitted to say that the amulet did a reverse translation of my sentiments for the listener, and that I really had no idea what I actually sounded like in the Latin tongue. Perhaps it was translating what I was thinking before I even said it! Nevertheless, he decided we should leave the wagon and horses attached for safety's sake, although it would take longer to get to Naples.

Perhaps we spent too long deciding, because the innkeeper was directly on our heels. He had an old heirloom sword from somewhere and was about to run us through when suddenly, out of nowhere, a white dog with dark spots appeared and snapped at him, biting into his sword hand. He turned to strike what he deemed was a filthy cur from the other side of the Styx, but the dog had somehow vanished and we were already at a steady gallop, thumbing our noses and making rather modern gestures at the two humiliated horsemen, who staggered back and forth in a belching cloud of dust and rage.

Our trying journey was not long in duration yet seemed interminable to my modern sensibilities. At last, we arrived at the mouth of a cave. And when I say a cave, I mean to say a massive palace, roughly hewn out of the mouth of that cave. At once, I recognized the impish face of Ganymede, the cupbearer of the gods, on one of the statues placed high above us. Beneath Ganymede, two equally stony guards stared us down.

"Strangers, state your business."

Then a dissipated man with a long beard stood up from his seat and hurried toward us.

"Hold off, men. I recognize that sly countenance. It could only be Mentulus. I thought as much. I had one of my twitchings. I always sit out here when I know someone is about to arrive."

A second man with a long beard, and hair as white as the first, appeared and shook his head in agitation.

"Kosmas, you lying fool, you were sitting out here because someone sighted a boat."

"Thrasyllus, you know you owe your life to sighting a boat. Let it alone."

At this point, I pressed forward with unbridled enthusiasm, anxious to verbalize the contents of the information pill I had popped upon my arrival in the baths.

"Thrasyllus, ah yes. You are the one who predicts the succession of your little Gaius. It is a pity you will not live to see the result of this final prophecy."

Thrasyllus looked at me apprehensively.

"Whaaa ... what? Is Tiberius going to throw me off the cliff? When? Today?"

"Do not mind her. She is toying with you, Thrasyllus."

"That's not very becoming, to tease her elder like that!"

But the one called Kosmas reached for my right arm and stroked my palm.

"Ah, but I am getting one of my twitchings. I think this lovely woman has the gift of reading the stars and foretelling what is to come."

Mentulus squeezed the arm of Kosmas with an air of affection.

"Then let her predict a table of dishes, for we have had a long and perilous journey and are positively famished. Now, allow me to introduce you to Diminuenda Anodyne Minoris …"

"Minoris?"

Kosmas smiled warmly, still stroking my arm.

"I knew your father, my dear. When he was the scandal of the bathhouse!"

"Now, where is our fair emperor?"

Thrasyllus looked around nervously and then leaned in with a hushed voice.

"He's brooding on the cliffs. And between you and me, I am concerned. He has put everything into the hands of that … Sejanus. I have warned him about that man, but he will not listen for the life of him. Ah yes, you hail from Rome. What are your thoughts about the state of affairs there?"

Mentulus waved his hands about indifferently.

"The usual, crucifixions and taxes."

"And Sejanus?"

"Am I to dine here, or cut out my own tongue and serve myself?"

"Quite right, we will set about making the preparations."

But Thrasyllus stopped.

"See that stone there? That stone fell from up there. And Sejanus, wily schemer that he is, threw himself over Tiberius to protect him from it."

"Are you suggesting Sejanus has some extraordinary power over stones and can make them fall at will?"

"If his will is in it, no doubt *that* man will find a means."

Kosmas squeezed my hand.

"ἠλύθομεν τόδ᾽ ὑπ᾽ ἄντρον ὑπόστεγον."

" 'And then we came upon a roofed cave …' "

"My, you certainly know your Greek. It's Empedocles, my favourite poet."

"So you are also interested in poetry."

"Indeed. I am really more of a poet than a prophet, if one thing is not the other."

Thrasyllus scowled.

"They are *not* the same thing."

"Assuredly not. Tiberius keeps me here to entertain him with my poetry. He keeps Thrasyllus here to tell him the sun is going to rise in the morning."

"Watch yourself, Kosmas. We never know when our own private sun is suddenly going to set. Especially in this place."

Kosmas nodded with a touch of solemnity, stopping in front of a statue of a warrior lifting his dead comrade out of the dust. Then, with his hand over his heart, he began reciting one of his poems from memory:

> Narrow are the gullies of our short life
> and as treacherous our preoccupations
> on this all too brief journey through.
>
> The will of the wicked, just like that of
> the good, turned back at every turning
> by the contrary elements of our world.
>
> We smile with sails full of squalls
> icy tumult cannot reach, or so we
> say, in saying we know everything.
>
> Yet the discreet truth of the future
> is broader than our narrow senses
> know, beyond our thwarted will.

It was then that a tall man with a shrewd face joined our company. His face was fixed into a crooked grin but his eyes shone with restrained anger as he answered in kind:

> It's more than a proper mishmash, Kosmas!
> You used to be satisfied doing nothing all
> day with your boy and girl. Now they've run
> off together, you philosophize about nothing
> and dictate to us about the nature of nothing
> What do I want from you, Kosmas? *Nothing*.

Kosmas sat me down beside him and clasped my hand with both of his.

"So it is, and often is the case, that a barbed tongue pricks itself and bids the mouth shout truth in surprise. I cannot deny my being a bit lonely on these cold nights ..."

Mentulus sidled up against me, reminding me he was definitely still there.

"Diminuenda, this is Ancus Valerius Libellus. You're not likely to get much more out of him than a dozen epigrams."

"Charming!"

Libellus, without altering his smile in the slightest, turned toward Mentulus with a raised voice.

> Who is that stealing in the door?
> Mentulus, I didn't recognize you
> by your loathsome features alone.
> Like Priapus, you enter *head*-first!

Thrasyllus shook his head and pointed his walking stick at the poet. "Take heed, Libellus! Your smart answers will one day be the end of you!" Then as he turned around, Libellus launched another epigram at his back:

> The last time he told the truth
> Thrasyllus got a sound thrashing.
> The last time he told twenty lies
> Thrasyllus got a sound thrashing.
> Thrasyllus is quite the soothsayer.
> He can always foresee a thrashing.

Thrasyllus lifted his stick, fully prepared to instruct Libellus in the brand of eloquence a real thrashing might provide, but hesitated at the sight of another man in a tattered tunic and ratty sandals. As this man joined our company, Kosmas pinched my arm and pulled me closer.

"This is the much esteemed Septimus Pomponius, although I warn you to take care. His mistress Crassitilla is no longer speaking to him. He claims she accuses him of creating false arguments and drama in order to complete additional volumes of poetry. I advise you to watch what you say, or else you may become the subject of his next eighty-nine elegies!"

The poet slowly approached, lifting a roll of *papyri* over his face and fanning his heavy sighs.

"Septimus, this is Diminuenda, the charming daughter of Minoris."

"Minoris? Praise his name and everyone so fortunate at love's cruel games! Ahh ... this Diminuenda has eyes like those of my Crassitilla, except darker, and her skin is a healthier shade ... but how can I even speak of another woman when I only want to talk of Crassitilla ..."

"He will carry on like this until we let him read his poem."

Septimus squeezed my hand and studied it with a glint of admiration in his eyes.

"Ah yes, my poem! That it would bring her back to me! She will no longer grant me an audience, so I must make do with emperors! She will no longer let me haunt about her door in even the foulest weather!"

"Are you so sure of your audience, Septimus?"

At this remark, Septimus dropped my hand and began to read from his roll of *papyri*:

> Muddy drunkards stumble along my road
> beating me with their grimy fists, howling
> insults, threatening fire, finally hurling up
> restless meals upon my threshold. Could
> a door recollect, I would certainly recall
> better times than these, perhaps as arch
> of triumph, or even beloved entrance
> in Etruria, where being a doorway to
> the dead would be a welcome chore.

> Nor can I apologize for my lady
> leaning out the window, egging
> on the concert of drunken cats
> downing a murder of squawking
> birds. She blames the murderous
> age, tempting them just the same
> save for the fool who with bitter
> complaints teaches me concern
> in spite of his insinuating songs:

> *Janus, god of stubborn doorways,*
> *you with the lone power to remove*
> *the one obstacle between me and*
> *the woman within, since I cannot*
> *coax this door to step away from*
> *itself, would you strike it down*
> *for me? Ordinarily I would lose*
> *sleep, even over the destruction*
> *of a mere door, especially if it*

were my friend. But I know this
door knows no pity for countless
tears of love warping its wood
and endlessly aging its joints.

Ah, if only you would fashion
a large enough hole, through
which both of us could find
some measure of satisfaction,
or if not that, a cleft, through
which complimentary breath
could pass, and reach the
burning ears of my love
and warm her everywhere.

Or at least force the door
and let me see if she is out.
Then I will know she lies
in the arms of the lucky
and that I am the most
inconsolable creature
to creep past her door
a shadow of shadows
moaning in the gloam.

He is the only one waiting
until the first bird of dawn
and I tremble to wait with
him, knowing only scandal
within and rumour beyond,
the most knocked of doors.

Libellus paused, which seemed a show of respect, before reciting another short epigram:

> Pomponius is puffed up in positive
> paroxysms of pleasure, like a little
> bark without an oak, spit from the
> foul storm, glad to still be babbling.

At this point, a rather handsome man in a very fine tunic made his way toward our party. He also appeared to have some writing ready to share at the first request. Kosmas sidled up to me again with even less of a grandfatherly air.

"This is Pollex Blandus. I suggest you trust him only a few drops less than Pomponius. His erotic verses are always attracting censure. Recently, his scandalous *Orgiarium* has landed him in a number of nasty situations."

Pollex paced up and down and pointed at a large and complicated marble that portrayed Scylla devouring the men of Odysseus.

"This is the story of women and their love! Look how the lovers crowd about her and look how she ruins each of them in turn! It is no different with my beloved Ambivia! She is coming to my reading with another man, although she assures me it means nothing. Well, this is what I have to say to her!"

With that, Pollex Blandus clung to the Scylla and read his verse:

> So, you are bringing someone to supper!
> Your lover? I will not be able to wrest
> my eyes from your every movement
> and when from my side of the table
> you hear growling, do not think it
> is on account of my empty belly!
>
> I have until now been immobile,
> man of marble and example to all
> yet you render me a milky Galatea
> with solid principles springing into
> passions, melting at a single word …
>
> O I am sure he is a splendid fellow
> although he bores me to tears with

long-winded harangues that never
reach their windy destination. Are
you claiming they reach your ears?

Tell you what. Why don't you smile
and nod at his silliest of suggestions?
Meanwhile, teach me the verboten
language of your body, and lend me
the complete attention of your eyes.

That braggart will hardly notice. So
let him talk the torches out of their
light, while you apply drink to your
lips, mouthing sensuous promises
across, of future nights to arrive ...

Rub my foot with yours and cry
out, calling it accident. Rub my
foot again. Yes, again, like two
lovers just getting acquainted
let us take our delectable time.

Let the wine be our language.
Even bibulous Antonius, who
died for love, could not imbibe
the entire outpouring of desire
between our disparate states.

But this triumvirate has one
too many heads, and I advise
driving out the emptiest head
drooping toward a deep sleep
that idiot sleep of inebriates.

Do not let him touch you
since the most brutal torture

is nothing to watching that
greedy ignoble hand, pawing
your wealth of lovely charms.

No, do not let him kiss you!
Push away his avaricious lips.
Make complaint of his breath.
As for things I cannot see
do not cheat under the table.

I know innumerable modes
of this kind of gratification.
This is my source of terror,
that of a torturer suddenly
attached to his own rack.

I know more than anyone
the secrets an open cloak
can procure, and private
entertainments enjoyed
beneath the finest tunic.

I do not wish the man dead
since he is half-dead already
and boring himself into a
permanent snore, leaving
time enough for our love.

However, ensure he drinks
double, triple, or quadruple
your measure. Then you rise
to go, abandoning that man
to find me in the confusion.

But what horror if his snores
wake him up and in a snit

he seizes your hand and
accompanies you home
before our hour is up!

Then perhaps he will taste
your lips, and perhaps more
than your lips. Only if you
must surrender, tell me in
the morning it was *terrible*.

This time, Libellus was hastier to react with his own short invective:

Antistius sucks while Sibellus sodomizes.
Turpia implores them to swap positions.
Everybody earns their keep but Blandus
who sponges dinners with their *leftovers*.

Kosmas eased his arm gently around my waist and coaxed me in the direction
of another giant marble sculpture. His voice was now a hushed whisper.
"My dear, look at this image of Odysseus blinding Polyphemus. The Cyclops
is a lesson to us all not to be too narrow in our views. Yes, the overwhelming
arrogance of Odysseus that follows is another lesson, since we should think
ourselves no better than frightened men hitched to the underbellies of sheep."
Libellus laughed and responded with yet another sardonic sally:

Kosmas is rather a shrewd old fart
so very wise even his farts are wise!
Whenever he is molesting fresh pupils
in the baths you can hear every bubble!

Kosmas was about to reply, but instead he fell silent with a wry grin. He put
his arm around my shoulders and looked at me with a sad, distant expression.
Then he appeared to improvise his own poem:

Forgive the insubordination of an old-timer ...
I am like a cracked dial that can no longer
read the angle of the sun without confusing it

with its own shadow. Forgive my muddy talk,
but what is it we are teaching the young? To
flatter, Blandus? To be pompous, Pomponius?
To smile and smile and cut a throat, Libellus?
Am I the only one to muddy the knowledge
of the past? If my philosophy is *nothing*, is
this not the fashion of our time, to master
the rhetoric of our masters to the point of
saying *nothing*? Do we expect instruction
in fantasy will endow our men with sense,
or expect ground flour from feeble chaff?
Will these sacks of wind fill the bellies
of our sons, leaving their minds fallow?
Then at the mercy of passing thieves
and *flamines* (is there any difference!)
at the whim of the slightest portent
or superstition, are we to call these
misguided and brashly flatulent asses
our upstanding examples of morality?
In the face of every conflict, we lift
our hands to the heavens and blame
the gods for our unbound bloodshed
and sacrifice our daughters to stone
and sword for the sake of old fables.
Who would watch their beloved be
wrenched away to her doom without
tears, in a state of perfect tranquility,
confident in the woodland goddess?
Heed not *flamines* and rhetoricians
who teach us to flatter the forgotten
names of creaky gods, and live by
their fickle codes, in dust and filth.
We humour these clay deities, only
to achieve our own twisted dreams,
and I do not expect times to ever
be worse than these. Yes, for this

reason, I am glad to be nearing the
end of my life, although nothing
ever truly ends, or was, to begin
with. A composition of *nothing*,
I will return to my origins about
us, to the long perpetual nothing
which never waits, yet simply *is*.

All of our company was speechless after hearing this poem, save for a poet
I later learned was called Priscus Rectus, who attempted an epigram in answer:

Kosmas is a dusty old tome indeed!
I need no philosophy in the mouth
of lovers, only a warm, able tongue
proffered by his tastier successors.

Libellus responded by giving Rectus a kick for his lack of respect and sending
an epigram after him:

Who can argue with the earthy verses
of Rectus? He is a poet composed of
elemental compost. Even the stinkers
cannot take the wind out of Rectus!

Then a team of strong, handsome lads appeared and prepared a place for us
to start feasting. I was surprised at the speed with which they worked. Their eyes
did not wander once and they did not say a word. Kosmas beckoned me to take a
place next to him and bid me lie down on my left side. Mentulus looked irritated
at the excessive amount of attention Kosmas was paying to me and nestled in on
my right. As for me, I was not used to being in the midst of such eccentric and
jocular company and did not really mind being sandwiched between these two
respected poets. I say *sandwiched* because Kosmas was gently stroking my back
and shoulders while Mentulus offered to feed me olives and honeyed treats from
the vast antepast laid out before us. Meanwhile, I could not stop ogling some of
the astoundingly beautiful slaves. I wondered if their lives were pure drudgery
or if this was in fact half-decent labour for them. I studied each face and tried
to guess whether any of them would be freed and one day become an owner of
other souls. They remained impassive and aloof and this made them even more

appealing to me. I also observed the hint of envy on the faces of the other poets sitting across from me and reminded myself that women were seldom invited here as official guests. In spite of this honour, my thoughts strayed to historical accounts of unsatisfied wives like Julia, who defied the law in her own name to consort with licentious poets and anonymously scour the streets, taking on dozens of lovers. I was rather piqued to imagine having that power and freedom to fulfill every fantasy to excess, to enjoy an erotic poem and immediately capitalize upon it. Also, it was hard to be objective with Kosmas casually stroking my skin and Mentulus urging me to sip more wine. Much to the consternation of the poets and philosophers, a few more men filed in and reached for some piping-hot sausages. They bit into them greedily, without much consideration for their scorched fingers or tongues.

Thrasyllus instantly began to shoo away the newcomers.

"You are welcome, Otho! But as for the rest of you legacy hunters and shameless informants, we have nothing but day-old mullet for you! Especially you, Vagnius!"

The sly face of the man named Vagnius looked up from his helpings.

"Thrasyllus, are you so troubled? I only offer admonitions about earthly matters. You inform upon the stars themselves!"

Kosmas knelt closer and told me that Rome was replete with these *delatores* who made their fortune spreading gossip and informing upon their neighbours and friends. You could not say a word at a dinner party without one of them distorting what you said into a vicious attack. My head had begun to swim with wine, and for this reason, I remember fragments of what was said, but not always who the speaker was.

"Isn't Tiberius planning to dispose of the *delatores*?"

"To what end? Without their false charges, Sejanus would have no one to toss into the Tiber!"

"Or to crucify!"

"And where is our most gracious host?"

"Probably brushing up on the naughtiest verses of Elephantis!"

"A fair and notorious poetess!"

"I warrant he is acting out every one of the illustrations!"

"Then his appetite will be barely whetted …"

Epigrams were launched between mouthfuls, including this one:

> You really chide a rutting goat
> chasing kids in the Caprineum
> while you fleas upon his back
> suck each favour second-hand!

"Are we so vile, for wanting to pay our respects and devour our free bowl of fruit?"

"But do not think our benefactor is so hard-hearted. After being forced to divorce Vipsania, he shadowed her in the street with tears in his eyes."

"May each man suffer who has the misfortune to fall in love with his own wife!"

"Well, it's hardly fashionable."

At that moment, I recall one of the legacy hunters waggling a pair of wine-soaked sausages in my direction and giggling maniacally.

"Treat this woman well. She is the daughter of Minoris."

"Ah, is that the same Minoris who wishes only to restore the Republic?"

"Rubbish! You know that's a filthy lie!"

"I should have recognized her by her sensuous looks."

"Perhaps she knows a few pages of Elephantis!"

"Yes, I am certain she could demonstrate each technique for a select few …"

Everyone fell silent as a tall, broad-shouldered man appeared in a loose-fitting tunic with purple stripes upon it. He did not speak for a long time and no one dared to break the weighty silence. I recognized from some of the statues and coins that this must be the Emperor Tiberius, although his facial discolouration and scrofulous appearance contrasted sharply with the noble profiles everywhere else. But there was something strong and slow and deadly about each of his movements, made even more primitive by the surrounding cave.

"Friends, do carry on with your conversation. A lofty subject, no doubt."

"We were just discussing this guest that Mentulus snuck in with him. Apparently, she is Diminuenda, the fair daughter of Minoris."

The Emperor smiled warmly.

"I would say Minoris is far too lucky at dice, except no one has ever made me laugh so much while taking my money! He is a paragon of desire, and his daughter follows after him!"

"You are really too kind."

"Talking of desire, who chopped up his own son and tried to feed him to the gods?"

"You are thinking of Tantalus, yes? He was punished and had to live with fruit and water out of reach, in a perpetual state of desire."

Tiberius frowned for a moment, then relaxed his face.

"You haven't been brushing up on your myths, have you? Some fellows have tried to find out what I'm reading beforehand. I despise cheaters. I had no choice but to toss them into the sea."

"I must have been lucky with that one."

"Just like your father. The bright are not always wise, and neither are they always beautiful, but you happen to be all three."

"Surely you flatter!"

"No, I hate those who flatter more than those who cheat. Now, what were you discussing? Did they shower you with love poems yet?"

"They touched upon the subject, yes."

"What about Otho? More wine! Why don't you read us something, Otho?"

The servants brought the wine while Otho, a sinewy man in his sixties, cleared his throat.

"I have some epistles here, and one broaching the subject of wisdom and the desire for a happy life."

Tiberius downed his wine in one gulp, purpling even more than before.

"When we were sorting out those Pannonian barbarians, the men used to call me Biberius Caldius Mero, because of my thirst for warm undiluted wine."

"How amusing, Tiberius!"

"All right, if you're going to read something, get on with it, Otho!"

Obviously, I could not recollect the words that Otho read, so I had to resort to the *Discreet Annals of Minoris*, where several versions of his epistle are presented. This is the best version that I could find:

> You accuse me of being wise, since I take ages to cultivate each thought and set each one down in a form that woos perpetuity, and often you ask for the secret of my wisdom and for a guide to leading such a life. Just as often, I am loath to provide an answer, for fear of offence, since one life is really the same as another, in the eyes of its owner, and mine suits me perfectly. I only know that I do not accost the builder of temples and ask him his secret when deciding the shape of the podium and columns and pediment. Nor do I expect to immediately understand the many intricacies of architecture in Greece or Etruria, or how this learning would apply to the nature of our own dwellings. Nor do I expect my hands to instantly possess the education of the builder, whose real teacher has been one heavy block of stone after another.

> So it is with me, since fate has afforded me with a love of philosophy and a love for reckoning the valve of expressions, like a merchant with his scales, trying to decide the value of one thing weighed against another. When I do discover something of worth, I take note of it in my book of accounts, with the aim of making this verbal list of balances available to more eyes than my own.

At first glance, this might appear an act of vanity, a notion that like an overripe tree still bears some fruit. But we do not apply this accusation of vanity so readily to the column supporting a frieze full of gods and beasts in the midst of their adventures. However, is not a well-formed thought or a crafted line of verse just as beautiful and worthy of exhibition? And is not this line of thought, whether dipped wet upon *papyri* or melted warmly into wax or beaten firmly into pumice, even more humble in its beauty to behold, in the face of some ostentatious memorial built under the fickle lash of a wealthy former slave without a whit of taste?

Then by mid-morning, you are yawning ferociously, and asking me why I rose so early only to scribble down my first thoughts when my nose was buried in a book until dawn. You ask me why I experience an abrupt attack of desperation in the face of a crowd, and suddenly wish to be alone. Still, you do not go to the games without expecting to see magnificent beasts and more than a few sanctioned murders. So it is with me, waiting in the arena of thought for a magnificent thought to arrive with its own fanfare, to the point that I feel alone in the crowd, held rapt by my own private spectacle. Afterward, I go crying through the streets like a madman, wanting to drop this shadow of an idea at every door.

Now, you wonder what such a life requires. Truly, the sustenance for any man is the same. I would advise periods of fasting, since prolonged feasting and drinking tends to make one sluggish and eventually devoid of desire to undertake any studious or serious task. Take each thing in measure and in its own time. For never was there a route to poetry or philosophy with too much traffic at the same time. If there is anything of merit, it most often comes to an attentive meditative soul, who, through years of self-discipline, learns only to listen for the apparition of his masterwork, which nonetheless arrives in mere scraps at a time. So, then, patience and labour are the *opus caementicium* that keep these materials together.

As for your questions about my immortality, whether my name will be remembered or not is irrelevant to me. The thought of being remembered is pleasing and yet, after my demise, completely useless to me. Since I shun the uncouth rabble who would not deign to approach my writings with any element of propriety, it is not any more probable I will be understood by anyone in the future, other than a soul bearing similarity to myself. Without question, it is a pleasing idea that someone might read my thoughts in the future in the manner in which I have read the thoughts of my predecessors, imagining for the moment that we two are fine, agreeable friends.

When you ask me what you should think or write about, I have no answer for you. The subject should be apparent to you based on your own passions and interests. I will only say that the politics and wars of the day will disperse like grains of sand and that society will never shy away from making the same mistakes for what seem to be different reasons in very different eras from ours. Then celebrate the interior world of your mind, and keep time to the beating of your own heart. For when you are at the end of your life, and the fashion of the throng has passed, and statesmen and despots have met their demise, this sound of your own heart and this world of your mind are the only effects you will have that cannot be wrenched away from your frail limbs. These gifts, in the company of an excellent book, will be your lifelong friends.

Otho put down his *papyri* and everyone murmured agreeably, except Tiberius. Even Libellus appeared moved by this finely wrought epistle and answered in kind:

> When pretty lips are loose with wine
> and when carousing heads are whirling
> Otho dilutes his overwhelming words
> with a clarity brighter than the Tiber.

Tiberius did not speak for a while. Then he clapped his hands together for more wine.

"Since you approve so much of this man, we cannot let his speech go unrewarded!"

"We only meant his words would come second to yours, Tiberius!"

"Nonetheless, prepare him for our dining entertainment!"

Two slaves led Otho away while another refilled our cups. Kosmas, who had begun to look worried, forced a smile and addressed Tiberius.

"Diminuenda has displayed an aptitude for divining the stars ..."

Just then, the main course was set down and the servants cut helpings for each of us. Tiberius stared at me rather stonily.

"Did you know we were going to fill our bellies with leftover boar?"

"No, Tiberius."

"Then do you have some prophecy for me, daughter of Minoris?"

"I am tentative about troubling you with it."

"Minoris always had an uncanny ability for reading the heavens. Come now, what is it?"

"Beware of Sejanus."

"Sejanus? But he's my most trusted man!"

"Then I will not speak ill of him, except to say that not long from now, you will receive a letter from Antonia. As I care for your well-being and that of Rome, I urge you to heed the contents of this letter without hesitation."

Tiberius did not reply and everyone returned their full attention to their bit of boar while a troupe of scantily clad young men and women surrounded us and began to dance suggestively. Mentulus informed me in a mocking tone that it was a rare privilege to meet the multitalented *meretrices*, who were more accustomed to awaiting imperial pleasures in hidden catacombs. However, as he ogled three glistening figures miming several acts of fornication, I could sense his brimming envy.

"Tonight they are certainly behaving themselves!"

"The oily antepast to the hindmost portion of a leftover goat?"

Priscus Rectus was so excited he sprang up and addressed the writhing, gesticulating figures.

> Let us celebrate these crazed artists
> encouraging their contortionist tricks!
> They make heads spin and flush flesh
> more than a whole amphora of wine!

Tiberius smirked at this feeble libation (while many of the more accomplished poets muttered maledictions into their cups) and seized a *meretrix* by the hips. The ageless man-boy took refuge in his lap and wiggled his buttocks obscenely, permitting the Emperor to fondle his scarcely concealed charms under a flapping cut of cloth. I recall that my attention was drawn to this aroused dancer when a scream was heard, followed by a sizable splash.

"There, daughter of Minoris! Did you know I was going to do that?"

"Do what, Tiberius?"

"Chuck Otho from the cliffs?"

"Err ... no, Tiberius."

"I had no issue with the wise old fellow. But you cannot go around saying whatever pops into your head, thinking you can do without wars and politics and statesmen. This kind of thinking, when it is left unchallenged, becomes deadly to the welfare of Rome. Now he'll hold his tongue before making such claims in future ..."

Kosmas asked quietly if Otho would be all right.

"A heap of bones or a broken skull ... how do I know? We all know our duty and how to best serve it through our unwavering discipline."

Priscus Rectus and Vagnius agreed that the best verses were found in poetry honouring war campaigns in full support of the outstanding administration. Meanwhile, the other poets and prognosticators tried to look less ill at ease.

"Let us dedicate something to Tiberius!"

"No, not now, friends. Let us retire to a more comfortable setting for more wine and more delectable pleasures, for I have never understood why these bloody entertainments excite me so!"

The nervous company moved carefully past a number of statues of lascivious centaurs and satyrs with outlandishly large parts. I was quite keen to steal away into the Emperor's bedroom to get my hands on that painting. However, I could see Kosmas was concerned about the tragedy involving Otho. Although I felt an impulse to commiserate with him, part of me was surprised and intrigued by what the Emperor had done, based on a mere whim. I was actually attracted, not to the rather repugnant Emperor himself, but to the brute power that ran through him, probably with the faint hope of somehow wresting it away from him. The notion of stealing one of his favourite treasures was even more thrilling. It was a rather sophisticated conceit to pinch a portrait that I had inspired in another era, and in spite of the obstacles he had created for me, for not the first time I admired my father's wicked sense of irony.

Naturally, I had formed the germ of a plan to sneak away from the others, but before enacting it, I was exposed to a scene which I must pause to describe, even in meagre detail. I had not given much thought to the Ancient Roman view toward buggery, but Tiberius was not backward about citing Julius as the conquered queen of Nicomedes who in the end wrenched Bithynia from his grasp with no other army than amatory forces. Speaking of which, an army of "reinforcements" was marching in through a number of connected rooms. My amulet was not shy about filling me in on the taxonomic divisions of incoming prostitutes, including *aelicariae* who handed out cakes in the shape of sexual organs, *ambubiae* who regaled us with deep-throated song, *bustuariae* who would solemnly take on all mourners during a ceremony for our departed Otho, *citharistriae* and *cymbalistriae* who were plucking and clanging their instruments as a form of foreplay, *diobolares* for the downtrodden who liked a bit of rough, *fellatrices* who were less impressive at this particular moment, *gallinae* who like the *fellatrices* reminded me of the painting in the bedroom and my need to nab it very soon, and *mimae* who silently acted out what was on offer. There must have been even more varieties of pleasure-bringers but my head was spinning at that point and I could not keep track. Tiberius seized a stripling with a rather demented look about him and used his waggling backside to incite his passion, which had like him the characteristic of being slow to action, and was, presumably, as powerful and deadly once prompted. It took no stretch of the imagination to picture him defiling his victims in turn and then tossing them from the cliffs as soon as he was sated, in the manner of a wastrel throwing away nibbled bits of fruit. I was again startled to find myself intrigued and overwhelmed by this idea, rather than horrified.

Suffice it to say that no one could remain entirely aloof to this procession of *show horses*, selected for their combination of beauty and expertise, who endeavoured to outshine one another in generous displays of lechery. Male and female youths were offering up their moist parts to more than one man at once. One adorable lady glared at me and gave me a playful kiss, whispering to me softly in an unknown tongue, before abandoning herself to three lovers who obeyed her every gesture and were swiftly encouraged to take their pleasure in whichever place they wished. Things went similarly with a tall, handsome Nubian man who followed suit by taunting me with a lingering kiss before surrendering to a short, determined couple, who attended to his immediate needs on either side of him. It is noteworthy to mention the sublime choreography that was demonstrated by each daisy chain of cavorting bodies. Once they had linked up, each unit in the chain maintained a steady rhythm and I felt put to shame for my own graceless experiences in the global voyeur game. I was particularly struck by pairs of male and female contortionists who curled up into perfect circles and tasted each other's dripping sexes in tandem. Many of the cries and groans evaded the translation protocols of my amulet and yet they all seemed to be part of a universal language.

Nor was the Emperor neglected. Tiberius simply stared at me while multiple men and women feverishly attended to his lower half with their lips and tongues and hands. I found it quite ironic that such a charmless tyrant could appear to be deified in this instant, especially while puppeteering two other squealers with his fingers. The woman moaned for every movement of his hand between her thighs and the man yelped for every rectal adjustment and variation. Given his terrible reputation, I suspected that Tiberius was showing a great deal of restraint where I was concerned, due to my illustrious family name. I was less fortunate with some of the *meretrices*, who pulled me into one of their writhing daisy chains, and it was quite the ordeal extricating myself before partaking in a number of scenarios more scandalous than any I had observed upon the walls of the *apodyterium*. However, once free, with my clothes more than askew, I took the left hand of Mentulus and the right hand of Kosmas and made a show of leading them off down a long corridor, which immediately engendered raucous laughter and deafening applause. One little deviant with a gargantuan organ watched us leave with a sickening cackle, never lifting his trembling paw from his undulating instrument, before most effusively ejaculating in the face of not one but five devoted supplicants.

Upon entering the Emperor's sumptuous bedroom, I emitted a gasp of surprise at once again seeing Parrhasius's painting of myself in a most compromising position, depicted as Atalanta upon her knees, attending to the ardent passion of Meleager after the invigorating boar hunt. Mentulus misinterpreted my reaction, perhaps suspecting that my delicate sensibilities were being wickedly challenged by the subject matter, when in fact the model and I had enjoyed several other acts which even Mentulus might have deemed cruel and unnatural.

"That painting never fails to shock its visitors. I understand it was bequeathed to Tiberius with the condition that if he were offended, he would receive a million *sesterces* instead. As you can see, he kept the painting, and you are as enchanting as the woman depicted in it."

While speaking, Mentulus sidled up to me and kissed my neck and shoulders, laying strong hands upon my breasts and massaging them in steady circles. My body began to react to his advances while my mind was wheeling elsewhere at great haste. While Kosmas watched with inert but interested consternation, Mentulus caressed and rubbed my charms, breathing soft verses all over me.

"Diminuenda, you know I have waited for this moment for ages ..."

"Yes, you have no idea how right you are. But surely you do not take me for one of those professional analists in the other room who promise one thing and then do another as soon as a higher price is fixed."

"No, of course not. Did you think I took you for one of the *forariae*? One of the *delicatae* or *famosae* at the very least! Or one of those temptresses who teaches us how to worship Venus. Properly!"

"Mentulus, look upon this lewd painting by Parrhasius, and know that I will do a thousand things more exciting, things that would even shock Elephantis to consider, so long as you do exactly as I wish."

"What do you ask of me, my lady?"

"I need your help to take this painting down."

"Take it down? Why?"

"I intend to steal it."

At the peak of his passion, Mentulus suddenly seemed to shrivel up. He looked at me imploringly for a minute before shaking his head.

"I cannot do that, Diminuenda. I have done many questionable things in my time, but stealing this prized work from my host would be too much for me.

I will not stop you in what you are planning to do, but with heavy regret, I must insist that we part company."

Mentulus left without another word and I watched him go with disbelief. Kosmas smiled sadly and clasped my hand tighter.

"Do not be vexed with him, my dear Diminuenda. He is a talented poet at the height of his powers and he needs all the social influence he can garner. He puts on a brash front, but he is by no means immune to the ill effects of having witnessed far too many of his peers tossed from the cliffs to their doom. I only wish you had asked me to help you instead. At my time of life, the company of a fickle Emperor cannot contest the company of the most enchanting young woman I have ever met. And yes, beautiful ..."

Kosmas embraced me firmly and began fondling and stroking me exactly as Mentulus had.

"Mmm ... then you will help me?"

"If you are offering me a thousand pleasures, how can I in any good conscience refuse?"

"I was actually lying to Mentulus. But you are a great comfort to me, Kosmas."

"We are both foreigners in this place. I am from Rhodes, originally, and before that, a vast desert. Therefore, I welcome the chance to encounter turbulent seas in your arms, my dear. Only, where are we to go?"

"First, we need to get this painting down on the stone where I can set up a rudimentary temporal insulation field."

"I am not certain I understand."

"Have no fear, Kosmas. I am going to totally blow your mind ..."

Seconds later, when Tiberius burst into his empty bedroom covered in sexual acrobats and sopping little *minnows*, to his surprise and anger, he realized that his favourite painting had utterly vanished.

V

There was a man named Hrafn, son of Ulf the Unpredictable and Freyja the Fiery. Hrafn was a dark and wilful man, and in his younger years he put his mind to freebooting and his dark sails became a scourge to stranger and neighbour seafarers alike. Yet no one could have foretold his freebooting days would end, or that he would return to his estate at Grimfjord with all his wealth and take Unnur to wife. And it was said of Hrafn that he proved a great holder of lands without sly dealings. He oversaw his workers and smiths with gentle laughter, and was not stingy with his wise counsel for those who sought it. Yet in the evening, he grew moody and ill-tempered, and even Unnur took care to step lightly around him. In Grimfjord, it was told of Hrafn that he was strong of shape and shared the changeling ways of his father, and that while everyone on the estate was sleeping, he enjoyed unspeakable mirth and mischief.

Hrafn Ulfsson and his wife Unnur had two sons. The elder was named Sindri, and the younger, Loki. They were both tall and strong enough, and Sindri was fair in complexion and cheery in manner, not unlike his mother. But Loki was swarthy like his father, with dark and incongruous features. He also displayed a gloomy disposition after dusk. Sindri had been named for his ease of birth, since he brought Unnur little trouble. But his brother brought his mother so much trouble at his time of birth that a lamp was tipped over and a small fire started.

"This does not bode well for us," said Unnur.

"He may be as great as the fire god Loki, who threatens all the gods," offered Hrafn.

"Then we should name him Loki," replied Unnur.

"I like that idea fine," said Hrafn.

Hrafn had a sister named Sigyn who dwelt in a simple home near the cavernous crags of Grimfjord. Most people of the Ulfsson estate regarded her as an eccentric who was more than set in her ways and they took great care to avoid her. Other desperate souls sought her out for cures and curses, since she was rumoured to be a seeress with magical abilities. As a boy, Loki enjoyed visiting her, and people of the region say she taught him many dark arts. One day they were concentrating over a wooden game board when Sigyn tapped him with her long stick.

"I have cast your rune," said Sigyn. "Would you like to hear it?"

"If something is on your mind, best make it known," answered Loki.

Then she spoke a verse:

> Son of Hrafn, you are dark indeed
> as the shadow of a crashing wave.

> Yet take heed! Your namesake is
> consuming fire that threatens all.
> In the arms of one kind woman
> you will find cool, still comfort
> but beware of the brooch thief!
> She will take far more than this.

"Sigyn, how does this feeble verse concern me?" demanded Loki.

"I cannot make sense for someone who makes no sense," replied Sigyn.

After this incident, Sigyn no longer asked Loki to visit her. She is now out of the saga.

The next summer, Loki was tending to some of his father's sheep when he noticed a girl observing him. He made strange faces and voices at her and made her laugh. Her eyes were lively and he chased her in an attempt to touch her. In the end, she swung a water pail at him and a broken iron binding scratched his left thigh quite deeply. Blood gushed from the cut and Loki gave up his pursuit.

His mother was tending to his wound with a cure she had learned from the seeress when Loki began to make inquiries.

"Mother, who is the strange girl gathering water near our sheep?" asked Loki.

"Adalbjorg is your foster sister from a match best forgotten," said Unnur.

"A man could do worse than betrothing her," replied Loki.

"It will come to trouble, but you never took advice well," retorted Unnur.

The next morning, Loki was waiting in the same place with his sheep when he saw Adalbjorg passing with her bent water pail. Then he spoke this verse:

> She cut deep and to the quick,
> this beautiful bringer of water.
> Look at this painful wound,
> no match for another pain!
> I suffer whenever she flees
> a fire in my raging blood.
> Were I to desire one wife
> let her name be Adalbjorg.

Then he reached for her and gave her a quick kiss. This time she did not withdraw or hurry away. She did not find Loki as irritating as he was reported to be.

That evening, Unnur crept up to Hrafn and told him of Loki's intention to select Adalbjorg for himself.

"I do not like it, but that boy is stubborn," said Hrafn.

"Some say he takes after his father," answered Unnur.

"I'm not keen about asking Atli until we know what kind of man Loki is," offered Hrafn.

"Let him travel with his uncle. Then he might forget about this girl," said Unnur.

"I don't want to talk about it any longer," said Hrafn.

Thororm Ulfsson was planning a voyage to Vinland, since these expeditions were considered a good source of fame and fortune. Hrafn asked that Loki accompany him for the rest of the summer and Thororm agreed, on the condition that his nephew not slow him down or cause any problems. A ship and crew were prepared and it was not long before they set sail. The journey was relatively easy and nothing else worth telling took place.

They were staying a few days in Vinland, in one of Hrafn's established houses, when Loki suggested they go hunting instead of living off their neighbours, who were already starting to tire of them. Thororm thought this a foolhardy idea, since they still had enough preserved candlefish for some time. But Loki kept pestering him, until Thororm thought of a way for them to find some food. Thororm picked up two axes and led Loki to the remotest part of Vinland. They went through the woods and soon saw other inhabitants. Thororm called them *Skrælings*, because they were dark in colouring and not fair like his kinsmen in Grimfjord. Loki, who was also considered to be dark and ill-favoured in complexion, did not mind them.

As Thororm and Loki came closer, they observed a few *Skrælings* gathering around a whale upon the shore. They were decorating it with some sparse plants and singing in their strange language. Thororm guessed that more of them would be on their way to help with the whale and this was their chance to take the smaller party by surprise.

"Hold your axe steady and then swing it deep into his back," advised Thororm.

"They live here and this is not a raid by sea," said Loki.

"Do what I say and do not cause me more trouble," urged Thororm.

"Uncle, you are a fool. There is neither honour nor renown in this action," replied Loki.

While his uncle was cursing his name, Loki approached the *Skrælings*. He was not certain what to say to them, so instead, he decided to recite a *drapa*. Then he offered them a small quantity of milk and cheese. All of this sat well with the *Skrælings*, who carved out a generous portion of whale meat and gave it to Loki, along with one of their furs. As he draped it about his shoulders, he noticed a woman staring at him from the edge of the woods. She had dark hair but her skin was lighter than that of the whale hunters. She stared at him with her bright eyes before departing in haste.

Back at their dwelling, they ate whale in silence. But it was not long before Loki asked about the woman near the woods.

"She is called Minordis, but you'd best forget her," said Thororm with renewed glee.

"You are done telling me what to do, uncle," retorted Loki.

"She has beguiled Cosmak the Crotchety, which is bad luck for you," added Thororm.

"Old men do not live forever," laughed Loki.

Then he spoke a verse:

> Today I tasted mighty whale
> without endless bloodshed
> and earned this warm fur
> curdling wit with words.
> No thanks to Thororm
> murderer of the herd!
> He lacks the strength
> to rob my mind of her.

Thororm did not speak to him for the remainder of that summer in Vinland.

At the time of this saga, Olaf Tryggvessön was ruling Norway. During the journey home, Loki and Thororm came ashore at No-Sleep Sound and found a chance to ingratiate themselves with the king's emissaries, who were trying to convince a stubborn group of landowners to pay a levy and to convert to the new religion. Thororm made a point of visiting each house and telling the inhabitants that if they did not agree to the wishes of Olaf the Fat, they would be fed living snakes and hacked into pieces, and he would do everything he could to help. Fortunately, one of the landowners, Dólgfinnr Ulfsson, was a relation of Loki's, and listened carefully to his advice. Loki pointed out that although it was undesirable to pay a distant monarch for nothing very substantial, the new religion was not going to go away and that it was best to take what new opportunities came to one, instead of being so stubborn as to get everyone killed. Dólgfinnr agreed that he did not wish any harm to come to his sons, nor anyone else in their community. Loki offered to travel with him to visit the king, so that their assent was seen as a tribute and not as a surrender. Dólgfinnr could not find fault with this idea, although Thororm assured him it was bound to go wrong in some way.

Then they sailed out to sea, and at last came to Norway. Loki presented Dólgfinnr to the king as a representative of landowners who wished to pay the levy and convert to the new religion. To mark the occasion, he announced that he had composed a *mansöngr* in the king's honour, which he then read:

> Since the handsome lad
> was sold for a rich cloak
> he has cast such a rune
> to amaze even Freyja
> and needs none of her help
> to wed the Swedish queen.

> Since the handsome lad
> was sold for a rich cloak
> out of love, lovely Allogia
> has paid his blood-money
> and in the worst of clothes
> he has won the hand of Gyda.

> Since the handsome lad
> was sold for a rich cloak
> he has pursued Haakon Jarl
> into the muck of a pigsty
> and won the kingdom
> by the head of a swine.

> Since the handsome lad
> was sold for a rich cloak
> he has roused the rebels
> at the thing in Trondheim
> after they chewed suet
> for their lack of prowess.

> Since the handsome lad
> was sold for a rich cloak
> he has been too potent

for Sigrid the Haughty
who torches suitors
just to keep warm.

Since the handsome lad
was sold for a rich cloak
he has cast such a rune
to amaze even Freyja
and needs none of her help
to bed the Swedish queen.

When Loki had ended his poem, King Olaf burst into laughter. He said that he had received many tributes from court *skalds* but none of them had made him laugh so heartily. He added that it took great courage for Loki to recite these things to him. Loki said women liked to take their time over things and that before long Sigrid the Haughty was bound to change her mind about converting to the new religion. The king accepted Dólgfinnr and his kin to be converted, and asked the man's two sons to serve him. However, he was unable to convince Loki to commit to the new faith.

"Will you not become my warrior *skald*?" asked Olaf.

"I must return to Grimfjord to be married," said Loki.

"Then will you not take the new ways with you?" pressed the king.

"I cannot forsake Odin, who fills my cup with mead," said Loki.

"You can still write verses in the new way," suggested Olaf.

"I would rather eat snakes and lose my ugly head," replied Loki.

"That will not be necessary," decided Olaf.

When Loki returned to Grimfjord, there was much talk about his dealings with King Olaf. People spoke with more care about the son of Hrafn and Freyja. What is more, Adalbjorg made it clear that he was less of a nuisance to be around than she had initially suspected. She began to accompany Loki in the evenings for long walks, and inevitably they ended up discussing his promise of betrothal.

"You once wanted to take me for your wife," reminded Adalbjorg.

"What you say is true and cannot be undone," replied Loki.

"And now that you consort with kings?" she asked.

Loki answered with this verse:

> These lovely fates of fair linen
> should not out of dire despair
> wring the shiftless promises
> of this proud-hearted man.
> Kings are fickle as waves
> rising and falling in the wind
> while my fiery desire rages
> for the hand of Adalbjorg.

"You speak well but I don't know what to make of you," said Adalbjorg.
"No less are you a mystery to me," laughed Loki.
Then they both went home.

The following spring, several families flocked to Grimfjord for the wedding of Loki and Adalbjorg. The dowry was agreeable to Loki, and in good faith, he pledged to her some of his gifts from King Olaf, including gold and jewels and a remarkable brooch that she consented to wear. Everyone was rather merry, except for Loki's uncle, who had remained on bad terms with his nephew since their voyage together. During the festivities, Thororm had too much to drink and made many improper suggestions to Adalbjorg. He insisted it was his right as an elder of Loki to *entertain* the bride in accordance with an ancient custom. Loki went over to the wall and unhooked a large gleaming axe.

"Uncle, you have insulted me for long enough. This is exactly what you are entitled to."

Then Loki swung the axe and without another word, Thororm fell. This killing upset all of the guests and divided them between those who favoured Loki and those who had never really cared for his sort. Adalbjorg and her parents were none too pleased by this turn of events. However, everyone agreed that this outcome did not bode well for the happiness of the two in question.

"What kind of life are we to have here?" asked Adalbjorg quietly.
"A better fate awaits us in Vinland," replied Loki.
"I do not expect to find any more joy there," retorted Adalbjorg.
"Your outlook does not change the situation," said Loki.

Directly after his wedding, Loki set sail for Vinland, accompanied by his wife and two of Dólgfinnr's sons, Fisk and Hogni. The brothers were undecided about the merits of this journey. Fisk was eager to see the new lands he had heard about but Hogni felt there was more glory to be gained in the company of their father and King Olaf. Loki pointed out that their constant bickering made a short voyage seem interminable.

Upon arrival, Adalbjorg and the Dólgfinnrson brothers were startled to observe the activity of so many strange people with dark features. They readied their weapons but Loki advised them not to trouble themselves over the *Skrælings*. They were local inhabitants and there was little to be done about that, either way. Then Cosmak the Crotchety and a woman named Minordis appeared with a small group of followers and greeted their party warmly. Loki accepted this show of affability and paid particular attention to Minordis. In her honour, he recited this verse:

> Goddess of the frothy horn
> many are the raven's lives
> before I could wipe away
> the memory of those eyes
> nor will the wave-gleam
> lure me from business
> with the bling-coffer.
> I am set on Minordis.

Adalbjorg and Cosmak did not take kindly to the nature of this poem. Thorolf Toothgrinder, also known as Thorolf the Fop, one of the men in Cosmak's retinue, expressed his immediate outrage and indignation. When Loki and Adalbjorg had reached one of Hrafn's dwellings and were putting it in order, she made her concerns known.

"Those men have the look of outlaws! Is this to be our life?" she wailed.

"We are also in exile and our choices are few," replied Loki.

By the time autumn arrived, the situation had not improved. Loki spent much of his time with the *Skrælings*, learning their ways and exchanging wares with them for food. The rest of his party did not care for them and thought that Loki was the worser off for trading with these suspicious little men. Finally, he accepted his wife's advice and began to search for small game in the nearby wood. However, for the next few days, they were still living on scraps of whale meat and the brothers made a number of remarks about Loki's ability with words being useless in practical matters. He had tried chasing game with a spear and had even resorted to a crude snare with bait, and yet the sparse creatures of the wood continued to elude him.

He was sleeping near one of his snares, in the middle of a troublesome dream, when suddenly he awoke to see Minordis dangling a few birds over his head.

"These are a gift to you," she announced.

"A hunter needs no gifts," he said.

"I am thanking you for your poem," she said.

She knelt beside him and he pulled her close and gave her a quick kiss. Then he spoke this verse:

> Five days perched in this wood
> the cruncher of cavernous skulls
> waited for the slightest stirring
> of a lame paw or broken wing
> without any hint of success.
> Who will now mock the luck
> of Loki's disastrous snares
> that caught him Minordis?

He kissed her again in a more than friendly manner and then she scurried home. That evening, Adalbjorg cooked the birds without comment and the Dólgfinnrson brothers ate in silence. After that day, Loki frequented the wood with renewed enthusiasm. He often crossed paths with Minordis and was never without a poem for her. One day she was pouring out some slop when Loki happened by and recited this verse:

> She does not shirk her duties
> the goddess of meadow-land
> but there is far more pleasure
> to be had in the scraggly wood
> with the fine hoarder of words
> than in pouring out pig-waste
> the way the climber of Ask
> pours want for her into me.

This time, Minordis responded in kind:

> If your dull spear-shaft
> is to catch any quarry
> find its point, or try
> night-duelling alone!

Soon after this incident, he came upon a place where she liked to bathe. At once, he averted his eyes and spoke through a collection of shrubs:

> I had thought sweet mead
> the richest gift of the gods
> until I saw the cold, light
> skin of nude Minordis.
> Never can I wipe away
> the memory of her look
> laughing in the water!
> I am set on Minordis.

Covering herself with folded arms, she made her reply:

> He has a very pretty wit
> the husband of another
> yet all his sly wisdom
> meets the wrong wife!

The next time Loki saw her, he redoubled his declarations of desire. Then he recited this verse:

> I have seen burning swords
> tempered in freezing rivers
> and high smouldering houses
> subdued with gathered seas
> but I am like a faint catch
> roasting over a cruel fire
> that never cools or fades
> unless I can soon settle.

"You are stubborn as a stone," said Minordis.
"A stone would not suffer," replied Loki.
"We belong to other people," she said.
"I would brave far more for your touch," he responded.
"All right, don't talk about it so much," she pleaded.
"I only speak of what I often think about," he said.

Loki pulled her to him and gave her a long, lingering kiss. Minordis told him it was getting late and that she had to return home. But not before she had had the last word.

"Tomorrow, Cosmak is going whaling with the *Skrælings*."

Loki scarcely slept that night, and Adalbjorg was disturbed by his tossing and turning and as a result of his troubled dreams. In the morning, over seal, she made her complaints to him within earshot of the Dólgfinnrson brothers. She claimed that spending so much time in the woods was playing tricks with his mind and that he was just like his father, who turned funny in the evenings. Loki announced that he was going hunting and left without eating.

"I think he goes to see that witch," said Adalbjorg.

"Things are bound to improve," offered Fisk.

"I never expected life to turn out like this," continued Adalbjorg.

"Maybe you should divorce him," suggested Hogni.

"That wouldn't help anything," replied Adalbjorg.

When Loki arrived at the lodgings on the other side of the wood, he opened the door and found Minordis waiting for him. They lay together and both were well satisfied in doing what they had both been thinking about for some time. They embraced and were merry for a long time, before sharing a sense of sorrow.

"What is to be done?" asked Loki.

"I am not certain," answered Minordis.

"We would be happier together," insisted Loki.

"I really should make a decision," said Minordis.

"I want to pledge myself to you," offered Loki.

"I have seen your wife wearing a brooch," she said.

"I can give you finer things," boasted Loki.

"Would you ever lend it to me?" she pressed.

"How would I explain its absence?" asked Loki.

"Such is the pledge of poets!" she exclaimed.

Loki left the dwelling, pleased but not best pleased with Minordis. Outside, he ran into Thorolf the Fop, who eyed him with increasing suspicion.

"Northerner, what is your business in there?" bellowed Thorolf.

"Outlaw, I can go wherever I like," retorted Loki.

"You better keep clear of Minordis," warned Thorolf.

"Cosmak's wife can make her own decisions," replied Loki.

"She would never want to see you," said Thorolf.

Then Loki answered him with this verse:

> In this place of pastures
> hogs do not grow to size

but it is a shameful joke
to see this grunting pig
runt of a diseased litter
still attempting to suckle
the tits of his neighbours
while oinking out advice.

"I don't care for your poem either. Now stay away from Minordis!" yelled
Thorolf.

"It is unwise for you to threaten me," glowered Loki.

"You'll see what happens," replied Thorolf.

Talk began to spread among the settlers in Vinland about Loki spending an
inordinate amount of time with Minordis, thus confirming the suspicions of
Adalbjorg. The Dólgfinnrson brothers wondered aloud what she would do, and
she promised them that such deeds would not go unanswered. One night, she
brewed a heavy draught and pressed her husband and their guests to drink heavily.
Once they were all asleep, she crept out of their dwelling with Loki's broad-axe.
Adalbjorg was aware that the *Skrælings* kept caches of food in the woods for
ceremonial purposes, guarded by carvings of their gods. She smashed the idols with
the axe and scattered the food, leading a trail back to the lodging of Cosmak the
Crotchety, leaving scraps of seal and whale meat and bits of wood and soapstone
figures outside their door. Then at daybreak, she roused Hogni and told him it
was Loki's wish that he go into the woods and sound his horn to initiate the start
of their morning hunt. He was the least bright of the two brothers and he did as
she asked with no small amount of grumbling.

"What is that noise?" asked Loki.

"I wish I knew," grinned Adalbjorg.

"Your smile troubles me," said Loki.

"Your oats are getting cold," said Adalbjorg.

The *Skrælings* awoke at the sound of the horn and hurried into the wood to see
what was happening. For them, it was like the sound of terrifying spirits. Then,
they saw their idols and caches of food had been despoiled and followed the trail
back to Cosmak's lodging. When Cosmak answered the door, he was nearly run
through with a harpoon. He locked the door but they persisted with their war
cries. Some of them ran to fetch a large ballista, which they used to hurl stones at
the door of the dwelling. Thorolf came out of his lodging to complain, but he was
hit in the head with one of the stones and then lay still for a very long time. Loki,
Adalbjorg, and the Dólgfinnrson brothers peeked out of the woods and watched

the attack in silence. Loki was eager to intervene but Adalbjorg reminded him of what had happened to Thororm the last time he had acted without thinking.

"We should assist our neighbours," insisted Loki.

"Are we to be exiled from here too?" asked Adalbjorg.

"They would sooner come to our aid," said Loki.

"That is where you are wrong," replied Adalbjorg.

The door of Cosmak's dwelling was starting to split and everyone expected him and Minordis to be slaughtered in their own house. Then something strange happened. Minordis opened the door but she was not alone. She had her arms wrapped around a Uniped, who hopped upon its one leg in front of her. The *Skrælings* were startled to see this gleaming creature and fled in terror as it began to fire lightning at them. A few of them were killed instantly but the rest escaped.

"This proves she is a sorceress," said Adalbjorg.

"We should drive her away!" growled Hogni.

"Only to remain in this difficult place?" asked Fisk.

"Whatever the case, she is not short of courage," said Loki.

After this incident, Loki thought about Minordis even more often than before. He returned to the woods. When they met again, they embraced and lay upon the ground, mindful of nothing but their overwhelming lust. Loki began to unfasten the knots of her clothing but Minordis deterred him with a baleful glance.

"Are you unhappy?" he asked.

"I wish I had some token of your word," she said.

"There is a reindeer comb I have in mind," he suggested.

"That is indeed a thing you understand," she admitted.

"I will bring you the brooch you seek," he replied.

"That would establish trust between us," she said.

He responded with this verse:

> For certain the necklace-tree
> has plenty for her branches
> and the bold caster of spells
> will gain this token of truth
> since Loki proffers his oath
> urged on by mighty longing
> to unravel the linen-goddess
> and lie with lovely Minordis.

"I really should reach a decision," she said.

Loki parted with Minordis. On his way back to his lodging, he encountered Thorolf the Fop, who shoved him roughly.

"What are you doing in these woods?" he demanded.

"My business is my own," answered Loki.

"I told you to stay away from her!" yelled Thorolf.

"What concern is it of yours?" asked Loki.

"And leave her out of your libellous verses!" roared Thorolf.

Then he reached for his sword, but Loki struggled with his opponent and bit his fingers with much ferocity, gaining the upper hand. He held the blade to his enemy's neck and recited this verse:

> In the wood of meadow-land
> the son of Hrafn was hunting
> the scent of particular game
> but nosed the stink of doom
> about the quivering hind
> of meddlesome Thorolf.
> The berserk bit him well
> and bled his nonsense!

Then Loki raised the sword and dealt Thorolf his death blow.

For a time after this episode, things were peaceful. Loki had put off the matter of giving his wife's brooch to Minordis, although she appeared to him in dreams and asked him many times for this token. He was barely sleeping and neither was anyone else in his company. If he did sleep, he would awaken in a sweat, recounting his nightmares. More than once, Adalbjorg asked him about the dreams that were troubling him so much. In answer, Loki spoke a verse:

> Thought and Memory·alighted
> from the Mead-Maker's arms
> tugging at a contorted twig
> burning with a feeble flame.
> They fought over this wood
> snapping it into tiny pieces
> and stamping out the flame
> until the midland went dark.

Then he spoke again:

A fair server of herb-surf
beguiled me with glances
then poured out poison
and bid me to imbibe.
I fell upon the floor
ransacked of strength
and with blood paid
this brooch bearer.

Then he spoke yet another verse:

A wolf was snarling over
the remains of a fresh kill
and the sound of a horn
brought many hunters.
They chased the wolf
deep into these woods
and behind a nurse log
there was no way out!

"Dreams don't mean anything," said Adalbjorg.

Meanwhile, Loki's elder brother Sindri had returned to Grimfjord from raiding. His parents welcomed him warmly but he was surprised to find himself otherwise greeted with many unfavourable murmurs.

"They have a long memory for the life of Thororm," he said.

"They are kin to Thorolf, who lies without a grave in Vinland," explained Hrafn.

"Is this Loki's doing?" asked Sindri.

"They want compensation for Thorolf Toothgrinder," said Unnur.

"Let them seek their blood money elsewhere!" shouted Sindri.

Thorolf the Fop had three brothers remaining, named Thorstein, Thorgeir, and Thord. They were quite offended by Sindri's complete indifference to their dispute. But Thororm had also left a surviving brother named Orri. He took the Toothgrinder clan aside and calmed them down, revealing to them a devious plan. Orri reminded them that Loki was an outcast in Vinland with only a few followers. He would sail with them and they would take their revenge without any fierce opposition. Sindri overheard what they were saying and informed his parents at once.

"They mean to murder Loki," he said.

"What do you intend to do?" asked Unnur.

"I must hurry to warn my brother," stated Sindri.

"He is stronger in all things except listening," said Hrafn.

"Yes, and he was a more than troublesome birth," added Unnur.

"The odds are bad, but my rune is already cast," said Sindri.

"Nothing good can come from this," replied Hrafn.

The Toothgrinder brothers celebrated their revenge pact with Orri into the evening and were sluggish to leave Grimfjord. Sindri, on the other hand, set sail at dawn. He was quick to reach Vinland and rushed directly to Loki's dwelling. Adalbjorg greeted him and asked him why he had come during the onset of winter. Sindri told her immediately about the men who were on their way. At once, she set the Dólgfinnrson brothers to work with an axe, in keeping with what she had in mind. Then she ran to find Loki, who was emerging from the woods with a handful of birds. She told him about the assassins and he said that it didn't surprise him, given his dreams. As a precaution, he took her brooch from her, insisting that the Toothgrinder brothers would only remove her head to take it. They took shifts sleeping and kept watch for days, until finally they saw a ship approaching. Night was drawing in and the intruders expected everyone to be eating or fast asleep. Adalbjorg had suggested chopping holes in the backs of their lodgings to provide a means of escape. The Toothgrinder brothers stood outside with the idea of setting their dwellings on fire and flushing them out. But as they stared through the smoke of the blazing wood, they failed to realize that Loki and his party had snuck up behind them with swords and axes. There was no time to react and the Toothgrinder brothers were cut down at once. Orri tried to flee, but Adalbjorg tripped him up with a long spear and lanced him where he lay.

"They soon learned that killing Loki is no easy thing," said Loki.

"Our house is gone," wailed Adalbjorg.

"I will check on our neighbours," announced Loki.

"You and that witch are the reason for all this angst," said Adalbjorg.

"They may be in similar trouble," replied Loki.

"Know that when she lay with Cosmak, Thorolf lay with them!" she cried.

"Such calumny is unfit for your lips and my poet's ears," he answered.

Against everyone's advice, Loki went alone through the wood to visit Minordis. He was unsettled to see the number of bodies about her dwelling. He came upon a dead man with white hair and when he turned him over, he saw in the moonlight that it was Cosmak the Crotchety. Suddenly, Loki was overtaken by two assailants and knocked to the ground. But he was able to lift the blunt end of his axe and smash in one of their skulls. An ordinary man would have met his doom then and there, but Loki often displayed the properties of a berserk at night and surprised his second attacker with more than one vicious bite before swinging his axe into the man's chest. Under the moon, he could now see they were the outlaws living with Cosmak. Then he spoke a verse:

> How these shivering hinds
> leapt upon a cornered wolf
> and in the furor of the kill
> lost their nerve to frenzy!
> The brewer of word-ale
> would not abandon him
> to such cowardly beasts
> not the smith of verses!

Loki finished his boast to the night air and then heard a nearby noise. He saw Minordis emerging from her dwelling. Beside her stood the hideous Uniped. Before Loki could say a word, the Uniped fired multiple arrows at him, piercing his groin and chest. Minordis raced over to him and saw that in his open hand he held the brooch he had long since promised to bring her. He groaned and recited this verse:

> I hurried back to hollowness
> of a fruitless meadow-land
> denying any deadly danger
> lay hidden in this goddess
> slow to reckon the number
> of cocks in the bleak coop
> or studs in the dark stable
> eager to mount Minordis!

"This was not my intention," she said.
"Either way, I will not see morning," he replied.
"You have missed many wonders," she sighed.
"I have just what fate pledged to me," he laughed.
Minordis took the brooch from his hand. He smiled and spoke a verse:

> Since the first breath of Loki
> fatal runes have been written

that he should be consumed
by his own fiery disposition
that he should be watchful
of a beautiful brooch thief
yet he lived without fear
and died without regret.

So then Loki died. He was found the next morning among the bodies of a number of invaders, outlaws, and inhabitants. Minordis was nowhere to be found although some people thought they had seen her turn into a mink or sea otter. For a time, this was a great mystery. But soon, everyone began to lose interest in this affair. Adalbjorg returned to Grimfjord with Sindri and soon became his wife. The Dólgfinnrson brothers remained in Vinland and failed in all their attempts at farming and hunting. After more than one skirmish with the *Skrælings*, they were attacked by a whaling party and died at sea.

Thus, here ends this saga.

VI

I must admit to the reader that it was a relief to have fled inhospitable Vinland and to have reached my own time again. I put the brooch in the family vault at once and spared a fleeting thought for poor Kosmas (reinvented as the unfortunate Cosmak) and Loki, who had sacrificed their lives in order to guarantee a lifetime of high maintenance for yours truly. After a lengthy session beneath the powerful blast of the Minor *corps bidet*, I selected a silken gown from the guest room and went downstairs to scrape up something to nibble. However, I could hear muffled cries from behind a wall of the library. I shoved the painting of my father aside and peeped through the viewing portal to see Master Fuddlemuck and Timothy Gimmick in mutually compromising positions with a number of imported adolescents. I was a trifle miffed to witness their abandon and degree of glee without their professed Queen of the Night. I wiggled the better half of the leftmost statue of Priapus and appeared in the opening.

"Gimmick!"

"Mistress! We did not expect you back so soon!"

Then a uniquely endowed man-boy strutted up to me and displayed his fleshy wares while a pair of girls gushed over me. They were all clearly eighteen and a half.

"Yeah that's right. You like that, eh? That's right."

"Look at her she's so pretty and I mean hot."

I smiled at the group of young people, charmed by their dialect. I could tell at once they were mountain folk from the surrounding cliffs. I coaxed them into a corner before clicking my rump-me-pumps together. The floor opened up underneath them and they plummeted until the echo of their screams could no longer be heard. Timothy Gimmick was in a state of demi-undress, and now quivering, was unable to control the better part of him. I laughed and turned to Fuddlemuck, helping him out of his airborne conveyance.

"I hope your confidentiality clause covers this one!"

"I confess to having a soft spot for you. Trap doors are a turn-on!"

Then our own amorous demonstration roused Mr. Gimmick out of his post-coital stupor and he vociferously pleaded with us to grant him the honour of attending to our lubricity. I informed him that while at present part of me remained inaccessible (in theory), this was by no means the only route to the same destination, since a part of me remained hidden like a long-fossilized animal, only waiting for his omnipotent piston to liberate such light sweet crude. Forgive me, but this kind of talk was necessary for Mr. Gimmick to rise to the occasion without further delay and in both this department and that, he proved no amateur at going about his business. Nor did Master Fuddlemuck seem any less spry, especially after crawling back into his bobbing chair and treating me to diverse mid-air acrobatics, the nature of which I dare not repeat to another living soul, or without a decent vintage handy. During this administration, he would only refer to me as *Spinning Jenny*, which perplexed and nevertheless excited me.

It was not until we were utterly spent and clean as slightly used whistles that we retired to an intimate corner of the banquet hall for a meal prepared by Mr. Gimmick.

"In homage to your light sweet crude, I have prepared some crudité!"

"Mmm … these cucumber spears remind me of Rome!"

"Are they ripe enough? I dispatched those young people to fetch a few items."

"Then it is a pity they are now dispatched!"

"And the pork tenderloin? On occasion, your father would throw a kosher wobbler."

"I like my white veal well enough, provided there is a generous helping of sauce."

"There is more than a dollop, mistress, and more where that came from …"

"Look at these yam yummies!"

"I say, are these hen's eggs to your fancy?"

At this point, we burst into uncontrollable titters.

I must have regaled them with several time-tripping tales before they began to grow bored of the onerous history involved in getting from here to there. Gimmick started in with wicked rejoinders made during years of service, and Fuddlemuck with the long and short of countless triumphs for clients up to their neck in it. I took this opportunity to remind them that I really had to resume my adventures at once if I was to have any hope of becoming the inheritrix. Master Fuddlemuck seemed a tad miffed at my sudden disinterest, and told us it was all the same to him, since he was on the clock. This was the only note to sour the otherwise splendid ambience of our lavish ménage.

I was feeling a bit logy after supper and the bottle of wine had gone to my head. To paraphrase Boccaccio, this carelessness *lifted me out of the frying pan and dropped me right in the fire*. I had been very careful about my choice of costumes for each epoch but on this occasion I threw caution to the wind. I called for Aiutetta, one of the pool-party attendants, and asked her to find me something amusing on the double. She laughed nervously, dropping an inflatable device at my feet. I nearly shed a tear, since I had not seen one of those toys in months, and with the addition of my leapfrogging through time, not in centuries. It was a state of the art novelty vulva in the shape of a seashell, incidentally one of the most popular items during my fishhole days.

Aiutetta, who had been privy to more about my travels than I would have wished her to know, began to lecture me on the unconscionable ramifications of introducing a synthetic substance into an earlier period of history, an act that might at the very least ruin a great deal of novelty vulva congloms. I waved her away, informing her that I was the *scion* in uncon*scion*able and coming to the conclusion that Heraclitus was right. When we drink too much, we are easily led about by children of the world. Not that Aiutetta condemned my grapey breath. On the contrary, she took each playful slap like a good sport and then set about preparing a fresh chamber for our nocturnal activities. But my mind was already made up and I flung her from me in the middle of a kiss. Without another word, I leapt upon the vulva and activated the amulet.

Had I adhered more strictly to the rules of sipping and spitting in accordance with the sensible advice of former sommelier Timothy Gimmick, I might have second-guessed the folly of appearing completely naked in the middle of the Arno River, with nothing to cling to but a novelty flotation device. To drown in such a fashion was just the sort of ending to befit a wayward member of the Minor dynasty. I realized that I would also be making good on the empty threat of the tiresome heroine in that overplayed aria from *Gianni Schicchi*:

> *Sì, sì, ci voglio andare!*
> *e se l'amassi indarno*
> *andrei sul Ponte Vecchio*
> *ma per buttarme in Arno!*

Such a musing caused me to giggle to the point that bubbles came out of my nose, just as I struck the tempestuous waters of Florence, circa 1478.

It was a great struggle for me to seize a fistful of FloateX and paddle toward the bank of the Arno. All the same, I was not unaware of my quarry, the devout in his prime praying to a clump of clouds. I would have been at a loss to make the connexion, but the NGF I had just popped informed me that the man's face bore a high percentile of similarity to the lone face that looks outward in his *Adoration of the Magi*. I was seeking none other than Alessandro di Mariano di Vanni Filipepi, whose first-hand concern was rapidly converted into squeamishness as I rose out of the water and balanced upon the undulating novelty vulva. I made heroic efforts to cover the parts that were so offensive to his senses, but this only seemed to agitate him even more. I could not resist a smirk as our renowned friend, known to everyone as the "Little Barrel," rolled about the riverbank, shielding his eyes from my wet skin and at the same time interrogating the heavens in feeble verse.

O what devil arises from the depths of hell?
O what woman wavers upon a cockle shell?

I assured him that I was neither a devil nor any ordinary woman. That did not mean I was accustomed to undertaking seaward voyages on bivalve molluscs. I pointed out that if he were really the gifted painter of reputable intellect, a veritable Apelles in our time, he would surely appreciate the type of accident to befall a lady on occasion, when confined to crowded vessels teeming with brigands, scoundrels, and cutthroats. I implored him to imagine the wretched fate I had managed to escape that had left me to face the mercy of the indifferent Arno. By the time I introduced the lascivious company of players singing Germanic shanties and the merciless intervention by theatrical pirates, my new friend was near tears. He removed his threadbare coat and wrapped it around my shoulders and body, trembling as he did so.

"Forgive me, lovely lady of the sea! I should never have put your chaste life in question!"

"Why did you think I was a devil?"

"I am subject to unclean ideas. I thought you were sent to tempt me at my weakest hour."

"Surely the temptation itself is what tests your integrity."

"These are decadent times when men run amok, and without spiritual rule."

"Surely the only rule necessary is to rule oneself with a suitable degree of self-control."

"But the flesh ... the flesh is weak!"

"Fear not. I will not bite."

"But you are an example to us all! You have survived countless misadventures with your virtue intact!"

"Something like that."

"And now you have emerged from the sea. It reminds me of some of the imagery of Lucretius in *De rerum natura*. The only part that makes sense, in fact."

"I beg to differ! His views on the abolition of superstition and human sacrifice are worth burning a thousand candles over!"

"You have read Lucretius? You are a marvel! And look how you rise from the sea as lovely as Venus herself, shyly covering her ..."

"You know that whole Venus thing has been done to death."

"Your manner of speaking is alien to me, although I am entirely beguiled."

"I have risked innumerable perils at sea to reach these shores, in order to find the great thinkers who profess to follow the teachings of Plato."

"Savonarola warns us against the false idols of Plato."

"Did you ever consider that your precious Madonnas might never have existed without a Venus as their stolid foundation?"

"You present arguments that trouble but also tickle me. Were I not already enamoured of a lady, I think I would wish to become an instrument of your beautiful intelligence."

"You mean Simonetta? What does she have that I don't?"

"How did you know that? Does everyone in Florence know?"

"Of course not. Your secret is safe with me."

"She only has an eye for Giuliano."

"What if he were out of the way? That would clear a path for you."

"Devil! What talk is this?"

"Calm yourself. I am here in search of knowledge ... and art."

"What do they call you where you are from?"

"I will reveal this shortly, but only before the man I seek."

"For whom have you endured such perils and hardship?"

"*The son of the sun.*"

Alessandro took my hand and led me to a small unassuming dwelling. Then he knocked on the wooden door nine times.

"Yes?"

"We are here to see the Magnificent One."

Upon entering the main chamber, I was taken aback to see a group of men lounging in quasi-Roman fashion, with their choice of lovers resting at their feet. It should not have surprised me to observe the Florentine attempts to evoke their historical ancestry mixed with their adopted philosophical dispositions like water with the wine. This was the first time I realized that history was destined to repeat itself, except with different window dressing. That is to say that, however secretly, men (and women!) will gather to behave in relatively the same manner in any time and place.

As they noticed my guide, a steady chorus of his mocksome moniker echoed about the room.

"Little Barrel! Little Barrel!"

"Has the Little Barrel come here to rein in our behaviour, or to whip us onward?"

"Has the Little Barrel come to tell us we are destined for eternal hellfire?"

"Where is the boy you are keeping, Little Barrel?"

"This is not my purpose, but since I am here, I must admit that I am witness to much avarice and excess of appetite! What would Savonarola say?"

"What would Savonarola say?"

"The Little Barrel tells us how to live and then he runs home and paints every filthy thing he sees."

A man with dark hair and a bent nose smiled and put a finger to his lips before speaking.

"There is space enough in this city for the passionate of spirit to live among whiners and wailers like the *Piagnoni*. They are merely afraid of themselves and who can blame them? I will not say a word against them, nor the reputation of our friend, who is, as you all know, a fine painter. But let me resume where I was interrupted before attending to the business of our friend, at the risk of exposing this delicate person to … ahem … sinful practices."

"Indeed, let Lorenzo finish! He was reading from his satirical collection of sonnets."

The man with dark hair eyed me curiously before reading his poem.

> For each extremity of fettered flesh
> in which sibling senses may relish
> rough clarity of my young butter
> I scrape out a soft refrain of Love.
>
> Flustered night was nearly spent
> wringing out every starry droplet
> from her damp and tangled train
> and I shudder to even remember.
>
> Love felt inside his purple mantle
> and with fervour groped my heart
> where my drowsing lady also lay.
>
> Laughing, he prodded her awake
> and with a plate of fiery sausages
> she ate that heart. Then she spat.

"Brilliant! How witty and amusing!"
"I have never heard anything so moving."
"Dante could not do better!"
"Riveting! Read it again!"
Only I could not hold my tongue and protested against their overweening praise.

"With respect, Magnificent One, though this sonnet is a worthy and amusing imitation, do you truly expect it to rival *La Vita Nuova* by itself? Surely you cannot claim a poetical doctrine of equal merit hides inside this short poem?"

There were a few gasps.

"Who is this glowing lady ... with opinions?"

"I am known as Diminuenda di Minori."

This time everyone in the room gasped. Lorenzo nodded with enthusiasm.

"So learned and so lovely! I should have known you were one of the Minori at first sight."

"I am here to give you good counsel, Magnificent One."

"Yes, I think I know. I have heard tell of your arrival. A woman named Minori would come to me and deliver a dire prophecy. Then I would lose my heart and not quite listen and forget all about it and so on. Such is life ... short and so full of uncertainty!"

"Enough chatter! Read us another poem!"

Lorenzo threw back his head and laughed.

"What of the carnival song of the fruit pickers?"

"A taste, Magnificent One! Just a taste!"

So Lorenzo read:

Watch how you weave through the valleys and arbours, for we are the lusty boys who pluck the plentiful fruit of your bountiful gardens. Sometimes we scamper up the loftiest branch to nab what we are seeking and sometimes we crawl on hands and knees to chase our tumbling quarry. Beneath the overbearing heat of the sun, the taste to our dry lips of the soft green catch is juicier and more delicious but also wanting the refined and subtle character of the overripe choice as autumn approaches. In other words, no matter the prize of occasion, we so love to eat whatever we find, because this treasure is the gift that makes our short lives seem terribly rich. Yet beware! Watch how you weave through the valleys and arbours, for we are the lusty boys who lie in wait munching delectable selections to their very marrow and sampling the collected sap of halcyon seasons. We ask you, what is a more entertaining pastime than picking the most sumptuous of purple grapes and vigorously trampling them underfoot, in order to press and squeeze out the precious wine that makes us merry and more than wanton? We have long bottles and short bottles that are brimming over with every taste imaginable, whatever your pleasure. We promise the energetic surprise of youth or the patient persistence of age. Or you can try more than one at once, whatever your fancy. We cannot tell you precisely how to find and seize your pleasure, only hurry while the season lasts, and watch how you weave through the valleys and arbours, for we are the lusty boys who pluck the plentiful fruit of your bountiful gardens.

"*Bravissimo!* Another triumph!"

"Petrarch wishes he had written that!"

I could not resist a giggle, although I noticed Alessandro had covered his ears and was rocking back and forth on his heels, wailing a dolorous hymn.

Lorenzo held up his hands and shook his head in mock protest.

"Friends, we have drunk more than our fair share of libations to please Bacco a hundred times over! And neither Plato nor Apollo would be outraged at our exchange of words! But now I must attend to a most rigid matter of state!"

The Magnificent One slid his arm about my waist and muttered a few phrases through gritted teeth that evaded the translation capabilities of my amulet. The revellers rose with and stretched amid a polyphony of yawns before slowly trickling out. As soon as the doors were closed behind us, I saw Lorenzo's face adopt a stern impassive look.

"Please forgive me. The news you have brought me is not fit for their ears, but why should they even hear it?"

"Then you will take me at my word."

"Certainly. I have been waiting for a Minori woman since I was only a boy. It's a family prophecy."

"Then heed my warning, Magnificent One. Beware of the Pazzi."

Lorenzo squinted and stroked his chin thoughtfully.

"Magnificent One, you do not believe it!"

"No. What you say makes sense but is also curious, since it is one of the Pazzi who warns me about trusting the Portinari too much, since they take half of our profits from any one of our wool transactions."

"They are pulling the wool over your eyes?"

"What an uncanny expression! Now, I warn you, it may turn up in one of my sonnets."

"The Pazzi family presents a very real danger to you."

"I am quite familiar with their threats. What was more offensive was to hear they also believe I will be ruined by debt. They think the Pazzi bank will triumph over the Medici bank, due to our overlending and extravagance. So all I really have to fear is a banking crisis!"

"Has Montesecco come to see you?"

"Yes, this is true."

"He came to Cafaggiolo for the sole purpose of identifying the man he is to assassinate. But in spite of being a mercenary, he lacks either stomach or heart to complete the deed."

"Who do you expect will try to *complete the deed*?"

"I cannot tell you everything. It is … forbidden. But if you place your trust in me, you will emerge from this calamity even better and stronger than you already are."

"Calamity? I see I have no choice but to trust you."

"Magnificent One, do you remember Imola?"

A shadow crossed Lorenzo's face.

"Why speak of this?"

"You tried to prevent one party from purchasing Imola."

"Dio! What if there is something in what you say?"

"You trusted your rival not to advance said party the necessary funds."

"I am still listening."

"Now that you have altered the inheritance laws, coincidentally in favour of a particular Medici over a Pazzi, might you not speculate that more than one party has an interest in the Pazzi bank controlling the interests of everyone?"

"Those lunatics?"

"Madness, assuredly. However, it only takes a fistful of madmen to aspire to the folly of revolution."

"You are a lovely member of the Minori, and yet you speak with the cagey diplomacy of a Medici. You make me wish that Lucrezia could advise me in these delicate matters."

"Magnificent One, are you on your way to see her tonight?"

"Ah … you must have heard the others joking. They say that Lorenzo wears himself out, riding to see Lucrezia every night and then riding back. They say that Lorenzo wears himself out, always riding …"

I felt this juncture was apropos for the removal of Alessandro's threadbare coat.

"Even if you are to go *riding* tonight, is there nothing you can find first with which to warm me, for I am very cold."

"But is this to be my last night upon this bountiful earth?"

"Place your faith in me. It need not be."

At this point, I noticed Alessandro rather sheepishly peeping out from behind a curtain.

"Well, if you don't have to run back to that boy you are keeping, why don't you join us?"

Instead, he fled at once, startled out of his wits.

Then Lorenzo took hold of me and brusquely set about giving me the business, and like a boss who knows about banking.

"You must not be too hard on our dear Apelles. Soon he will give you an exquisite painting of your incomparable beauty and all will be forgotten."

Il Magnifico was not shy about demonstrating his strength and stamina, bringing me to the point where his severe features scarcely mattered to me. We had barely drifted into a state of repose when I realized he was once more reinitiating me with indefatigable ardour.

"Is this not more amusing than riding to and fro?"

"If it is my last night, I have more than made use of it!"

As I dutifully applied the diverse skill set of my former vocation, in spite of his initial astonishment, he soon surrendered to every luxurious temptation as if I were the Goddess herself. We reclined in spent glory and noted the dawn light arising with renewed hope.

"You are rather magnificent after all."

"Apelles could not imagine such a scene!"

"Now you must ready yourself. You must be alert."

"I am sated and brimming over. But also famished!"

"There may not be time. Soon it will be time for Mass."

Lorenzo dressed quickly and hurried away, directing me to join him later at the church, so as not to arouse any suspicion. However, he soon returned, complaining that the wretched boy cardinal was nowhere to be found. He caught me investigating the presumed closet of his much-lauded mistress and tried to suppress a smile I knew by now all too well.

"*Scusati … Diminuenda.*"

His sudden use of the familiar reference was telling and in spite of being rankled, I was doubly flattered by the hunger in his eyes. I had deactivated the amulet's translation function for a while to enjoy the roughness of his native tongue while he was at the height of passion. He in turn lost the capacity to understand me, and simply assumed that I was excitedly berating him with Gallic curses from a northerly region.

"*Cattiva strega!*"

At one point, when the Magnificent One was most intensely engaged in proving the exemplar totality of his manhood to me, I could not resist a few outbursts of wicked laughter, to consider how shocked the boy Rafaello would be to learn how many edicts we had managed to defy in one night, not to mention how meagre this was in comparison to the murder attempt he was presently being dragged into. I cried out the name of the young cardinal to let Lorenzo in on the joke.

"*Povero ragazzo!*"

"*Poverissimo ragazzo!*"

Afterward, I felt a bit peevish in the presence of his sudden piety. No one had ever begged for celestial forgiveness after a night with me, let alone fifteen minutes. I reminded Lorenzo that they all more or less had it in for him, but he merely shrugged his shoulders.

"And now?"

"Time to collect our cardinal."

I accompanied him at a distance, having no wish to compromise either of us, nor to create too large a hiccup in history, or even a temporal burp sizable enough to go unexcused. My eyes drank in the smooth ashlar and contrasting rustication of the walls of the Palazzo Medici. We were discussing the charming kneeling windows and delectable aedicules when the boy appeared.

"Rafaello, do you forget your duty?"

"*Scusi, Magnifico* ... I was transfixed by the bronze of David."

"Only do not stare at him too long, Rafaello. Your relations will say I am corrupting the purity of your devout senses."

"Surely there is no harm in enjoying such treasures as I have seen in your home. Yet this image of the young hero is different than I am familiar with, and sparks the imagination ... the sensuous pose ... his foot touching the head of Goliath as if giving a caress to a sleeping giant ... the blatant invitation of his buttocks ... *come sfanciulli* ..."

At this point, I was extremely grateful for the NGF I had popped, because I launched into a short lecture concerning the dialectic between dutiful repression and homoerotic desire as represented in similar examples of art, although I no longer remember a word of what I said. I do recall that the young cardinal Rafaello was somewhat perplexed.

"But this enjoyment in such acts, even in the mind ... that is a sin!"

"One must also consider whether the complete use of our faculties, whether mental or physical, are homage and tribute to our ingenious maker, and not anathema."

At my prompting, Rafaello smiled shyly.

"I confess to having very strange thoughts at times ..."

"My father is known for this saying – *do what you will, only don't get caught.*"

Lorenzo laughed and Rafaello turned red and we shared an awkward silence for the rest of our walk. Then as we admired the Duomo, I asked about its origins and Lorenzo happily told us of the eggshell half Brunelleschi had used to demonstrate the unique properties of a shell structure and thus win the contract. My own novelty vulva shell crossed my mind but I remained silent. Upon entering the cathedral, I directed Lorenzo to the southern side of the altar. There were some murmurs among those present about my appearance there, and he assured them I was a cousin he had promised to entertain during the festivities. Then Lorenzo's brother Giuliano entered from the opposite side, supported by Francesco de' Pazzi and Bernardo Baroncelli. Giuliano was feeling ill and the pair had done him the *good turn* of escorting him to church. The Mass bell sounded and we stood in place, ready to make the sign of the cross. I noted that the priest Antonio Maffei was slowly reaching toward Lorenzo's shoulder from behind, with knife drawn. Stefano da Bagnone was also inching closer.

"*Traditor!*"

Lorenzo whirled about, wrapped in his cloak with sword at the ready, surprising his attackers, who were only able to wound him slightly. However, Maffei was about to deliver the *coup de grâce* when out of nowhere the familiar spotted fire dog appeared, snarling and biting and putting him off balance. Maffei's blade only grazed Lorenzo's neck. I was less surprised to realize that the dog had disappeared just as abruptly. In addition, I must admit to being thrilled at the way the poet Poliziano and two of the Cavalcantis rushed into action, forming a human shield around their leader and friend. Unfortunately, the bank manager and diplomat Francesco Nori was stabbed to death by the raving Baroncelli. Lorenzo leapt over a low wooden railing and led our way through the wicket of the choir and into the new sacristy. Once inside, we slammed shut the heavy doors behind us. I embraced the whimpering boy cardinal on his knees and tried to reassure him.

"Looks like sodomy is the least of your worries!"

"Those men were priests … murdering in church!"

Lorenzo nodded at me with newfound awe.

"Did you see what happened to Giuliano?"

I had no answer for him. Poliziano said that he might have been wounded but Lorenzo's knowing brother, he must have used his wits to flee and survive. Then, after seeing our agitation, Poliziano proposed that we tell stories to one another to pass the time until we received a signal regarding the restoration of our security. Perhaps due to the foreknowledge I had provided, Lorenzo took this idea in stride and asked what type of stories they should tell. Poliziano suggested that since the Pazzi family of crazy folk were behind this attack, it would be fitting for each of us to spin out a yarn involving someone named Pazzo. We thought this to be an excellent idea and without delay, a visiting poet and satirist Uccellino began his tale:

> You must have heard something of Perrolito Piano and how he became known as *Il Geloso Pazzo*. If not, then I must tell it at once!

All was well with Perrolito. He was a merchant who found no trouble in spinning a veritable fortune from cloth. It was not so long ago that he made great gains from our conquest of Volterra and its quantity of alum. One could only wish his talent with mordants had been extended to holding together his marriage equally fast.

Fiammetta had wed him in her youth and soon discovered that she was bound hand and foot to a busy bore of a husband. Note that it is a trial for any lady from the country to remain unfazed and to not be dazzled by the glittering leaves that surround our native trunk – Fiorenza!

Hence, like flies to a honey loaf, attentive fellows flocked, but she gave them no sign of encouragement, save for one in particular who struck her fancy. This was a poet named Braggoluce who used to caterwaul his latest verses outside her window and toss her notes about the depth of his affection for her. She found him to be quite remarkable, when in fact you couldn't throw a stone without hitting another poet just like him.

Every day, while Perrolito was dyeing silks and fashioning garments, Braggoluce was offering the same items as gifts to the poor fellow's wife. To her credit, she resisted all of his advances and would not let him too close, until finally he lay down in the middle of the road and implored the nearest palfrey to trample him, since he had nothing to live for but the delicious lips of Fiammetta. However, once Braggoluce had been dragged inside and once she had sampled the delectable joy of having a young robust lover to entertain her, she became impatient for his return and would wait anxiously by the window for their next chance to embrace each other.

Now, there was an acquaintance of Braggoluce, a rival poet named Severino. He had no love for Braggoluce and did not like the way he put on airs and bellowed his silly poems all over Florence. One day they were comparing poems about their respective lady loves when Severino began to criticize Braggoluce for his uninspired sonnets. Braggoluce retorted that he could not write while his hands were otherwise occupied in pleasing the lady in question, doing her double the service of his poems. Then, without much prodding, he confessed that Fiammetta was his delight from daybreak until sunset.

Severino sped straight to Perrolito's shop and told him of Braggoluce's sinful boasts, embellishing wherever he felt it was necessary to complement his poetic abilities. Once Perrolito had recovered from his initial shock, his heart turned to flint and there was nothing on his mind but revenge. Fortune was certainly smiling upon him in his hour of need, because Braggoluce found his amusement in purchasing gifts from the cuckold's shop to present to his wife. Perrolito took the earliest opportunity to strangle Braggoluce with an emerald scarf. Then, with unusual zeal, he cut out the man's heart and wrapped it in some layers of selvage.

Perrolito took this prize *heart of a pig* to a cook named Nestore, and paid him a healthy sum to apply his magic with spices and talent with preparation in order to produce a magnificent meat pie. Fiammetta was thinking only of the absent Braggoluce when her husband came home. He told his wife that a mysterious friar named Braggoluce had given him this heart as a gift and as an apology for missing their saintly appointment earlier the same day.

Fiammetta laughed outright at what she imagined to be a jest by Braggoluce, since no friar would be so generous and free of avarice to give away a meal he could surely gulp down himself. Likewise, her husband laughed at her impatience to dine upon the baked heart of her lover. He waited until she had swallowed every single bite before revealing the ghastly truth about her repast. At once, the happy burps of Fiammetta became sorrowful wails.

This tale should end here on this tragic note. However, after some weeks had passed, Fiammetta considered that her husband must truly love her to have done something so verboten, and little by little her coolness melted into renewed glints of affection. Now he only wondered what he could do to please her and make her his wife again. At this point, Fiammetta confessed that although she was not indifferent to the chatty charms of Braggoluce, she was even more ashamed to admit that she had never enjoyed having him so much as within the crust of that heavenly pie.

Most marriages are based on more than a few oddities in common, and this one was no exception. Perrolito took comfort in this admission, and before long, their home was a haven to visiting poets from every part of Italy. They were even egged on to flirt openly with the lovely Fiammetta. But beware! Anyone lucky enough to be chosen by her as a mate would soon suffer the most intolerable anguish before becoming another of Nestore's prized creations.

At some point, people began to wonder about all of these missing poets, not to mention the contents of Nestore's meat pies. It is rumoured that the couple fled to Pisa, where people cannot taste the difference, no matter what they put in their mouths. But to their credit, they are still very excited by their gruesome activities and love each other more than ever.

God grant that we may also enjoy ourselves.

We all found this tale rather curious and felt quite the overweening appetite for another to follow it. I was eager to give it a go and with the blessing of the others, I improvised a fresh yarn that was inspired by a true event:

In one of the rural regions near where I am from, there is a nunnery of great renown which I shall refrain from naming for fear of soiling its impeccable reputation. At this convent, the abbess and nine nuns are all young in years and understandably subject to many temptations on the prickly road to heaven.

Now, at this place, among men, only a friar was permitted to visit. This was one Pazzolino Gentile, a scoundrel who would sooner slit a throat than recite a single prayer. But as with many folk, once he began to weary of shedding blood and performing evil deeds, out of sheer convenience he found his true calling. Yet he was considered an asset due to his booming voice and penchant for doling out ferocious admonitions. Indeed, no home was safe from the rabid invectives of Pazzolino!

In spite of his irascible nature, Pazzolino was by all accounts a man, and it was not very long before the nuns had reached an understanding with him that was more than agreeable to both parties. Let this be a lesson to us – while we are quaking with fear in our own abodes, afraid to have another helping of wine or cuddle our very own spouses, these houses of God are shelters for the most arcane iniquities!

I have no inkling whether Pazzolino attended to the untenable desires of each nun in orderly fashion or all at once in the same breath, but I am confident that unlike hordes of the poor with their empty soup tureens, they never went wanting. His own jaded appetites had scarcely been whetted when Sixtus IV called upon him to be of service to one of his vile nephews, and this created a vacant situation.

It happened that an acquaintance who was aware of Pazzolino's exploits prodded him for his blessing to visit the nunnery. This was a big, strong fellow named Doppio who had received this nickname on account of the fact that he did everything with the combined might of two men. Pazzolino admonished him for such a wicked suggestion, although he realized it was better to entertain the nuns with a devil he knew rather than one he knew from Adam.

Prior to embarking on his holy mission, Pazzolino brought Doppio to the nunnery, explaining that he had been cursed from birth and could not speak or hear, nor make use of his limbs. He implored the nuns to take pity on this lummox and to care for him as they would a stray orphan in dire need. The abbess and her nuns held to this promise and treated Doppio exactly in the manner of a stray waif. That is to say they took advantage of his helplessness and insulted and berated him at every opportunity, when not in the mood to beat him senseless in order to alleviate their boredom. Doppio endured each blow in the hope that tenderness would follow. But due to a certain reserve on the part of the nuns, an entire week had passed before they advanced to more outrageous infamies.

They filled their nights with speculation, comparing Doppio to a tree with dead limbs that had retained a healthy, solid trunk. The youngest nun suggested that so long as he had eyes, he was surely not insensible to their charms. In addition, in order to compensate him for each affliction, the Almighty might have bestowed him with an immoderately insurmountable pride and joy. The nun in charge of bathing Doppio admitted that she had borne witness to no small miracle in that part of the idiot's anatomy. With a laugh, the abbess volunteered to try out this hypothesis and before long returned to them with a glowing report. They concluded that the Lord never closed one door without promptly opening another!

Hence, the nuns, being more chaste and goodly than other women, needed ten times the attention and activity in order to check their repressed cravings. They were pleased enough with Doppio to stop deriding him and to grant him a new moniker, *Font of Our Perpetual Delight*. As for the man in question, he was at the mercy of their incessant demands and he soon began to waste away from sheer exhaustion. He realized that he was like a child who had been whining for a single dessert, only to be made to eat this dessert ten to twenty times a day instead of once.

This being the case, he was secretly relieved when Pazzolino returned from his mission. The nuns, however, were nowhere near as interested in him as they had been, having become enraptured with the apparent immobility of their fresh man-toy. They informed Pazzolino that his religious services were no longer required, which caused him to fly into a fatal rage.

He wasted no time in finding Doppio in his quarters and restraining him before depriving him of his hands and feet. Then, taking great joy in the irony, he performed a number of acts upon his former friend that were forbidden in all his speeches. Thus, it goes to show that our men may enjoy one another without harm in our city, while in these remote parts, these hypocrites only revel in the foulest of crimes. Pazzolino would have sliced off the ears of his victim, save for the fact he wanted to tell him the tale of Doppio's illegitimate offspring and precisely how he had cared for each of his daughters at the nunnery, since at least three of the young ladies were known to be Doppiolinas. And Doppio's horror was so great that he died of shock on the spot.

At first the nuns questioned the strange disappearance of Doppio, but within a month they had entirely forgotten him. Once again, they warmed to Pazzolino, and after working out a sensible itinerary, he resumed his former duties with the grace, gusto, and generosity befitting any man of the cloth.

At the end of this story, the very good-looking Giovanni Cavalcanti nodded with an air of solemnity, agreeing that these stories were examples of crazed excess in contemporary times. Then in response, he wished to tell the tale of a Pazzo who learned the art of silence:

I must as prologue remind you that our city was once celebrated for its customs, its sense of decorum, and its self-restraint, before the hefty rats of avarice began to nibble it to the marrow. One of these customs was merely to greet those you respected, and to withhold salutations from those to whom you had never been introduced and those who had never done a single thing for you that sprang from the generosity of their souls. Although in hindsight it was a blunder for the banker's daughter to withhold her famous greeting from Dante, she was merely adhering to this custom when smiling at him only after he had traversed the depths of hell and beyond.

Now, I do not know for what reason, but there was a Messer Pazzo who strived day and night to receive a greeting from the noteworthy Delicato, who excelled in everything he did, whether in singing during carnival or jotting down verses or in wooing esteemed ladies or in expounding his arcane philosophical discoveries. Though Messer Pazzo and his company possessed neither skill nor interest in any of these activities, they became increasingly anxious for this aloof fellow to take notice of them and pay them an undeserved homage.

Henceforth, Messer Pazzo and his friends began to follow Delicato. Wherever he went, they appeared and foisted their ungainly opinions and obnoxious manners upon him. Whether ensconced in the libraries of munificent *condottieri* or hidden deep in the mausolea of fine dynasties or perched in a garden outside an alluring lady's window, they would pounce on him, and Delicato would only interrupt his studies and songs to give but one reply:

"Gentlemen, you have the authority to say whatever you wish in your own place."

They did not modify their behaviour, yet whenever they surprised him, the poet would give them the same reply. Messer Pazzo and his companions could make neither head nor hind of this remark, and asked many people what Delicato meant by repeating this nonsensical utterance, unless it was nothing more than a sign of madness that afflicted bachelors of a certain age. Finally, a travelling cabbalist named Smeraldo, who had just returned from visiting Delicato, stopped for long enough to explain this subtle gaffe.

"You are the madmen, if you cannot descry his meaning. This is neither riddle nor enigma, and believe me, I deal in ancient puzzles that would permanently drive you out of your wits. He is saying that wherever you go, crawling from decaying garden to dusty library to lugubrious graveyard, you belong there, because without the light of intellect, you are perpetually in the dark and therefore worse off than the dead. You feed like leeches upon the living and worms upon the dead. He means that you revere dead things so stupidly that you ignore the living and seek the name of Delicato as a name upon an epitaph that has gone cold. You are so preoccupied by this mad pursuit that you fail to appreciate the vivid brilliance of those living among you. Since you are like the living dead seeking the dead, why should he trouble himself to honour you with even the smallest token of his acknowledgement?"

After hearing out Smeraldo and giving him a sound thrashing for his impudence, these men felt suitably ashamed for having treated Delicato with such indelicacy. From that day forth, Messer Pazzo practised the arduous art of keeping his mouth closed, which to this day is the best that can be said of him.

We applauded Giovanni for reciting this tale and were about to tell another when we heard galloping hooves and shouting in the streets.

"Popolo! Popolo e libertà!"

"Palle! Palle!"

Lorenzo's face was at first grave to hear the sounds of revolution and then reassured to hear the defiant cries of the Florentines in support of his family. The people were screaming for *balls*, the familiar pawnbroker symbol on the Medici coat of arms – I could not resist a weak smile to think whose balls they were indeed screaming for. Then, as Lorenzo's entourage was escorting him to the Palazzo della Signoria, I took the opportunity to slip away with only a small twinge of regret, since my father's business was uppermost in my mind. A man bumped into me and I was about to pelt him with abuse when I recognized his peculiarly handsome face. It was none other than Alessandro di Mariano di Vanni Filipepi, virtually out of breath.

"My adoration for you knows no limit."

"Are you mad? Haven't you heard what's happened?"

"Do you mean the Passover plot?"

"What else?"

"Savonarola said this would happen. I am not surprised."

At that moment, Francesco de' Pazzi was thrown from a window. He was still bleeding from where he had cut himself while stabbing Giuliano. He was twisting and struggling upon the noose around his neck when the demonic figure of the Archbishop Salviati was flung down to join him. Salviati writhed upon the end of his rope and managed to swing far enough to reach the dangling body of Francesco. He sunk his teeth into the chest of his co-conspirator and then bit into his noose like a rabid beast. Together then, in this infamous position, they died. Alessandro was already rapidly sketching each macabre movement. I pressed him gently to do a sketch for me, and to dedicate it to me. He briskly complied without a word, and in offering it, gave me a sketch he had done of me floating on the Arno the previous evening. Once everything was in order, I begged his pardon and took my leave of him, promising to return that afternoon. The last thing I saw was Lorenzo appearing at a window of the Palazzo with a bandage around his neck. The crowd roared with approval. Assured that his reign was secured and having what I required, without delay I reactivated the amulet.

VII

The Music of Time

Personnages ·

    FOLDEROL, a playwright
    SMADRIGALETTO, a musician
    FILOMOTTE, a witty wife
    DIMINUÉE (DE LA CHAÎNE), a sly consort
    NEZBEAU, a gentleman of the court
    CHERCHETTE, a high-strung beauty
    PLEURINE, a sensitive minx
    SONORE, Diminuée's servant
    BRAIE, a faithful servant

The scene is the stage of the Royal Theatre at Versailles.

Prologue

After the exhausting conquests and glorious exploits of our august monarch, it is fitting that all those who lay claim upon the varied ranks of letters toil in order to achieve the spoils of his praise, and perhaps to sound victory for having given him pleasing diversion. Let us then attempt, nay, do better than attempt, to achieve the praise of this great prince who grants *The Music of Time* an audience, since it was created to give him some relief after such noble endeavours.

ACT I

Scene 1

CHERCHETTE. So that is how the matter stands.

FILOMOTTE. Yes, I see. But where did this wooing *sans pareil* take place?

CHERCHETTE. At last night's *comédie-ballet*!

FILOMOTTE. My dear, that simply will not do at all.

CHERCHETTE. Whatever can you mean, madame?

FILOMOTTE. The man has no taste!

CHERCHETTE. Why, the work was penned by Folderol himself!

FILOMOTTE. Precisely.

CHERCHETTE. But madame, he is your husband!

FILOMOTTE. Naturally, so I know what I am talking about.

CHERCHETTE. He also has the strongest royal support.

FILOMOTTE. Support? What does he know of that?

CHERCHETTE. Madame, I assure you, this was the perfect backdrop for a most studious courtship.

FILOMOTTE. I consider his comedies rather inauspicious.

CHERCHETTE. Even those you perform?

FILOMOTTE. This is my wifely duty, to portray the very clown of myself!

CHERCHETTE. Madame, I believe you are afraid to disclose your true feelings.

FILOMOTTE. Go on, then. Tell me more of your paramour.

CHERCHETTE. The music stopped, and there I stood, transfixed. Then, out of nowhere, I heard the most beautiful voice, and suddenly it seemed the music had not stopped, and since that moment, it seems the music might never stop.

FILOMOTTE. Who was the owner of this beautiful voice?

CHERCHETTE. He was masked, in costume. One of the players, surely.

FILOMOTTE. He is on excellent terms with discretion, then.

CHERCHETTE. Because he was afraid to appear frightful in the wake of my great beauty. At least that is what he told me, and many other things of wondrous charm, so many that I reel to recall even one of them.

FILOMOTTE. Is it, as they say, an awful bore for a donkey to make love to one?

CHERCHETTE. This was no donkey, madame. Rather more lordly and made up like a sultan.

FILOMOTTE. O dear.

CHERCHETTE. He kissed my hand and was anxious that we meet again. Tonight, in fact!

FILOMOTTE. Ah!

CHERCHETTE. And how is it with you?

FILOMOTTE. Hmm?

CHERCHETTE. You sound like you just pricked your finger and then sat on the same needle.

FILOMOTTE. Ah ... ah ... there is no end to this wretched drudgery! Then it is His Majesty's pleasure that I stage my marital woes at a frequency that beguiles the mind.

CHERCHETTE. There is something else, Madame. Tell me.

FILOMOTTE. Just that your "sultan" sounds too familiar to me.

CHERCHETTE. Now I am the one on the business end of a needle!

FILOMOTTE. Nor are you the only one to meet that needle!

CHERCHETTE. Please, I must know what you know.

FILOMOTTE. Have you not heard of Smadrigaletto?

CHERCHETTE. By reputation only.

FILOMOTTE. That is saying more than enough.

CHERCHETTE. Wait ... surely you do not mean ...

FILOMOTTE. Precisely.

CHERCHETTE. Ah, I am undone!

FILOMOTTE. Do not despair. Unlike my husband's, this farce may turn out in our favour, but you must place your complete faith in me.

CHERCHETTE. I am indebted to you, Madame.

FILOMOTTE. I am at your service. Though keep in mind, I would rather deal with two dozen dozens of donkeys than cross this man.

Scene 2

> BRAIE, *alone onstage.*

BRAIE. Do my eyes and ears deceive me? Surely this is the devil's workshop! Pray tell, what are those unsettling sounds directly after dinner? Why do they not cease? Whomever I encounter, I must take courage to tell everything I know, even if it takes an eighth of one hour. Yet from what I have learned, it is most certainly a sin to listen. In this little room, the scribbler Folderol writes his offal with blood and bile, or so the fiddler Smadrigaletto tells him with alarming frequency. Our souls are not safe while these reprobates are at liberty to ply their sordid trade, although there is not a day on which the gods have failed to smile down on their malevolent antics! Ah, they are returning! I must make myself scarce and wait until they ring for me.

(*Enter* FOLDEROL *and* SMADRIGALETTO.)

FOLDEROL. Ah!

SMADRIGALETTO. Ah?

FOLDEROL. Indeed. Ah!

SMADRIGALETTO. Sweet Grumbles, what is your complaint on this lovely night?

FOLDEROL. A night like any other.

SMADRIGALETTO. The usual, then?

FOLDEROL. Ah, you mean my disgust with the way of court, and town, and all that staggers between their ornaments and false fronts? Ah, you mean my disgust with the way we all leap and hop from bed to bed and cover up our crimes with smiles? Ah, you mean my disgust with the way we wring out our ecstasies and sorrows for public jeering dipped in foul phlegm?

SMADRIGALETTO. Something else, then?

FOLDEROL. You will laugh if I tell you.

SMADRIGALETTO. I will laugh if you tell me!

FOLDEROL. I am most desperately (*sighs heavily*) in love.

SMADRIGALETTO. (*Stifles laughter.*) Is that not your usual complaint?

FOLDEROL. This time, I mean it. This time it is for real.

SMADRIGALETTO. *In vino veritas!*

FOLDEROL. Mock all you want. It was a lovely night when she appeared in front of a font, and when she lifted up her shining eyes they were full of unbridled admiration. Smadri, she knew me by my real name and had allegiance for every triumph and hid knowledge of every disaster, reciting my own words back at me.

SMADRIGALETTO. A pretty face that speaks so plainly! Surely you can do better.

FOLDEROL. Mock all you want. It was a lovely night when she appeared in front of a font and touched upon the theme of wedlock, touting its virtues and its fine embroidery.

SMADRIGALETTO. Beware of proposals in the dark. They are often more fatal than mockery.

FOLDEROL. She did not propose. However, I took her subtle hint. If I were to ask for her hand she would not tarry one hour to surrender up her balmy freshness!

SMADRIGALETTO. This very fresh balminess is locked up inside a young lady, then?

FOLDEROL. Yes, she is half my age and yet she makes me feel twice as young.

SMADRIGALETTO. At least your sums add up to new problems. Are you not leaving out one very tiny detail? Talking of wedlock, I mean.

FOLDEROL. In answer, I would speak of my own cursed union, were it not to speak ill of the dead.

SMADRIGALETTO. I thought I saw Filomotte last night. She looked very much alive. Of course, her mouth was full, overflowing with your bitter complaints.

FOLDEROL. That is not my fault. She only takes part in my comedies to keep an eye on me.

SMADRIGALETTO. Is that not a sign of devotion?

FOLDEROL. It is no easy thing to accept counsel from such a "paragon of virtue."

SMADRIGALETTO. You should know, for your own pigheaded good, that your wife is entirely unassailable. Folly though it be, her only thought is of Folderol!

FOLDEROL. Am I to measure her virtue by the extent of your vice, then, master of music?

SMADRIGALETTO. Aha! You admit she has virtue. But only just the one?

FOLDEROL. You are free to mock my predicament, since you have never been in love.

SMADRIGALETTO. Unless one can be in love with love, as the saying goes. But you are correct in your estimation. I do not know love in the way you mean.

FOLDEROL. One day you may learn, my friend.

SMADRIGALETTO. Ha! How they would rejoice to see me suffering and behaving like blocks of ice heaved upon an open fire! Even now, there is an audience queuing up to see this kind of love lampooned and its fool festooned, swaying in the grip of his own enchanted music!

FOLDEROL. Ah, you are proud, Smadri! You are already ablaze in the open fire of yourself!

SMADRIGALETTO. Braie!

FOLDEROL. You are incorrigible. There is still more work to do.

SMADRIGALETTO. Braie!

(*Enter* BRAIE *out of hiding place.*)

BRAIE. Master, you called for me.

SMADRIGALETTO. Your feet are far slower than your ears.

BRAIE. Master?

SMADRIGALETTO. My room needs tending to. Go at once!

BRAIE. As you wish, master.

FOLDEROL. You keep the strangest company. Braie? Is that even a boy or a girl?

SMADRIGALETTO. I will let you know, presently.

Scene 3

CHERCHETTE. Ah, monsieur, I just left your wife.

FOLDEROL. They say fortune often smiles like a brilliant sun through empty air.

CHERCHETTE. Excuse me ... what is that?

FOLDEROL. Your presence is like a brilliant sun, beating and beating and beating down on me!

CHERCHETTE. What! Are you here to see Madame de la Chaîne?

FOLDEROL. I must confess, it is her domicile.

CHERCHETTE. I believe you are having a spot of fun with me. Is that not just like the whimsical creator of engaging comedies? Last night was a triumph, surely?

FOLDEROL. It was and it was not.

CHERCHETTE. What can you mean?

FOLDEROL. If I were to give voice to those voluminous outpourings that reside within me, it would set your ears aflame and scandalize whatever remained.

CHERCHETTE. Ah! Then are you here to see Madame de la Chaîne?

FOLDEROL. I insist, you first, mademoiselle.

CHERCHETTE. Could we see her together? Should we see her together?

FOLDEROL. La Chaîne is our sun, after all. If we do not make a home of her sitting room, we may miss our chance to make use of her grand illumination.

(*Enter* DIMINUÉE.)

DIMINUÉE. Cherchette, how pretty you look! And Folderol too! There is not audience enough to pay you your due. Last night's entertainments were perfection to any who claim to perceive.

FOLDEROL. Yet you are the very audience I am seeking.

CHERCHETTE. That is what I was about to say.

FOLDEROL. My dear Diminuée, you are the perfect touch to perfection ... *sbleque*!

DIMINUÉE. Folderol, what on earth is the matter?

FOLDEROL. Forgive me, Diminuée! I am a plain-speaking man and the niceties of court tend to stick in my throat and then I come out with all manner of stuff and nonsense and even bizarre sounds like *sbleque*!

DIMINUÉE. There is nothing to forgive. Even if we scowl at your rough talk by day, we eagerly flock to hear it at night!

CHERCHETTE. How true and how apt. I would wish to speak plainly but the words are stuck.

DIMINUÉE. I expect it is impolite to ask precisely where they are stuck?

CHERCHETTE. Please, madame, have mercy. I am seeking your wise counsel.

FOLDEROL. Indeed. I am also seeking your wise counsel.

DIMINUÉE. Children, children, one at a time! Or since we are among friends here, may we not share one another's troubles? In that case, out with it!

CHERCHETTE. I am most desperately in love.

FOLDEROL. I am most desperately in love.

DIMINUÉE. In love with each other?

CHERCHETTE. No, madame!

FOLDEROL. Ah no, anything but that!

DIMINUÉE. With whom, then? You first, Cherchette.

CHERCHETTE. I only know he was at last night's *comédie-ballet*! He wore a mask, you see.

DIMINUÉE. An excellent first impression! Tell me more.

CHERCHETTE. The music stopped, and there I stood, transfixed. Then, out of nowhere, I heard the most beautiful voice, and suddenly it seemed the music had not stopped, and since that moment, it seems the music might never stop.

FOLDEROL. Are you not at all curious to hear about my secret love?

DIMINUÉE. I know a great deal about your secret love.

FOLDEROL. You are indeed wise, madame, if you already know of this.

DIMINUÉE. Her name is Filomotte, I believe.

FOLDEROL. How you mock me, madame! You talk of the complete opposite.

DIMINUÉE. Come, monsieur. You love her and you do your level best to keep it secret.

FOLDEROL. Then my news will shock you. I am speaking of a woman who appeared in front of a font last night and pledged her most ardent affections to me. Since that moment, my life has not been my own.

DIMINUÉE. Yet this garish spectacle is not the wittiest of your comedies! You have just met her, and already you cannot sleep. You have spoken to her with the largest of eyes and there is no direct answer, since she is a heroine of the last century, and already you are losing patience with her, since you have had to suffer, what ... two or three or perhaps even several hours in the grip of those grand and noble sentiments? I dread to think what storms will blow over you. What set-tos I foresee! How many vexations are in the works and how often will your own hot air flutter the sails of your pitiful boat, in threatening to leave her? Is this the curiosity you bring to me, that an ingenious specialist in farces is now the hero of a grand romance?

FOLDEROL. I confess, madame, that you read more than a mere prologue into my affairs.

DIMINUÉE. Far be it from me to lecture you on the subject of entertainment, but for the sober-minded, is there a spectacle more amusing than the spasmodic contortions of a man in love? Now, mark my words, monsieur. This emotional tumult will quickly become the fortress in which you are imprisoned, and not for misappropriation of state funds but for crude mishandling of your own feelings. Will you never believe what I have told you a hundred times? Love is a veritable caprice, involuntary, even in one who experiences its pangs. It may be that this creature of the night has everything to subjugate you, and to inspire you with something I hope will be for your happiness, but so far, I cannot believe this to be a very serious attachment. You are certainly very strange, you men. An attentive woman soon wearies you, and the first woman in ill humour to cross your path wins the most heartfelt declarations at peril to the lot of you. At the risk of doing terrible injustice to my own sex with this hasty comparison, I must say you remind me of the fable about the dog who dropped the bird in his mouth to contest the dog with a bird in his mouth in the water below him, losing the apparition of a bird and the very real bird at once. Then have you found, perchance, everything you require in the little mistress who is the cause of your dolorous martyrdom?

FOLDEROL. Madame, as usual, your wit and insight give me pause for thought.

DIMINUÉE. Monsieur, I will address Cherchette's confusion until you come out of yours. Now, Cherchette, who is this fine suitor you speak of?

CHERCHETTE. Ah, I dare not. O but I must. I have reason to believe his name is ... Sm ...

(*Enter* SMADRIGALETTO.)

DIMINUÉE. Smadrigaletto, what a delightful surprise!

SMADRIGALETTO. I trust I am not disturbing you.

FOLDEROL. How could you think such a thing ... *sbleque*!

CHERCHETTE. I am undone. (*Swoons.*)

DIMINUÉE. Monsieur, kindly take this poor woman out into the open air, and while you are at it, you may clear your own head of more than a few cobwebs. I have a lesson with this master.

FOLDEROL. A lesson with this blackguard! There is only one lesson he can give and besides, I do not believe it! When your fingers are so nimble at play and your voice is more sublime than the music of the spheres ... *sbleque*! You may be right. I will take my leave.

(*Exit* FOLDEROL and CHERCHETTE.)

SMADRIGALETTO. What a fetching jumble of words.

DIMINUÉE. Pardon him, monsieur. Surely his wealth of eloquence upon the stage leaves him impoverished in other circumstances.

SMADRIGALETTO. It would appear that I have interrupted quite the conference.

DIMINUÉE. I wish it were not so. I have need of both of you.

SMADRIGALETTO. Quite the novelty, madame!

DIMINUÉE. Make light of it as you will, although a passing cuckoo could tell you what it thinks of two men of genius behaving so stupidly.

SMADRIGALETTO. Two men of genius, madame? There is but one of us here.

DIMINUÉE. If only you could put yourselves to work! Instead you wear yourselves out working at your leisure. Therefore, to solve the smallest of trifles, I must first bring down the behemoth that appears to be torturing you all.

SMADRIGALETTO. It is not like you to speak so abstractly, madame.

DIMINUÉE. Cherchette.

SMADRIGALETTO. Cherchette?

DIMINUÉE. Do you not have eyes? The woman is clearly infatuated with you.

SMADRIGALETTO. If that is the case, I know nothing about it.

DIMINUÉE. Did you not wear a mask and serenade her last night?

SMADRIGALETTO. Do my fellows really get up to those kinds of escapades? Shocking, madame, truly.

DIMINUÉE. You are playing me for a fool, monsieur.

SMADRIGALETTO. Can one so wise be played for a fool? That is news to me, madame.

DIMINUÉE. If you are my friend, you will dissemble nothing.

SMADRIGALETTO. Ah, madame, but you wound me by reminding me that we are friends, and can only ever be friends. Have I hidden my deeper affections from you, or for that matter, my most ardent longing for you?

DIMINUÉE. If your lyrical air is over, please return to the recit at hand.

SMADRIGALETTO. Let us say there is a man in a mask who serenades the ladies. Could he not be behaving this way only to disguise his real suffering? I mean to say, a woman that is the true object of all his feeling does not receive him in the way he would wish, and there is not a night he manages to sleep fitfully on account of the overwhelming passion he has conceived for her, an everlasting flame that will never be extinguished. What is more—

(SMADRIGALETTO *pulls her chair closer and kisses her hand.*)

DIMINUÉE. My, my, my. Will this poor knave never be able to sleep again?

SMADRIGALETTO. His road to redemption is a thorny one.

DIMINUÉE. How sad. But would this penitent strike a fair bargain with the object of his affections?

SMADRIGALETTO. He is not known to turn away from decent terms.

DIMINUÉE. But what if he finds them to be indecent?

SMADRIGALETTO. As I was saying, he is most agreeable.

DIMINUÉE. Then come to me this evening.

SMADRIGALETTO. I am here presently at the breathing time of day.

DIMINUÉE. There may be far more breathing this evening.

SMADRIGALETTO. (*Bows.*) As you wish, madame.

DIMINUÉE. Sonore!

 (*Enter* SONORE.)

DIMINUÉE. Kindly see that monsieur finds his way out safely.

SONORE. Yes, madame.

 (*Exit* DIMINUÉE.)

SMADRIGALETTO. I heard you humming earlier. What a lovely sound you make.

SONORE. Yes, monsieur. I mean, thank you, monsieur.

SMADRIGALETTO. But what do you do for amusement?

SONORE. Amusement, monsieur? I'm not sure I understand.

SMADRIGALETTO. Does serving madame leave you no amusement, nothing to call your own?

SONORE. I dare not say, monsieur.

SMADRIGALETTO. I implore you, please speak freely. Let us be friends.

SONORE. I am not long for service, monsieur, for I am spoken for.

SMADRIGALETTO. Does madame know of this?

SONORE. Not a whit, monsieur. But I beg you not to tell her.

SMADRIGALETTO. As you wish. Now, hum something for me.

SONORE. What should I hum, monsieur?

SMADRIGALETTO. Do you know anything from a *comédie-ballet*?

SONORE. Yes, I do.

SMADRIGALETTO. Well, hum it, then.

 (SONORE *hums a few strains.*)

SMADRIGALETTO. Well, what do you think of that?

SONORE. Of what, monsieur?

SMADRIGALETTO. The tune, my angel. The tune.

SONORE. Well, it's the last thing in my head. From last night, I mean.

SMADRIGALETTO. That is all you have to say about it?

SONORE. Forgive me, Monsieur. I know little of music.

SMADRIGALETTO. I see.

SONORE. What I love are the farces, and Folderol's most of all! What a gift that man has!

SMADRIGALETTO. Ah yes. I believe I can find my own way out.

Scene 4

PLEURINE. There you have my troubled tale.

DIMINUÉE. I sympathize, truly. But do you think it wise to give your heart to a man of the theatre? In other words, an impresario, a master of illusion?

PLEURINE. Who is more true to the eye and ear? Who is less reluctant to take the stage and cough up his own clever words? Who is less afraid to challenge the flimsy hypocrisies and continual pretence of court?

DIMINUÉE. I am not unmoved by your argument. My admiration for Folderol knows no limit. However, that statement could very well extend to the inimitable Filomotte.

PLEURINE. *Sbleque*! That name! That woman! Surely you know she is the cause of so much angst and unhappiness!

DIMINUÉE. Yet in her place, you would be different, another story with a fresh page?

PLEURINE. Yes! I would not mistreat a man of greatness!

DIMINUÉE. I do not think it. Sadly, another act in the same worn drama.

PLEURINE. I have said my peace to him. Then he wobbled this way and that, before closing his eyes and kissing my hand.

DIMINUÉE. You closed your eyes as well, I suppose.

PLEURINE. Of course!

DIMINUÉE. I can picture you both, closing your eyes to all circumstance. It is not uncommon. Even in the dark, he kissed your hand in the open air, advertising your mutual affection to the night, if no one else. You should be keenly aware that a woman is always balancing between two irreconcilable passions that continually agitate her mind: the desire to please, and the fear of embarrassment. Even the most shy and retiring woman would not scorn an audience in love with her charms. This is what enables us to shine even at the height of notoriety. Our slightest infraction that stems from our love, we brandish like another gewgaw upon a string of gemstones. But how often is a woman permissive in love confused with one who takes payment for love? Therefore, a reasonable woman always prefers a good reputation to celebrity. Yet are you prepared to attach yourself to this public man, to take the place of poor Filomotte in becoming an object of derision upon the lips of anyone who can find their way to the *comédie-ballet*? Take care, my dear, because if what you say is true, then you are understudy to this role and no other.

PLEURINE. Madame, you have a way of putting things so that one is left speechless.

(*Enter* FILOMOTTE.)

FILOMOTTE. How strangely you both look at me!

PLEURINE. My apologies. I have another engagement and must not be late. How sorry I am to not enjoy the pleasure of your company even a moment longer. Farewell, mesdames!

(*Exit* PLEURINE.)

FILOMOTTE. How sorry she is!

ACT II

Scene 1

FOLDEROL. Ah!

SMADRIGALETTO. Ah?

FOLDEROL. Here I was with the worst case of spleen you ever heard tell of, and Madame de la Chaîne set me to rights with a few pretty words. She embodies the spirit that should move the empty-headed court.

SMADRIGALETTO. As the fortune teller said, pretty words will come to you, and pretty bodies, too, but that is not all that I see in your ill-used palms. Now, I trust you are at last ready to wring out your spleen onto the page, so that I may correct each garish drop with one of my more salient notes?

FOLDEROL. Yes, I can feel it now! The naked Muse is tickling my nethers with her quill! A doctor—

SMADRIGALETTO. The spleen of inspiration, struck down by the flame of gout!

FOLDEROL. No, the character is to be a lunatic doctor. No, on second thought, a nagging wife. No, a finance minister out of his depth—

SMADRIGALETTO. If your spleen is sluggish, we could take a look at *The Music of Time*.

FOLDEROL. *The Music of Time*, always *The Music of Time*! Another bit of fluff coughed out by yet another hack!

SMADRIGALETTO. Always the same answer! Madame de la Chaîne speaks most favourably of the author, who wishes to remain in the shadows.

FOLDEROL. Like all tyrants, he begins as a shy flower. All right, Smadri, let's take a look at *The Music of Time*.

(*Enter* NEZBEAU. *Upon entering, he brushes aside the compositional materials of* FOLDEROL *and* SMADRIGALETTO.)

NEZBEAU (*to* FOLDEROL) I just spoke with your lovely wife, and she told me you were here, and at once, I felt my heart would not be still until I had told you of my high regard for you, the highest regard that one can regard. I knew my life would be worthless until my wish was granted and I was counted among the number of your friends. Of course, as a person of some small influence, save for those who call it large, I am surely to be given a hearing and not turned away without at least making some argument in my favour.

FOLDEROL. A ridiculous dandy!

NEZBEAU. Pardon?

FOLDEROL. We are at work, mulling over ideas. So, you came here to fight, hmm?

NEZBEAU. On the contrary!

FOLDEROL. Ha! Filomotte loves a good fight. You had words with her, did you?

NEZBEAU. She was the epitome of charming and she encouraged me to pay you my most humble respects.

FOLDEROL. Me! Her tone was not like a tainted unction then?

NEZBEAU. I do not understand. The whole world owes you tribute. Most humbly, I am here to give you what tribute I can.

FOLDEROL. Sir.

NEZBEAU. Our whole kingdom is nothing without you, a dazzling gem, no, the most blinding jewel upon our crown!

FOLDEROL. Sir.

NEZBEAU. Now, I beg you, give me your hand, so that you may swear me eternal friendship.

FOLDEROL. Sir.

NEZBEAU. That look in your eye! How can my heart's idol turn away in horror?

FOLDEROL. Sir, you do me too much honour. Friendship is a sacred thing, and I would reckon, a rare thing. Why it sprouts up over time, almost like a weed, in the strangest of cracks in our feeble wall, no one really knows. We must see what takes root, if anything, and if there is something, we must tend to it with a candid demeanour.

NEZBEAU. I should take that down. No, I will remember it forever. Let us leave our sprouting to time, then. Meanwhile, I am on an excellent footing with the king, so you should let me know if you have need of my influence at any time. Also, in the name of our noble sprouting, I would very much like to read you this poem I am thinking of making public.

FOLDEROL. Sir, you are nipping at the wrong heel.

NEZBEAU. Why, what do you mean?

FOLDEROL. My penchant for truth and critique of all that is false has given me the reputation of being a loathsome idealist. In other words, I would tell you what I think, and that might be fatal for you.

NEZBEAU. The very thing I ask, that you should tell me what you think!

FOLDEROL. I suppose—

NEZBEAU. "Sonnet." This is a sonnet. A lady flattered my attentions, thus leading to this homage to the amplitude of her eyes. These are not windy or overblown phrases. You will find that the subject is treated with the utmost delicacy.

FOLDEROL. The kick is in the trifle.

NEZBEAU. What's that?

FOLDEROL. Let us hear your sonnet called "Sonnet," then.

NEZBEAU. The style may strike you as limpid, which is to say the matter is not overwhelmingly heavy in nature.

FOLDEROL. One of these days, this prologue will end!

NEZBEAU. Something I dashed off, actually, in less than an hour, when the flattery of the lady in question caused me some unrest in the middle of the night.

FOLDEROL. Like intestinal distress.

NEZBEAU. Hmm?

FOLDEROL. We cannot master time, for time is our judge. Anyway, let's hear it.

NEZBEAU. (*Reads.*)

> Lady, you looked my way,
>
> drowning me in distress
>
> all night and all day,
>
> dogging your dress.

SMADRIGALETTO. There's a pleasing turn of phrase.

FOLDEROL (*to* SMADRIGALETTO). You have the gall to say this is good.

NEZBEAU.

> In your eyes I found hope,
>
> crowning my many woes,
>
> and not a long thick nope
>
> or a bouquet of no's.

SMADRIGALETTO. That's an interesting image.

FOLDEROL (*to* SMADRIGALETTO). I could call you worse than bootlicker.

NEZBEAU.

> This is my terrible torment
>
> like a foaming foment,
>
> to be gripped by passion
>
> because you are fair
>
> then you are not there
>
> in all your fine fashion!

SMADRIGALETTO. That ending surprises and delights!

FOLDEROL (*to* SMADRIGALETTO). *Sbleque*! Is it worse to create or celebrate this offal?

NEZBEAU. You flatter me.

SMADRIGALETTO. No, I do not flatter you.

NEZBEAU (*to* FOLDEROL). And you, sir? What is your sincere opinion?

FOLDEROL. This is a delicate matter. The author asks the opinion of others, seeking praise, rather like a fool surprised by his own echo in a cave. As for the critic, even if he does not wish for the favour of the author of this kind of work, he would prefer not to make an enemy of him, and to maintain the yeasty jellied substance that society is. I would say that writing is an itch we should scratch, but not always in public, or even in front of our closest peers. Instead, leave it to age in a dark cellar, the deepest darkest cellar you can find, in a place where no one ever dares to go. That is my advice to anyone with your well-meaning aspirations.

NEZBEAU. Are you telling me to bury my work in the earth, then?

FOLDEROL. I don't say that. I am thinking of a friend who sought my advice. I thought that he should apply as much attention to his writing as he did to his costume, and to allow his verses to consider their own countenance before going out of doors, if you will accept this creaky analogy. The great bard puts it nicely. Barren spectators may be induced to laugh at anything, but that only makes the judicious grieve. Indeed, a wise friend of mine has advised that one must laugh at what one takes seriously, instead of taking seriously what everyone is laughing at.

NEZBEAU. Then you did not care for my sonnet?

FOLDEROL. I don't say that. I have often thought that we start out by aiming to please, like lovers in love, but soon end up like lovers who sell their love. All I am saying is that it might be better to stash your love in a deep, dark cellar where you can keep an eye on it.

NEZBEAU. I feel you are trying to tell me something. Is it that my work is not to your liking?

FOLDEROL. I don't say that. I am wondering aloud, in the general sense, what drives some books into print? Are we then martyrs to those who must write for their livelihood, suffering to put second helpings into their mouths, or mistresses into their second beds? In your case, it would seem unnecessary folly to sacrifice your reputation at court. Is it not enough you will make that lady in question suffer with the apparition of your love? Must the public also suffer to hear about it?

NEZBEAU. I am almost certain you are trying to tell me something. Is it—

FOLDEROL. Sir, you do not know me, and that is vexing for a start. In these situations, the work must recommend itself and stand in place of your presumptuousness. It is often the case that someone who puts so much industry into his flattery in conversation is like a spendthrift suddenly out of pocket the instant he sits down to write a few lines. It is also often the case that the scribbler finds and follows the worst models, compounding the problem. It is like shovelling dung onto a heap of offal and hoping for improvement. You combine sheer affectation with feebleness of expression to the point that sincerity and form are both killed by your cross-purposes. Are you really *drowning in distress* or *dogging her dress*? By the way, what on earth is a *foaming foment*? That is borderline nonsense. I do not blame you with all the vehemence I might muster, since this poem has got the tune of the time and apes perfectly the wretched taste of the age. If apes could do better, I would not be surprised. Instead, for our benefit, here is a little ditty by my wise friend.

> Pale suitors, if men have sense,
>
> let them cease their nonsense,
>
> unless such noise repents
>
> its own dreary impudence
>
> and word-weary coincidence
>
> dies an eighth death in sheer nonsense
>
> far from the truculent succulence
>
> your ladies find truly immense.

True, this is overtly ornate, rather in the manner of medieval antiques, but do you not see how its syllabic undulations reach a satiric point in the simplest of rhymes? It is straight to the point, in terms of its critique of a plethora of other awful poems, and also in what it is saying, dressed only with the lightest hint of wit.

> Pale suitors, if men have sense,
>
> let them cease their nonsense,
>
> unless such noise repents

its own dreary impudence

and word-weary coincidence

dies an eighth death in sheer nonsense

far from the truculent succulence

your ladies find truly immense.

This is what a real woman might say, and this is what a wise woman might say in response to your poem. Surely you see that.

NEZBEAU. This woman is a friend of yours?

FOLDEROL. One I respect to the skies! What is more, her way with words is exceptional.

NEZBEAU. As for my own verses, they are very good.

FOLDEROL. Then we do not agree.

NEZBEAU. It is enough for me that others praise them.

FOLDEROL. They are fools or flatterers or both.

NEZBEAU. You have all the wit, then?

FOLDEROL. Yet not enough to praise your work.

NEZBEAU. You should write a poem, then, to edify me.

FOLDEROL. I could do just as poorly, and keep it to myself.

NEZBEAU. You are certainly full of yourself!

FOLDEROL. You would run to a quack and ask him to change his diagnosis.

SMADRIGALETTO. Gentlemen, this silly business has gone too far. Now make amends.

NEZBEAU. Then I withdraw my complaint. I am your servant, sir.

FOLDEROL. And I, sir, am your most humble servant.

(*Exit* NEZBEAU.)

SMADRIGALETTO. Most amusing. Your sincerity certainly got you in hot water.

FOLDEROL. Leave me alone.

SMADRIGALETTO. Just now, there is *The Music of Time* to think of.

FOLDEROL. To the devil with you and to the devil with *The Music of Time*!

SMADRIGALETTO. Let us make the bed first, before we complain of discomfort.

FOLDEROL. All right, where were we? Ah yes, a ridiculous dandy was about to ask advice of the court fool. I know just how to phrase it. There might be something in that.

SMADRIGALETTO. These complicated *pensées* of yours are not exactly drawing in the crowds.

FOLDEROL. Then pack the gaps with pretty tunes and they will applaud.

Scene 2

FOLDEROL. In faith, where are they?

SMADRIGALETTO. I sent them away. You are having one of your episodes.

FOLDEROL. Smadri, you know we must rehearse! Our impromptu is due!

SMADRIGALETTO. My music will cover those patches of empty air.

FOLDEROL. Sugar over, you mean. Far too sweet is the taste of our time.

SMADRIGALETTO. Do soften for the tune of our time. To have the world whistling French melodies and breathing French airs is no frugal feat, my friend.

FOLDEROL. We are hardly friends. Acquaintances at best. We have the same employer.

SMADRIGALETTO. You set fire to the ship then saw away the gangplank.

FOLDEROL. Granted, you do have too much wit! I have a mind to jot down that line.

SMADRIGALETTO. Your antics grow worse every day. Why did you start up with Nezbeau? Now he will go public with your severe critique and try to sink our little production.

FOLDEROL. Sir, he started up with me! Has the world gone mad? Must he take legal action to compel me to say his poem is good when it is abysmal? What is more, if abysmal poems are all the rage, then why involve or pester me?

SMADRIGALETTO. There are times when your idealism is a hair's breadth from intolerance.

FOLDEROL. You sound just like my wife.

SMADRIGALETTO. You speak of another kind of injustice, one that causes general suffering on behalf of one so charming and winsome.

FOLDEROL. What am I to say, Smadri? However full of spleen I am, there are words I could use to describe Filomotte that would go well beyond praising her to the skies, but I swear to you they would not be heard or understood by these casual sufferers. Marriage is an institution of such unfathomable mystery that it requires its own language, an argot that is only understood by inmates within its particular walls.

SMADRIGALETTO. I often ask myself if Molière and Lulli went through similar trials before becoming so successful and beloved.

FOLDEROL. You should never envy another man without knowing what it is like to wear his hat or ... I was about to say *go to bed with his wife*, but that is something you do grasp in an amateurish way. However, since you invoke these peerless celebrities, I will concede that Molière writes most eloquently of these complex relations. It is a losing battle, to wage his tireless campaign against hypocrisy, the sweetmeat of society, and still he keeps up a valiant front. I would venture that he is not quite understood by his fellows, poor man!

SMADRIGALETTO. All the same, each philosophical dissertation would be a bitter pill to swallow without the musical interludes and comic interjections of Lulli. You cannot deny that he has changed opera forever! I understand that the *filles du roi* hum his tunes when they arrive in New France.

FOLDEROL. Ah yes, but those long overtures! They are just to signal that the king is getting ready to sit down, I think.

SMADRIGALETTO. Then the farce itself is the signal that he would like to leave?

FOLDEROL. I have had enough of criticism for one day. The point of our discussion was surely that even these inimitable men of genius have their own struggles and problems to work out.

SMADRIGALETTO. Molière's rivals stop at nothing to scandalize him.

FOLDEROL. Yes, that is what I was getting at. It is one thing to judge one's works but quite another to criticize his work based on his conduct. As much as people want to believe that the character of an artist is the same thing as the quality of his work, this is seldom the case. Take that barbarous Lulli, whose beautiful airs are the opposite of the way he behaves. I hear he kicked out Corelli, along with his *gross concerts*, because they sounded far too good! I could say more, but I have no wish to scandalize him!

SMADRIGALETTO. The same goes for Molière. There are pamphlets before every performance about the unhappiness in his home.

FOLDEROL. My heart goes out to him, truly. If you will indulge me, I will make a great confession now, and you must promise not to tell anyone, lest it unfork even a few tongues.

SMADRIGALETTO. Me? Ha! We are hardly friends.

FOLDEROL. Filomotte is entirely suited to me. I love her more than life itself, and she cannot help reciprocating this sentiment, although sentiment is not even the right word. Am I disgusting you yet?

SMADRIGALETTO. If that is the case, then why do you carry on like you do?

FOLDEROL. That is the mystery I was talking about. A common error is to approach the institution of marriage as if it were a pie one were continually afraid of eating or dropping. I admit, it is the most peculiar of bonds that can withstand the worst inferno and the ravages of time, and then like one of your enchanting tunes, there it is again, shooting up like a bright weed in the cracks. You suffer because your attempts to escape only make you more of a prisoner. You are bound to the pain it causes, as well as the unfathomable mystery it creates. If I were Molière – but no, he writes comedies and never about love as it is. It is not a subject fit for the stage!

SMADRIGALETTO. Given all that I know, you are right. I do not understand you.

FOLDEROL. Ha! If I were Molière, you would give me leeway to behave how I liked!

SMADRIGALETTO. Ha! If you were Molière, what then? What would you do?

FOLDEROL. I would tell her my exact feelings in no uncertain terms and then pick up and go.

SMADRIGALETTO. Go?

FOLDEROL. Away, away from here, anywhere, or even out of this world!

SMADRIGALETTO. That makes no sense, my faux Molière.

FOLDEROL. To a land full of sunflowers. To a flat, clean place. Some lowly lowlands, perhaps. No, it is impossible, I know. Our stupid pantomime must continue, perhaps until we are no more. I know this to be the truth, although I will never understand why.

SMADRIGALETTO. Have you tried ... well, what about a love letter?

FOLDEROL. A facility with words is the flagship of mistrust. The more sincere I am, the more she believes I am making an idol of her out of wax. She only listens when I rant and rage at her. In fact, she enjoys getting a strong reaction out of me. That is a real woman for you, who measures your pulse by the size of your heart attack. Still, I admit, it is the same for me. She is most exciting when she is most in a fury!

SMADRIGALETTO. You are disgusting me a little now.

FOLDEROL. Ha! If I were Molière! Then I could burrow into the holes in my plays and say exactly what I mean.

SMADRIGALETTO. Sir, that would be the cowardly way out.

FOLDEROL. No, I talk freely of my troubles, and that is life. It is not a *comédie-ballet* where we can be carried off by the nimble feet of dancers and the tremulous voices of singers ...

> (*Mournful dancers appear, flanked by a lone singer who resembles Pierrot.*)

> *Cruelle douleur, redouble ton ombre;*
>
> *Soudainement, tu vaincras par le nombre,*
>
> *Tu ne peux pas me distraire*
>
> *De mes soucis infinis.*
>
> *Moi je continue sans espoir*
>
> *Aux ombres de moi-même,*
>
> *Je ne dois plus toucher ce que j'aime*
>
> *Je ne dois plus bousculer les ténèbres.*

Scene 3

DIMINUÉE. Once again, we are alone. Are you now in a mood to discuss the business on everyone's mind, including that of our shining sovereign?

FOLDEROL. There are constant interruptions. The impromptu goes this way and then another way. I am not certain it will be ready in time.

DIMINUÉE. Have you reached the heart of the matter yet?

FOLDEROL. Only around the middle of the second act. To be frank, the subject of the work you gave me confounds me. There are a few characters and there is a definite atmosphere, but I cannot for the life of me unravel what it is about.

DIMINUÉE. Why must it be about anything?

FOLDEROL. There is a scribe of dubious morals and a rogue of a musician. Various women, too, although I cannot quite get a sense of them, except for the terribly clever one. Her name escapes me at the moment.

DIMINUÉE. So it should, for she is based on a lovely lady at court.

FOLDEROL. Now will you tell me who wrote this uneven extravagance?

DIMINUÉE. The author of this work asked to be known only as M.

FOLDEROL. Ah! That gives me an idea! But why entrust me with this work?

DIMINUÉE. Perhaps it is an experiment.

FOLDEROL. I would suspect trickery, were it not recommended to me by you, madame.

DIMINUÉE. Will you return *The Music of Time* to me and permit me to go over your changes, and then offer my opinion? Also, with your signature, as a precaution? There are such rogues about.

FOLDEROL. Certainly. In fact, I would be much obliged!

DIMINUÉE. I know you can forestall the royal audience with another of your entertainments. I have a long journey ahead of me, but in the interim, I hope that you will improve your behaviour and that you will show your wife more tenderness than you have, thus embracing the dignity that rightfully befits the name Folderol.

FOLDEROL. For your sake I will try, madame. I need not remind you how we theatre people are viewed and what my reputation must therefore be! In this topsy-turvy world, when I am most virtuous, I am most maligned. Nor was I fortunate enough to win the hand of Madame de la Chaîne!

DIMINUÉE. Sir, I would take you with me, if I did not have complete confidence in your talent and what would appear to you providential assurance that your destiny is here.

VIII

For your sake, faithful reader, I am inclined to interrupt the flow of this narrative from time to time to point out the various lacunae in my story. After my journey through human history, in the course of my studies, I discovered other accounts of my adventures that left me green to the gills with invidiousness, due to their striking brand of eloquence. In cases where I have managed to locate a particularly intriguing version of what was wearying to me at the time, I have included it on the basis of its literary merit rather than its adherence to the dreary facts at hand. I sometimes offer you a rendition that tells you what could have been said or thought at the time, rather than the events that actually happened. Forgive this trait of mine as you would the duplicity of a friend whom you cannot help but adore. What is more, if you are able to adore, by all means, please do.

June 5, 1833

My Dear Frond. You leaf through the Newspapers for word of your young Lioness – you are gravid with twin Melancholy & Longing to learn of her quantity of Satin & Tulle &c – she did not collapse during the Presentation in spite of anxieties sprouting like weeds about her before the Dukes even arrived. Her delicacy is said to have survived Straightforward & Surefooted, Ill-spoken & Ill-conceived & Creamy Charm, in that Order. –

See how I tease you with twaddle about ball dresses! – You are assuming this is the only matter to occupy my mind henceforth. – On the contrary, uppermost in my memory is an intimate party after the Court Ball, by no means a gathering of distinguished persons, but rather more to my Personal Taste, since each Man bravely bore a scientific turn of mind like a gleaming medal upon his forehead. –

According to Mama's Calculations, Mr Charles Babbage is relatively the same age as she & while she expected him to speak in Naughts & Crosses, this "finical dodderer" was, in her opinion, very light on the earth & addressed nothing but trifling concerns. – You are now dangling in suspense, asking as Mr Babbage must have, when we might be matched & if Mama approved, or if she did not, what the resultant Quantity might be. –

If you have not heard, Mr Babbage was fumbling about behind the scenes of The Rake Punished, seeking to apply some mathematical principle or other to the trap-door system, when the platform began to rise & he faced the shameful incongruity of appearing with a pack of devils on stage. Fortunately, he leapt off in time & avoided the fatal call of the Commendatore. I relate this brief tale to amuse you & to demonstrate what type of caller he may become. There could never be passionate display, save where the mind imposes limits upon an infinite series. Soon, I hope, he shall agree to once again tutor me, & cultivate the seedling within my uncanny brain that before its season feels well beyond ripe. –

At this stage, I cannot confess to you my primary interest in Mr Babbage, but I shall very shortly. Before long, you are to know my future & what is more, the future of Everything! –

Yours affec^{ly}
A. Ada Byron

Frond. Surely you will have difficulty believing what I am about to tell you, but today Mama & I went to see the <u>thinking</u> machine. – We know not what other moniker to lend it. Not infrequently, Mr Babbage refers to this friendly Beast as his Engine. It raised several Nos. to the 2nd & 3rd powers and extracted the root of a quadratic Equation. The most common operation is a form of brisk counting applied to variable ratios, which appeared to many an Occult principle of change indeed. –

Each member of our party was struck dumb by this demonstration, although I cannot confess to sharing their bemusement. – Call the moment Fatidical if you will, but within those unseen workings I felt an intense stirring up of my entire being, not to sully my perception with prophecy – observe sleeping within me & that prodigious machine this desire to relate an evident purpose of the Utmost Import! –

Sadly, I must close, since I am anxious to inform Mr Babbage of the fullness of my understanding & to candidly discuss with him the most immediate means for enacting their practical application. –

Yours affec^{ly}
A. Ada Byron

My Inimitable Frond. I have been remiss. Forgive me! I know you will.
I have been writing extensively, almost exclusively to Mrs Somerville,
with regard to these stones that form clusters & shower from the heavens like drops of rain. – As a Man, you will suspect our fair sex is merely
capable of arranging petals, but if you knew the Great Things we wrote
of! – By way of contrast, your letters are full of Rumour and Humours,
which is to say rude Appetite. – I am inclined in these instances to set
you like a pointer on the hunt for some silly minikin dangling Miss,
instead of after the One you shall never quite comprehend. –

You will say you do not understand exactly what I am speaking of.
No – you do not ... But I am trying by degrees to work out my ideas ...
It is time I made you aware of my unfathomable amount of intuition ...
I have sometimes used the expression that <u>I have a little bit of another
sense</u>. I have long felt conscious of this; & my course & plans & objects
for my life are led by this, if not driven! –

To prevent any Doubt on your part, I must enumerate the Qualities
I have observed during an intensive study of Self over a course of
many moons. – This sounds an exercise in conceit, although I can
assure you, it is not! To be frank, I believe myself to possess a most
singular, a most particular, combination of qualities precisely apt
for initiating me into the <u>hidden realities</u> of nature. I come to this
conclusion almost against my Will, and not through wild enthusiasm
or a preference for spells of self-exaltation. I have been slow to admit
such a blinding Truth, but there comes a time when one's modesty
must go wanting out of courtesy to a higher purpose. – I will reveal to
you the remarkable faculties in me that, when united, will permit me
to see & know anything that a living being can see & know ...

Firstly – Due to a refined peculiarity in my nervous system, I am
subject to perceptions of things which no one else can confess to have.
I do not know what to call this faculty of mine, this little gift that gives
me an <u>intuitive</u> perception of things beyond the rudiments of our common sensorium. That is to say hidden things, things hidden from eyes,
ears, & the ordinary senses ... You may not believe that I can observe
you this very instant, but I assure you, I am not wholly insensible to
what you are doing, to the curve of your eye & the impression of my
ink upon it. I confess to sensing what you must be thinking, presently;

Secondly – My unparalleled reasoning faculties;

Thirdly – My concentrative faculty. I do not mean my ability to throw my whole energy & existence into whatever activity I choose, but my bringing to bear on any one subject or idea, a vast apparatus from what might be deemed esoteric, irrelevant & extraneous sources. With every ray of the universe finding a common point in me ... well, you can imagine the potent amount of focus that would be applied directly to ... let us say, the problem of Mr Babbage's Engine. Decidedly, most people would find this a remarkably mad letter, & yet it is an example of some of the coolest, most rational, most logical, not to mention one of the finest, pieces of composition that was ever penned by a living mortal;

Fourthly – When opportune, my vast capacity for modesty;

Fifthly – The expanding nature of my concentrative faculty that alters whatever enters its radius. These changes may be small & even immeasurable, but my intuitive senses assure me they are vital to the progress & understanding of Man. I feel that my slightest idea, particularly where the Engine is concerned, will be far reaching, certainly well beyond the scope of your imagination. To consider the degree to which my every Thought & Action will traverse the laws of Time itself is astonishing and leaves me quite short of breath;

You now have a glimpse of the plans & objects of my life. You may consider me enthusiastic, or incomprehensible, or perhaps in a degree conceited. But I do not <u>think</u> you will.

Yours affec^{ly}
A. Ada Byron

February 26, 1841

My Dear Frond. Forgive your Debtor of Letters. I owe you more than to admit to enjoying <u>Mathematical Weeks</u>, & by that, I mean specifically the expansion of the field of my <u>Imagination</u>. The progress of my studies has come to a halt for the present. A matter has come to light & I would place every confidence in you & yet my hand will not shape the letters that spell out a most <u>strange</u> and <u>dreadful</u> history! Steady my nerve – be my recondite champion! Invest your good self in my endeavours & do not be shocked if in due time, I become a <u>Poet</u>.

    Yours affec^{ly}
    A. Ada Byron

March 23, 1841

Frond. Pinioned by <u>Court Dresses & Trains</u>, & all the vanities of life. I think they will be nearly settled in a day or two. I am arranging all my dresses & coiffures for the season, & then I shall have some always ready, & no more plague about it. My train for the 9th is said to be one of two velvets, & both are so beautiful I cannot decide; one an emerald green; the other a very rich pure purple; the dress will be my Coronation petticoat, white & gold. Is this for what I am meant – to spend my days in this Fashion, in wanton idleness? I do not always think it.

Yours affec^{ly}
A. Ada Byron

My Dear Frond. Tomorrow sees me off before you will receive this letter. – I am most vexed, having pledged & entrusted to Mr Babbage the exclusive use of my head, that the rest of me must journey at once to act as the most harmonious Muse to help bring into the world a Welsh harpist of thirteen years. – In spite of its goodly Merit, this task is not best pleasing to me, since my Work on the Engine is to be interrupted indefinitely. –

Sometimes I long for the carefree days when I merely wanted to construct fairy wings and flutter across the country. Mr Babbage helped with the flaps for my Flyology book then too.

This is rather disappointing, since the extension of Algebra ought to lead to a further extension similar in nature, to Geometry of <u>Three Dimensions</u>; & then again perhaps to <u>further extension</u> into some unknown region, & so on <u>ad infinitum</u> possibly. – I have informed Mrs and Mr Morgan of my continual discoveries, since they are sympathetic to my penchant for the application of metaphysical properties to what is immediately available to my every Observation. –

That is to say, the immeasurable beyond what is measurable. – What is beyond the limits of our paltry existence is perhaps beyond our understanding & possibly out of the province of any mortal to grapple with it. – This limitation does not directly affect me, since I often have a queer sensation as if I had died, & as if I can conceive & know <u>something of what</u> the change is. – This translation is one upon which I sincerely hope to elaborate. – My remarkable intuition & tact shall guide me to this ultimate Discovery, for the purpose of elucidating it for Mankind. – I have sometimes used the expression that <u>I have a little bit of another sense</u>. I have long & increasingly felt conscious of this; therefore the direction of my life & what boon is to arrive afterward is soundly decided.

Once I have combined a high & deep knowledge & philosophy with my peculiar temperament & instincts, the potent combination of these two will be apparent to any soul I take into my confidence. – Every day, I am garnering more training toward this inestimable goal, although the process creeps forward by slow imperceptible degrees. – Yet in the humblest sense of the word, the years shall reward me with the necessary quantity of what I call <u>capital</u>. But I care not what I go thro'; – I am enterprising; & the greater & harder the work; the greater my spirit of enterprise.

I hope before I die to throw light on <u>some</u> of the dark things of the world. I may do so; or I may not; but at any rate I shall do great good to myself & my own mind, if I do nothing else. Thus, do not despair for me or for yourself, since if what you claim is true, you will one day be known as the man who wholeheartedly loved a Genius without parallel.

Yours affec^{ly}
A. Ada Byron

Frond. I must confess martyrdom to my wondrous Science, in the face of loathsome malady. I have been suffering from gastritis & severe intestinal trouble. My breathing is shallow & I fear wasting away into a wisp or ghost of myself. Mama has been most helpful in this regard, recommending frequent bleeding sessions with her doctor. She had kept me on generous doses of opium for some time, although this had the irritating habit of making me logy, so I have been advised to take the stimulants brandy & laudanum to counteract this drowsiness, which is far more useful in assisting me with my sums. –

This is absolutely vital, since Babbage spends a great deal of time feasting & flirting in luxury & ease at his sumptuous repast, while I, poor little Fairy, dote upon his every whim in eternal service, mind & limb, on behalf of his beloved (& sometimes nearly wretched) Engine. You may suspect this <u>Fairyism</u> of being entirely <u>imaginary</u> ... but nothing could be further from the <u>Truth</u>. The coinage of my brain is by no mean counterfeit. That racing brain of mine is something more than merely mortal; as time will show (if only my <u>breathing</u> & some other et ceteras would make rapid progress <u>toward</u> instead of <u>from</u> mortality).

No one knows what <u>awful</u> energy & power lie yet undeveloped in that wiry little system of mine. I say awful, because you may imagine what it might be under certain circumstances. Forgive me, but Lord L—— sometimes cowers and cries out what a General I would make. Had worldly matters – power, rule, & ambition – been my line, what a formidable force I would have unleashed! Desperation would have mingled with sheer Prudence to form a union that would have given me unlimited sway & success, in all probability. –

Fortunately, my realm is limited to merely ethereal matters. On this note, & as a token of my trust in you, I share something miraculous that I have not even told my husband. On several evenings, while enjoying the stimulating system recommended by Mama, I have been visited by an otherworldly creature in the form of a woman. There are many oddities about Her, namely her form of dress. She does not wear a gown or anything I would deem <u>feminine</u>. She most often appears with but a yard of strange material about Her middle & a bodice that strikes me (I must admit) as <u>awfully</u> immodest. Frond, if you saw Her, your eyes would pop out of their sockets and what is more, you would perhaps forget me at once. To be frank, I should not care to entertain company of Her sort, were She not so very Ephemeral in her bearing

& so rife with understanding about the Engine. In fact, we speak of little else. I did not expect to develop such a sympathy for Her, & in response to my ardent attentions, my mystical apprentice has made me aware of the pleasures that only spirits enjoy, in addition to curious & improbable Charms that may bind an excellent Man to one. But I digress – more importantly of all, I am making great haste with my Calculations for the Engine.

His dinner downed & well-digested, Babbage will be pleased.

Yours ephemeral[ly]
A. Ada Byron

Frond. I continue to toil for Babbage in veritable reclusion. He appears to enjoy pestering me about pusillanimous trifles – particularly his quarrel with government officials – to the point that I have taken to calling the first of his original inventions <u>The Differences Engine</u>, much to his chagrin. He is so fixated upon winning this argument & righting imaginary slights against him that I feel it is often a detriment to the success of his remarkable machine. I wish he would come to understand the service I am performing for him & his fine work.

Hark! Do not think I overstep my modesty! I am acting as Fairy to more than one mind at once, and doing my Utmost to provide interpretation for the encompassing Idea – through me, this magic is bubbling and churning – & dare I say, through the brilliant charms of my <u>Night Visitor,</u> who does much to inspire and encourage the most frail of my notions.

Yours affec^{ly}
A. Ada Byron

Good Frond. You will agree that mortals have different types of minds. One constituted of no more than old cabbage & another of the finest quartz. It is in this spirit that I seek to filter a few of the scientific ideas that have preoccupied me for your benefit, acting as a gem refracting rays of sunlight for an inclined plant.

There are two sections of the sciences that directly concern the Engine & its <u>Importance</u>. One is the inexorable set of rules that govern the mechanical, subject to the general operations of matter. The second involves the intervention of reasoning, which is to say, our common understanding & how we interpret these rules & use them to our goodly advantage. The machine that Babbage proposes to build would be fully capable of transcending mere calculations & applying principles of analysis based upon known methodologies. However, the machine is not a thinking being, but simply an automaton which acts according to the laws imposed upon it, although my night visitor, the <u>Enchantress of Number</u>, suggests to me that we will have these engines one day, capable of such things few could fathom possible.

Consider a vertical column consisting of an indefinite number of circular discs, all pierced through their centres by a common axis, around which each of them can take an independent rotatory movement. Upon each of these discs is inscribed our numerical alphabet, what my friend calls our ten digits. The first disc is used to represent units & the second tens, & the third hundreds, & so on. To perform an arithmetic operation upon two columns, we may combine them accordingly & obtain the result on a third column. I will step through any of the operations as in the article, except to point out that the machine is divided into two principal classes: Variables & Operations, where the Variables are represented by columns & the Operations define the relationships among them.

The mill is a special apparatus that contains a number of columns similar to those of the Variables. When two numbers are to be combined together, the machine effaces them from the columns where they are written, that is, it places zero on every disc of the two vertical lines on which the numbers were represented, & transfers the numbers to the mill. Once the operation is completed, the result itself is transferred to the column of Variables which shall have been indicated. All fractional & irrational results can be represented to the degree of approximation made available by the number of discs in each column.

The mechanics of this machine are derived from Jacquard's apparatus, used for the manufacture of brocaded stuffs. The <u>woof</u>, or transverse thread, is conveyed by an instrument called the shuttle, which crosses the longitudinal thread, or <u>warp</u>. A system of levers is used to regulate each group of threads according to the pattern of the design being implemented. A rectangular sheet of pasteboard is used to determine which parcels of threads are to be raised by levers & which threads are to remain where they are at any given point in time. A series of cards can be used to reproduce a given pattern, enabling the manufacture of brocaded tissues with a precision & rapidity formerly difficult to obtain.

Similarly, the Analytical Engine uses Operation cards to prepare the machine to execute any determinate series of operations, such as additions, subtractions, multiplications & divisions. In addition, Variable cards are used to indicate the columns upon which the results are to be represented. The cards, when put in motion, successively arrange the various portions of the machine according to the nature of the processes that are to be effected, & the machine executes those processes by means of the various pieces of mechanism of which it is constituted.

There are immediate advantages to this machine: rigid accuracy, economy of time & economy of intelligence. That being the case, imagine how many observations remain practically barren for the progress of the sciences, because there are not powers sufficient for computing the results! Think how the prospect of a long & arid computation might hinder the mind of a man of genius, who demands time exclusively for meditation, & who beholds it snatched from him by the material routines of tedious operations! Thus, the idea of constructing an apparatus capable of aiding human weakness in these researches is a conception that, once realized, would mark a glorious epoch in the history of the sciences.

I call to your attention that the Difference Engine can in reality do nothing but add; & other operations can be performed by it only just to that extent in which it is possible, by judicious mathematical arrangement & artifices, to reduce them to a series of additions. Take into account that while the Difference Engine can merely tabulate & is incapable of developing, the Analytical Engine can either tabulate or develop. This new engine may be considered to be the material & mechanical representative of analysis, & that our actual working powers in this department of human study will be enabled more effectually than heretofore to keep pace with our theoretical knowledge of its principles and laws, through the complete control that the engine gives us over the executive manipulation of algebraical and numerical symbols.

I have arrived at a rather pretty description that appeals to all who hear it, pointing out that the Analytical Engine weaves algebraical patterns just as the Jacquard-loom weaves flowers & leaves. Babbage & I believe this is the only proposal or attempt ever made to construct a calculating machine founded on the principle of successive orders of differences that is capable of also printing off its own results. This engine surpasses its predecessors, both in the extent of the calculations it can perform, in the facility, certainty & accuracy with which it can effect them, & in the absence of all necessity for the intervention of human intelligence during the performance of its calculations.

Of vital interest is the storehouse, which contains an indefinite number of columns of discs, where each disc represents units or tens or hundreds, & so on. The columns are intended to receive the variables and constants in an analytical formula. With much enthusiasm, the Enchantress of Number refers to the storehouse as memory, although I bristle at the thought of applying any kind of human principle to a machine. I did not understand Her at first, but over time She pressed me to appreciate the possibilities for this storehouse system with mechanical improvements that are currently beyond our ability to effect. She has convinced me of her playful fancy that all the columns I could ever wish for would fit upon the head of a pin, although I sincerely feel that two hundred columns ought to be enough for anyone.

I have been in a veritable fever to transcribe these notes for you. Do not beat your brains about too much, Frond. Writing to you has roused a fiery lucidity in the core of my body & mind.

Yours affec^ly
A. Ada Byron

Frond. I regret not being able to make our Assignation, if that is the word. Do not take it hard, since I am very poorly and in truth up to very little. – Tomorrow I may perhaps try a little ride out, if the weather is mild. As you well know, the slightest excitement affects my nerves & drives my brain wilder than the most generous helpings of wine & stimulants. No more Laudanum, although I cannot envision another day passing without it. I become so easily excited, & my eyes water & burn. I am being put on a small quantity of Porter, diluted with twice the amount of Soda Water ...

My desire remains unquenched. I am frequently awake many hours at night, with feelings of exhaustion and a hunger that cannot be satisfied. We think a little Malt Liquor before bed-time may obviate much of this. I saw Gamelen today & told him everything about my wretched state for the past six months, except for those splendid visitations by the Enchantress of Number, which are in every sense beyond explaining. In his presence, my brain began to turn & twist, & my eyes began to burn. I dread recounting the history of my health, lest the impression of horror be revived with other forms of exertion and excitement. I learned much about my constitution & my temperament, & we identified many causes contributing to past derangements that I shall in future avoid. One ingredient (but only one among many) has been too much Mathematics.

There has been no end to the manias & whims I have been subject to, & which nothing but the most resolute determination on my part could have mastered. The disorder has been a Hydra-headed monster; no sooner vanquished in one shape, than it has sprung up in another. I have even considered that due to the way the Enchantress steals in & out of my delirium, She must be merely the coinage of my brain. If this is the case, then She has access to my own prophetic genius & expounds upon future times with surety and a sense of accuracy that is delightfully terrifying.

She whispers into my ear of my name in the future, of my doing more for Science than my father ever did for Poesy. She speaks of the importance of my work with the Engine, and how it will lead to concepts I can scarcely fathom. I have been unwilling to concede that the Analytical Machine might have any relation to modes of human behaviour, other than instructions we supply the machine with, thus providing its functionality. The Enchantress argues this point with me, insisting that advancements in a time to come will lead to the creation of an artificial <u>person</u>. The mechanics to which She refers are admittedly beyond even my great capabilities, but she insists the principle of the thing is almost exactly the same.

My head is certainly vastly <u>better</u>. But it needs <u>rest</u> & <u>peace</u>. I am rather lorn about so many I would wish to see, & cannot. Yourself, most of all.

Yours affec^{ly}
A. Ada Byron

Nov 17, 1844

Dear Frond. I am feeling an immense sense of clarity about All Things. For there have been many Things to make do with, including the good doctor's attempts to relieve my congestion of the head by frequent bleeding. When they remark about the strange effect wine has on my temper, they say I look affronted. I am inclined to think that instead of ordering Claret some months ago, Locock might have advised Laudanum or Morphine. I think he has got the thing at last.

My original suspicions were that Opium disagreed with me. But I now understand how & why it deceived me in this manner, since I was all the time taking wine & stimulants, perhaps dashing their humours upon its own sublime Majesty; & these elements combined to bring about a terrible jumble ...

The Good Lady Opium has a remarkable effect on my eyes, seeming to free them, & to make them open & cool. Then it makes me so philosophical, & so takes away fretting eagerness & anxieties. This sound Deliverer appears to harmonize the whole constitution, to make each function act in a just proportion (with judgment, discretion, moderation).

I have certainly suffered for all this interior luminosity, & yet I have my hopes, & very distinct ones, too, of one day getting cerebral phenomena that can be put into mathematical equations; in short a law or laws for the mutual action of the molecules of the brain (equivalent to the law of gravitation for planetary and sidereal worlds). I am proceeding in a track quite peculiar & my own, I believe. There are great difficulties but at present I see no reason to think them insurmountable.

The grand difficulty is in the practical experiments. In order to get the exact effects I require I must be a most skilful practical manipulator in experimental tests; & on materials difficult to deal with; viz. the brain, blood & nerves of animals. Fortunately, the Enchantress recognizes my enfeebled physical state & is most eager to assist me in my experimental manipulations.

In time I will do all I dare say ... I hope to bequeath to future generations a Calculus of the Nervous System.

Yours lucid[ly]
A. Ada Byron

Frond. Do you know it is to me quite delightful to have a frame so susceptible that it is an <u>experimental laboratory</u> always about me, & inseparable from me. I walk about, not in a Snail-Shell, but in a <u>Molecular Laboratory</u>. This is a new view to take of one's physical frame; & amply compensates me for <u>all</u> sufferings, had they been even greater.

By the bye, Faraday expresses himself in absolute amazement at what he (I think most happily & beautifully) designates the "elasticity of my intellect."

Even from the little <u>correspondence</u> we have lately had, he seems quite <u>strangely</u> impressed with this characteristic; & says that he feels himself a "mere tortoise" in comparison. As far as regards <u>himself</u>, he is so humble-minded that I cannot take <u>his</u> estimate of his powers – could he throw his whole life and existence for the time being into whatever he wills to do & accomplish the thing like myself – could he WILL things into being like a <u>Byron</u> – I think not. As regards <u>me</u>, I see the <u>fact</u>, that he is (justly or not) in great astonishment. It is evidently his impression that I am the <u>rising star</u> of Science.

Fortunately, I am equally humble-minded, even to a fault. I am simply the <u>instrument</u> for the divine purpose to act <u>on</u> & <u>thro'</u> ... wherefore should Angels descend upon me with beauteous rapture & press the forbidden coal to my lips. Like the Prophets of old, I shall speak the voice I am inspired with. I may be the Deborah, the Elijah of Science.

The only <u>merit</u> that can ever petal at my feet is that of putting myself & maintaining myself in such a state (physically & mentally) that God & His agents can use me as their <u>vocal</u> organ for the ears of mortals ...

I am a <u>Prophetess</u> born into the world; & this conviction fills me with <u>humility</u>, with <u>fear & trembling</u>!

I tell you my views because, <u>unless</u> I do so, it is scarcely giving you fair play (in <u>your</u> peculiar relationship to me, that is). If you know not the <u>colour</u> of my mind you may speak <u>inappropriately</u> to me. Was not that <u>my</u> early, & for a time, <u>fatal</u> error toward you?

As to my relations with the Divinity, such as it is or may <u>become</u>, neither you nor anyone else can alter or modify these, nor have you <u>any concern with</u> it. However intensely I may love certain mortals, there is <u>One</u> above whom I must ever love & adore a million-fold as intensely; the great All-Knowing Integral! –

None can ever again come between <u>me</u> & <u>Him</u> – To <u>Him</u> & to <u>His Will</u> have my truly <u>virgin</u> affections been given, at length & for ever. – (Awful words & sentiments!) ...

I tried to <u>serve two masters</u>, <u>God</u> & <u>The World</u>; until the warning voice of pain & suffering <u>recalled</u> me ...

Happy those indeed, who are so <u>imperatively</u> commanded ... Tho' <u>more yours</u> than I ever was in my life, yet I am <u>less yours</u> too. You will understand this.

I joyously await every ministration of the Angel dispatched to wave open my eyes, the radiant soul of finery I call <u>The Enchantress of Number</u>. As I said to Lord L——, what we do is our affair, sanctioned by the very cleft of heaven & by my station as Prophetess among unseeing unhearing mortals. With all the humility in my heart, I forgive them their lack of understanding.

Know that I no longer desire to shun the silken carpets of the rich & luxurious of the earth. Can I not bring to light a spirit to penetrate even the deadening blunting vapours of aristocratic self-indulgence?

Are not <u>these</u> ones most in need of a Prophet of God?

One must <u>study</u> them, for it is not by <u>direct</u> speaking & suggestion that one can do good to such. But, they may be <u>mesmerized</u>. You must depend on it; I am a great mesmerizer ...

"Crede Byron"
A. Ada Byron

Dearest Frond. They say <u>sleep is the highest accomplishment of genius.</u>
I could not agree more, since I have been tossing and turning all
night, scarcely able to demarcate the division between fancy & real
stuff. When I consider the extinguished orbs & rayless cheerless road
I thought I tread, I recoil with a shudder of horror & not a little bit.
Perhaps my aspirations to Godhead have been premature. Perhaps I
have wronged the heavens with what I have seen happen.

I had only settled into bed with my Opium and my spirits, having
worked out the right dosage for an excellent send-off, when whom did
I observe but the lovely Enchantress of Number, drawing me from
any promise of repose. It seemed that Lord L—— was roused &
defiantly obstructed our path, but the <u>Enchantress</u> gave him a <u>Swift
Kick</u> with Her riding boot and left him cowering in a corner after a
series of licks with her lash. I felt more than a drop of pity for him,
but I remained faithful to our divine mission & everything it would
entail. A carriage awaited, and we leapt inside. The steely beasts knew
no bar to their wild & impetuous flight.

We hastened through the night at incredible speed, at times sailing
over rooftops and tiny figures below. When we came to an abrupt
stop, I was horrified to see the entrance of a foul charnel house. But
as the <u>Enchantress</u> led me through heaps of stinking flesh, and as my
senses grew accustomed to this stench, I found that I was increasingly
interested in everything I saw. That is to say, as I had a natural aptitude
for mathematics, I without question had an innate understanding of
natural philosophy, for in a scientific pursuit, there is continual food
for discovery & wonder. It was one matter to consider the workings of
a calculating intelligence, even a helpless machine fed instructions by
mortal whims. But the Enchantress was brashly introducing me to the
decay and corruption that resided beneath the blooming cheek of life.
With the help of a shadowy footman, She drew away body after body.

We then retired to a nearby cellar in which She was to operate
upon sinew & bone. While working merrily, She spoke of ways in
which she gained knowledge without knowing anything. She also
spoke a great deal about time & its fickle intricacies to the point that
I began to wonder about the distant world she claimed to inhabit. Was
time indeed only a substance that stretched & shrank in the face of
our puny manipulations? My brain was in a fever as I watched Her
assemble something resembling a human frame & connect various
wires to it. But it did not take me long to succeed in discovering the

cause of generation & life, nor to perceive how animation was bestowed upon lifeless matter.

The mealy Thing, it twitched like <u>The Modern Prometheus</u>, while the Enchantress explained how the workings of the loom in my research were not so different from the workings of a mechanical intelligence. I could appreciate Her inkling that one day we will write instructions to manipulate artificial or animated life as easily as I write you these brilliant letters. The Enchantress claims there will be methods of writing these instructions that are named after me, not to mention artificial beings that also share my name. I had barely come to grips with these notions when the guilty Thing pulled free of our electrical harness & raced off into the night, with scarcely the apparatus to do so. If only Faraday could have seen our experiment before things went abominably wrong.

We could hear screams & both of us were aware of the unslaked thirst & unsated appetites of the dead <u>Entity</u> that we had unleashed upon our unsuspecting neighbours. I beheld horrific visions of the deathly wraith speeding home & taking swift revenge upon Lord L——, tearing him limb from limb & not leaving him a single working member, leaving me entirely exposed to the attentions of my admirers.

I was then shocked to find Lord L—— perfectly intact and my mother tending to me and calling for the doctor. Even as they applied the leeches & let my blood I could not forget what I had witnessed, even in dream. Surely I had written down all my thoughts in a series of diagrams that the <u>Enchantress of Number</u> had consulted with much encouragement. Are those sparkling papers still with Her then? Now, like a celestial pixie, She has once again vanished. Whither is She bound?

I wish you were at my side. I dare not write what underlies my meaning but you can surely fathom the juicy meat of the matter from the very <u>Morsels</u> of what I have not said.

Yours affec^{ly}
A. Ada Byron

IX

Hand in hand, we leap forward to the twentieth century. I had thought, like an overaffectionate tutor with an irresistibly marmish glow, to gingerly guide your hand and connect the geographical dots you shaded in so expertly, thus explaining the purpose of my journey. However, this would not be my place, since I am anything but a frustrated academic, although I assure you that before we are finished with one another, all of these indistinct mud-wrestling shapes shall be hosed down to a state of shimmering clarity. We now have innumerable accounts of various aspects of the Second World War, but none seemed to make such an ardent grope for the truth, nor succeed so deliciously in its fumblings, as the underground work of one Oskar Kunst, one of the pioneers of the *nouveau roman*. I have selected the chapter that most pertains to my own furtive involvement in this era, as cleverly depicted in his gripping thriller *Symplegades*.

László Löwenstein stepped out of a fog. Not a mental fog, for he was clear-headed and poised to take the shot if necessary, but a bona fide pea soup. He watched the subject down his stout and approach a woman at the bar. They exchanged a few words and within minutes, she was putting on her coat. László was very sharp and keen in the cold, mentally noting the pea-green colour of her coat and the *verkakte* brown of her scarf. The subject tugged at the soggy edges of the dark moustache that was incongruous with his greying temples. László concentrated on the man's face, trying to visualize the same kisser without facial hair ... younger and in some other place. But after an ounce of consideration, he decided against the overwhelming sense of familiarity that was stealing over him. The sad fact in this business was that people looked like other people. Even this fetching woman looked like twelve dozen others, and then thousands of figures throughout history. She was the same as ever. Yet he mentally jotted down the observation of her beauty mark, which also filled him with a sense of familiarity. He lingered as close as he dared, and shadowed them right to the door of a dilapidated flat. László considered the obvious implications, planning to gather any evidence of indiscretion and use it to influence the subject, perhaps even to the point of turning him. You never knew exactly what would turn the most smashing of chaps, although this method would be far better for the subject than various alternatives.

In less than a quarter of an hour, László heard footsteps and quickly hid. A woman's shoe. Clip of the shoes of a woman of pleasure. She sped by without noticing him. He tried the door, found it open, and slowly began to feel his way upstairs. But before he tripped, he had guessed the cause. He fumbled for a match and lit it, waving it over the bulging eyes of the subject. Then she had hurried off into the fog without her scarf. László sighed. People really looked like other people. Even the dead.

Friedrich Lang had not heard from his man at Bletchley Station. He decided to have a gander anyway. He looked around carefully before lifting the correct pot to uncover the spare key. Once inside, he perused diagrams of rotors of the machine, the kind of thing he expected to find. The fellow was brilliant, of course, but certainly with two strikes against him, not the sort of chap you can invite home to tea. Friedrich thumbed through some of his papers, keeping them in their exact pell-mell order. *Entscheidungsproblem.* More gibberish about ciphers. *A false proposition implies any proposition.* Now, what the devil did that mean? At last Friedrich noticed a crumpled note. *Reconvene with D.* It was likely they would find him at Bletchley Station, eager to reach his accomplice. *A false proposition implies any proposition.* The devil it does.

"Now, come along, love."

"I don't know."

Margaret Levy walked slowly through Hyde Park beside Harry Gurevich, looking up at the weeping beech as groups of long-tailed tits hopped all about them. In the distance, some pigeons lingered, watching.

"I'm glad it's stopped raining."

"You would be Mrs. Gurevich."

"Yes."

"Your mother likes me."

"Then why don't you marry *her*?"

The air raid siren began to wail. Harry seized her arm and began walking faster, tugging her along. She stopped and shook free of his tense grip.

"I'm not coming."

"Come along smartly, Maggie. It's the air raid!"

"I want to walk."

"It's the air raid! We'll get blown to bits!"

"Go then, if you're so keen on saving your neck."

"I sure can't stay here!"

Harry walked away briskly without looking back and then suddenly broke into a run for the nearest shelter. As she watched him go, she could not resist a smile. A stranger in the distance returned her smile weakly. His hand was in the pocket of his coat. Then the stranger turned away and tripped over a mound of earth and disappeared in an ear-splitting explosion.

Dick Denemy shadowed the prior shadow carefully, listening for his departure. He lifted the correct pot to uncover the spare key. With a trained eye, he examined the papers in pell-mell order, determining which had been moved and which had been left in place. Out of a sense of sheer superstition, he reached for a conspicuous page from the bottom of the pile. *If he knows what the speedy nancy knows. Best give it a once-over.*

```
The behaviour at any moment is determined by the symbols that
are being observed, and the state of mind at that moment.
Suppose a bound to the number of symbols or squares that can
be observed at one moment. More observing requires successive
observations. Suppose the number of states of mind finite. We
know the state of the system if we know the sequence of symbols
on the surface and the state of mind. The situation in regard
to the squares whose symbols may be altered is the same as in
regard to the observed squares. Assume the squares whose sym-
bols are changed are always observed squares. The new observed
squares must be immediately recognizable. Suppose they can only
be squares whose distance from the closest of the immediately
previously observed squares does not exceed a certain fixed
amount. Suppose each of the new observed squares is within L
squares of an immediately previously observed square.
```

Lovisa Gustafsson sat in the square, impatiently breaking off precious bread for alien pigeons. After that crude tussle in the Savoy, her subject had starting talking about his childhood and his interest in pigeons. She had expected to pump him for more information then and there, but his talk had only fluttered about the room like so many trapped birds. She had tailed him for a time afterward, decidedly stopping where he had stopped, in the square with the cooing birds. It was clear to her that one of these birds was an enemy pigeon. Nothing else made sense. A sallow-faced man smiled at her and she averted her eyes. She chanced the police box with her paisley scarf trailing behind her.

"Trafalgar. Tredegar. What!?!"

A false proposition implies any proposition. The codes had been reconfigured, already. If they were going to intercept a message, they were taking their bloody time about it.

Lt. Colonel Reginald "Rims" Whitehall refixed his steel-rimmed monacle before lighting his cigarette. No need for that. This was bound to be a soft touch. He opened the folder and consulted the papers inside. Papers full of type. Yes, very good. He stared intently at the photograph of a man with impenetrable eyes and a dark moustache. *Now I know what you look like, and that, old chap, is half the battle and by no means the war. Member of a jelly gang, hmm? This one'd take the sugar out of your tea before you'd even had a sip.* Leslie Thompson was led into the bare, colourless room. That is to say, the future Leslie Thompson was led into the bare, colourless room.

"Sit down."

"Please don't waste my time."

"A sizable quantity of gelignite was found on your person."

"Yes, I deny nothing."

"Then you turned yourself in of your own free will."

"Yes."

"Well then, how'd you like to work for the *Abwehr*?"

"You know I am already in communication with them."

"But do they believe it?"

"Do you?"

"You could find ways ... to convince me."

"I have come here to help you."

"You realize from where I'm sitting, your past looks a bit dodgy."

"All the better to convince the Fatherland."

Reggie Rims, or Rimsy, as he was known at the Diogenes Club, inhaled deeply and breathed outward, enveloping the freshly invented Leslie Thompson in a mysterious cloud of smoke.

"You came here to blow up a fortified meat factory, or so you claim."

"I still intend to."

"Playing the principal in the theatrical version?"

"That is rather what I had in mind."

"For all intents and purposes, your name is now Leslie Thompson. Welcome to Double Cross."

The agent known only as MUGGINS, "man of a thousand faces," moved closer and examined the painting in detail. His eyes studied the girl posing with laurel wreath, trumpet, and book. The book was said to be a work of Thucydides, and if so, then she was modelling as Clio, the Muse of History. He noted the rip in the map dividing the Dutch Republic in the north from controlled provinces in the south with more than a modicum of glee. The golden chandelier was a double-headed eagle representing the Austrian Habsburg dynasty, and given their intention for this painting, the allusive irony amused him. As with other aspects of the picture, the marble-tiled floor was out of place in an artist's studio, perhaps only another wry comment upon perspective technique. Apparently, the canvas was authentic seventeenth century, with paints mixed of white lead, indigo, cinnabar, gamboge, ochre, and lapis lazuli. The whole thing put together with badger hair. It was suspected he had then used phenol formaldehyde to harden the applied paints and accelerate the aging process by a few centuries. Then bake it, roll it, and fill in the cracks with black ink. It was supposed to be a self-portrait, but in this case ... of whom? Was there a difference in the artist with his back turned to the viewer, a difference so supersubtle that someone might be able to figure out that it was not the back of the original genius, but rather the back of a genius forger named Vanderspeigle the Minor? MUGGINS drew even closer and scrunched up his eyes. On the table was a death mask.

Dick Denemy joined the other rows of faceless figures standing uniformly in similar hats and greatcoats, seeming to bloom out of the platform at Bletchley Station likes sheaves of wheat. The key difference that was unknown to them and particularly to himself was the peculiar combination of his musings, based upon his very recent observations.

Simple operations must therefore include:

(a) Changes of the symbol on one of the observed squares.
(b) Changes of one of the squares observed to another square within L squares of one of the previously observed squares.

It may be that some of these changes necessarily involve a change of state of mind. The most general single operation must therefore be taken to be one of the following:

(A) A possible change (a) of symbol together with a possible change of state of mind.
(B) A possible change (b) of observed squares, together with a possible change of state of mind.

The operation actually performed is determined by the state of mind and the observed symbols. In particular, they determine the state of mind after the operation.

CRUMPET sprinted through the sparse copse, searching frantically for a place to hide. His mind reeled with circumstances, wondering who had compromised him. The agents swiftly raced through the meadow and along the trail of footprints and snapped branches, keen on his scent. For a moment, their respective loyalties seemed absurd. What could compel men like himself to become these merciless killing machines, scanning the trajectory of his flight with cold indifference? And what had he himself done to warrant this pursuit? CRUMPET had picked up the package even at the specified place and had taken the train to deliver it to its destination. Almost at once, horrific reports abounded. It was clear he was being manipulated, but by which side? He came to a stream and hesitated, deciding whether to hide or make his way across. He was already tired and out of breath. Even if he could manage to signal for help, to whom should the signal be sent? He had made his way to the other side when the gun sounded. One of the bullets missed, but the other two found their target. CRUMPET now lay crumpled in a patch of mud.

The men sped to his side. He was assuredly done like dinner. The sticky bit for their department would be the actual identity of CRUMPET and whether he was a formidable enemy or merely the victim of foul play. However, they were glad these questions were not their concern.

D MINOR directed the two agents into the room that looked like any other. They waited without a word for the tea to appear and for its bearer to disappear. She put on a gramophone record of a Haydn string quartet before pulling out a folder marked **URGENT**.

"Lads, welcome to Operation Gemini."

"Gemini? That suggests twins."

Hugh was talking out of turn again. Clym shot him a look of disapproval.

"Our information shows that enemy forces are putting a great deal of time and energy into occult practices. There is an undeniable parallelism between practices of prognostication and their subsequent steps in terms of engaging us."

Clym sipped his tea thoughtfully.

"Then I take it the idea is to plant false horoscopes to lead them astray."

"That was the original idea but it was rejected. It was then put to us that we were perhaps turning our back on certain techniques that would help us understand our adversary and at the same time give us similar attributes of intuitive fortuitousness ..."

"I say, absolutely not!"

They both glared at Hugh and he withered where he stood.

"Now, I have taken intensive training with our chief expert in the field and I have been assigned to the direct recruitment of multiple agents."

"You don't mean kooky old Crowley? Has he been sniffing around our toffs again?"

D MINOR did not answer. She discarded her rubber mackintosh and began to unbutton her crisp white shirt. Clym stared mutely into the checked pattern of her long woollen skirt. It reminded him of a tea towel from his childhood. He could have sworn the letters on her folder were dancing about. At one point, he thought the folder was marked **UNGUENT**. She ordered him to strip and he obeyed, almost without thinking. He felt he would do anything for her. She lay down on her back with her head at the foot of the bed and bid Clym to crawl between her thighs. Then she gave him a slip of paper to read.

" 'How my dry throat, held hard between thy hips / Shall drain the moon-wrought flow of womanhood!' "

She bid him tend to her insatiable need as she tended to his. Amid sucking and slurping sounds she gave out additional cues.

"Now you become Shiva and I become Shakti!"

"Indeed! O criminy, don't stop, Shakti!"

"I say, isn't this one called the *Fifths*? My wife is very fond of it."

Hugh pointed to the gramophone with a sense of futility. No one believed him. It was relatively public knowledge where he spent his Sundays but his colleagues turned a blind eye, wondering if they couldn't make use of him in other ways. Such was the game and he was playing it. Meanwhile, just as he had in dreams, *Shiva* had pinned *Shakti* to the bed and was driving her to the point of ecstasy with what was relatively known as *the wand* in sex magick circles. However, Clym was startled as she unfolded a decorative cloth bearing a swastika and spread it over her face.

"Do not be alarmed. This is a Hindu *svástika* representing the two forms of Brahma, both the evolution and the involution of the universe."

"Very well then!"

"Our magic will be better than their magic."

Meanwhile, Hugh concentrated upon the controlled amusement of Haydn and attempted to pry his eyes away from Clym's undulating buttocks. But there was no air raid warning for this one. Within seconds, just as he had in dreams, Hugh had assumed a most compromising position on top of Clym's intriguing rump and was making his naked ambition known.

"Hugh, is that you?" .

"I am the involution of the moon."

"But this is highly irregular, old boy!"

"Orders from the top. Just arch your back and think of England."

They spent the rest of the afternoon in this manner, switching posts and enacting the roles of various deities and restoring universal harmony to their tasks at hand. However, during the very climax of their assignment, the rubber mackintosh belonging to D MINOR spontaneously burst into flame.

The woman lay naked and immobile upon the sienna chesterfield with a great deal of red about her mouth, and what appeared to be a handkerchief or scarf placed over her pale neck. Her legs were slightly parted. A man with his back to her appeared unperturbed, directing his attention instead to a gramophone. His dark coat was draped over a chair. His grey hat was resting upon his coat. His reddish brown case remained closed upon the floor. In the background, beneath the azure sky and round silver mountains, three bareheaded men with open mouths peered into the window at the listening man and prone woman. In the foreground, on either side, two men in bowlers were waiting. The man on the right carried a net and the man on the left gripped a club.

Jean Assai climbed out of the trench and crawled upon his belly toward the mystery object. For all intents and purposes, the thing looked like a thermos but he wasn't expecting tea. Not just yet. The sun beat down on him as he applied the clamps. He used all of his strength to unscrew the lid and stopped, already exhausted. You would think Millicent would forgive him a quick nip of Napolean at such a moment. After all, it might be his very last. *It would be just like you to get yourself blown to kingdom come,* that's what she would say. Jean mopped his brow and examined the wires, second-guessing himself more than once. He told himself it was all for their imaginary child who wouldn't stumble upon this ghastly thing and get himself blown up like his damned fool of a father. Yet if his guess was correct, then he also had to unscrew the base of the device. At last, he managed it, but afterward he lay panting upon the sand. He wiped his sweating hands and then plucked out the charge. He leaned over and spoke into the radio.

"Best put this one on ice. Tell Millie to expect *Old Toes Up* for supper."

But the ground began to shake. Within a few yards, the neck of a bottle emerged out of the sand and peered around curiously. Then it began to grow in size until it towered over him. Jean could now tell it was the deadliest of enemies, a giant bottle of whiskey, and the expensive stuff too. He ran but it hovered briskly after him, accompanied by the unsettling sound of a theremin. When they found him, he showed signs of having drowned. Regrettably, this was the third time in so many weeks a sapper had missed his supper.

Hate. Maddox scrunched up his face with raw livid hate. There was no letter, no note. He could picture her matted hair upon the parquet floor, her sweating body so strong and vibrant and eager upon the spare cushion. He was jealous of that cushion and jealous of that hideous lamp that belonged to Lord Titchley. He was jealous of her dress and jealous of the hands that would remove it. He could picture her irresistible coquetry over the ugly table veneered in parquetry, over the ugly face of one of an infinite series of ugly faces, bearing the hideous powdered loneliness of their impassive ministry or their diffident flock, finding a vacant place with her upon the floor in one of the shiny herringbone squares. And the ugly hack writer like himself with a hideous case crammed with fears and conceits, entering from the back and making her laugh and laugh upon half a dozen freshly burnished lozenges. Maddox rationed his jealous hate into checked squares upon the parquet where she had surrendered to him, even with Lord Titchley still shuffling about upstairs and his hot panting breath still stinking with onions. Layer by layer, Maddox painstakingly began to peel the raw onion of his jealousy.

MUGGINS touched up the streaks of grey about his temples. There was no known photograph of Vanderspeigle the Minor, so he had to adhere to the common denominator of all known descriptions. He powdered his new beard carefully while examining another of the excellent forgeries. It appeared *The Little Square* was very closely modelled after *Het Straatje*. The observer was presented with a façade painted parallel to the frame in such a way that the individuals and their activities were rather obscured by it. Beside a green shutter to the left, two men were visible, standing beside a seated woman. Their dark squareness and her light roundness were likely indicative of sex, but their blobs for faces revealed nothing more than a sense of anonymity. To the right, beside a red shutter, one woman sat with her blobby head leaning against her hand, while behind her a serving maid was leaning over, peering into a cistern. Through the archway and gables of whitewashed brick resided the little square itself, divided into a series of visible squares. They seemed contrived, as if only an unbalanced architect would construct this collection of adjacent units. In the square, a woman was visible through a window. She appeared to be holding something, perhaps a letter. The back of a man was visible, as he made his way down the corridor toward the woman holding the letter. To the left of him, in another corner of the square, two men were standing with their blobby heads pressed together, perhaps in conversation. In front of the façade, two children were huddled together on their hands and knees. They appeared to have found something.

Jean Amar gave a silent signal to Edvard Hench before slipping into position at the window. The jalousie was shut tight but one of the louvres was mysteriously split, which left a crack through which Amar could continue his surveillance unimpeded. A woman was standing in front of a motionless man who lay flat upon the bed. The woman removed her crisp white shirt and walked toward the man in nothing but a long woollen skirt with a rich tartan pattern that reminded Jean of a dishtowel from his childhood. Strangely, the woman reminded Jean of a woman he had seen in a painting not long ago. The Muse of History. He could make out a tiny mark upon the small of her back, something that resembled a rather flowery swastika. The man was a man like any other, naked and presumably excited behind the moving screen of the woman's back. As the woman descended upon his body, Jean observed a blinding flash. He rubbed his eyes and when he looked again, the woman had vanished. But his expert training had already put together the circumstances of what had just happened. The glint could only have come from a monacle belonging to the only man who always wore one, even to bed. Jean swore under his breath, waking up Edvard, who had completely missed the cold and calculated murder of none other than the usually brilliant Reggie Rims.

Lovisa purred into a pillow with one eye open, with the taste of excellent tea on her tongue and with incessant cooing filling her ears. Strong and sweet, the Ipswich stuff. She had observed the madman in the square breaking off bits of unleavened bread for alien pigeons. Or she was the madwoman he was keeping under careful observation. It worked out to the same outcome, either way. This time it had been rather early with no one about. She had been standing under her umbrella and tearing off bits of bread when she saw him, well ahead of schedule. They had inclined his head to give her the impression of a polite nod. Then he had begun his slow approach and she had wondered whether he was in fact the infamous BISCUIT. She had been studying his crazed beefy not-bad-looking face when, with a sudden flourish, he had opened his coat, leaving nothing to her imagination. The room at the Savoy was already paid for and she purred with pleasure as he feverishly administered his special branch of the administration. With one eye open, she could see a lone pigeon peering inside. It was carrying a message.

A man known to many as Nippers entered the room. The agent known only as VOLE whirled about, surprised.

"Where's Reggie Rims?"

"Rimsy's dead, old boy."

"Blimey!"

"Can't be helped, old thing."

"Then Operation Neuter ..."

"Still on like a house on fire!"

"I see."

Nippers cleaned his nippers thoughtfully. He coughed. Then he spread out a series of leaflets for VOLE to examine.

"This is disruptive stuff they drop out of planes for our lads on the front."

VOLE studied each of the illustrations. Several of them were titled *The Girl You Left Behind*. In each case, while her boyfriend was fighting on the front lines, the woman in the illustrations was involved in a number of compromising situations for a lascivious Jewish war profiteer named Jacob Levy. Apparently, from what VOLE could initially gather, the title character was of shadowy Eastern European origins and had been impoverished until finding opportunities to profit through war contracts. He was also hand in glove with all warmongering officials.

"You know, sir, my mother ..."

"Don't want to know, old boy. Thing is, they target the *Chosen*, and it's almost equally disruptive to any side who dares to look. But whoever created him didn't count on some rather peculiar repercussions."

"Such as?"

"Jacob Levy has been sighted in London. At first, we took it for a lark, but apparently he is discussing very real war contracts and has formed a vast pool of computers and secretaries ... umm ... under him."

"So you think this is a form of counter-espionage?"

"Couldn't say, old thing. But your job is to go through these and to keep tabs on our Mr. Levy. We've got to get to the bottom of this on the double quick!"

"But isn't there a way to combat such lunacy?"

Nippers laughed, then coughed.

"Don't worry yourself, old stick. That's what Morse is for!"

The Girl You Left Behind

Poor little Joan! She is still thinking of Bob......

"Eeello ello!"

The package balked and turned to run from the man in the flapping raincoat. Finding his way blocked by another man in flapping raincoat, he tried a new direction, seeing enough of an opening to flee. The second man fired at once.

"Muzzle that, won't you?"

"Our orders are to interrupt his activity. Stop."

"You would interpret an encoded telegram that way."

"He is now well interrupted, you might say."

"Well, stop shooting now. Stop."

They turned the man over. He stared up glassily with a broad grin.

"Share the joke, old boy."

"I'm done for and I want to see your faces ..."

"Yes."

"... when I tell you."

"Yes?"

"You got it wrong. Your target is already moving."

"Good try. We know who you are. We know what you are working on."

"Nothing! I'm the decoy. A bit of steak and kidney to throw to the dogs ..."

"And the man we are looking for?"

"Gone. You know ... he runs incredibly quickly. You'll never catch him ..."

The decoy died, this time with a shocked expression on his face. The removal service would have to be called in. The two men paused, mulling the matter over. It was starting to look like a mistake had been made. However, they were glad these questions were not their concern.

"You'll never guess what I saw in Hyde Park!"

"I've had plenty of adventures in Hyde Park."

Anna stopped listening. Margaret couldn't say she cared much for her. On her first day, Anna had showed her the best way of cleaning the floor, simply to sweep all the dirt under the rug. Mr. Schmidt slept all day, so she could get away with murder. Once he was awake he would bellow grouchily for his tea. In addition, he had an obsession about the sugar bowls being clean and Margaret hated being chastened over a dot of sugar.

"This is my felluh."

Anna was holding the hand of a beaming navvy with a green muffler and leading him into the backroom of the shop. For Margaret, this peculiar practice was no longer any more unusual than working in a shop without any evident items for sale. She could hear muffled laughter and the creak of an old chesterfield.

"Filthy *shiksah!*"

She wiped down the sugar bowls with a damp cloth. It was nearly tea time. She did not even hear the agents steal inside. She was astonished to see her employer being strong-armed and led away by two men.

"What are you playing at?"

"This one's a Fifth Columnist, ehn't he? Been radioing the enemy all night under yer noses."

"Mr. Schmidt!"

Mr. Schmidt turned to Margaret and stared at her with bleary, irritated eyes. "Clean the sugar bowls! *Großreinemachen!*"

Following the roar of engines overhead, the picture fell out of the sky. *The Girl You Left Behind*. In the illustration, Jacob Levy was helping a girl who looked like a pin-up model put on a pair of nylon stockings while she examined a newly bought scarf. He was hunched over beside her, his glasses fogged up, clearly fascinated by her, grasping her tantalizing bottom and shapely thigh.

> *Today she will take home thirty pound.*
> *Two years ago, Beryl was still a salesgirl in a ha'penny shop*
> *getting six quid a week. Today she is getting thirty pound*
> *as the private assistant to Jacob Levy.*
> *Business is smashing and good ol' Jake is making*
> *quite a lot of dosh on war contracts.*
> *FOR HIM BLOODSHED MEANS BUSINESS.*
> *And he's getting to know Beryl better and better,*
> *while her fiancé, the tall and manly Cecil Smith, is at the front,*
> *fighting for characters like Jacob Levy. Beryl adores Cecil to bits,*
> *but she has no idea WHEN HE WILL COME BACK.*
> *Have you seen the other pictures of*
> *"The Girl You Left Behind?"*

A few of the men tore up these leaflets in disgust and despair. They climbed out of the trench with the intention of turning tail. The enemy was fast but their own commanding officer was faster. Soon their bodies lay still among the brilliant leaflets.

Dick Denemy waited on Piccadilly, not far from the explosion in Hyde Park. Nasty business, that. The notes he had recently perused continued to prey upon his mind. *Dilly took another hot bath yesterday. Had to force the door. Poor chap. He was literally up to here with abstractions, never mind knee-deep in hot water.* Denemy observed his contact and began to shadow him. This was one of those things, a possible red herring. Was the code cracker cracked? *The Enigma has twenty-six keys and twenty-six bulbs. Subject to alterations via wheels within the machine and plug-board, the depressed key corresponds to an illumined letter on the lamp-board. The enciphered letters are taken down and radioed by Morse. Machine on receiving end with identical settings agreed upon is used to type ciphered message and read by lamp-board into deciphered text.* The man disappeared into a public house. Denemy hesitated before following him inside. *Right in the middle, Dilly was always slipping up.*

Maddox sat in a pew at the back in shadow. Lady Titchley approached the altar and made a sign, lighting a candle and leaving a note beside it. Maddox was instantly jealous of the note that was not intended for him. He wanted to read it and then rip it to shreds, but he was determined not to lose sight of her. From the safety of his dark corner, he watched the sublime expression upon her face and trembled to think of the warm body beneath the fabric of her dress. Then at a distance, he followed her home. He wanted to lift the giant brass knocker and bang it violently against the door until she at last agreed to leave with him. But his plan was to lie in wait and watch. Yet he was the one ambushed by the approach of a diminutive man in formal dress, a dapper Jew with round rims, carrying a long rectangular box. Maddox averted his eyes and headed for the nearest public house, struggling to efface a series of repeating images from his mind. His bow tie loosening, his box opening, his small hands grasping flushed skin, her pale white body kneeling, her palms paddling herringbone parquet, her flesh aching and burning for his circumcised grotesque amid the distorted horns of triumphant Nibelungs. Goats and monkeys! He did not notice the man tailing him until he felt the gentle poke. Then, over a whiskey, almost at once, he agreed.

The agent known only as BUN stepped into the studio with care. However, he fought to hold back his excitement, since it was not every day one got the chance to meet a great artist. He smiled warmly at the man with the white beard.

"Vanderspeigle the Minor!"

"You are the man interested in buying some paintings."

"I am called Klaus."

He led Klaus to a back room where he could examine each of the paintings at length. He scrutinized the facsimile of *The Art of Painting* before moving on to *The Little Square*.

"I have not seen this one before."

Behind a green shutter, two shadowy men were looming over a frightened woman. To the right, beside a red shutter, another woman appeared to have been drugged, causing another woman to stare suspiciously into a cistern. There were a series of adjacent squares. A woman was visible through a window, reading a message that in all probability contained false information. A man was making his way toward her, clearly with orders either to turn or terminate. In another corner of the square, two agents were exchanging information. In front of the façade, two children were huddled together on their hands and knees. The body was about to be discovered under a bit of tile they were removing.

"How do you know this is not a forgery?"

"It scarcely matters, my friend. Is such a forgery not the most sincere assertion of Art?"

"You are a philosopher."

"A connoisseur with soul will know that beauty is in the eye of the beholder."

"What about this one?"

"A Magritte."

A naked woman lay dead. Her killer had his back to her, as he was receiving his next orders by gramophone. The spies were watching from the window in the background and on either side of the foreground. They were waiting for the first opportunity to pounce.

The man in the overcoat stopped running and nearly collapsed upon a bench in Hyde Park. Another man in shorts broke out of his team of runners and took a seat beside him.

"I say, fancy a drink? Water, I mean."

"Phfff ... that sounds divine."

"How about up the road? We'll make it, I think."

"Yes ... fine."

The two men walked slowly toward the Whistling Horse. They entered. The man in shorts ordered two waters and two bitters.

"I took the liberty."

The man in the overcoat gulped down one of the waters.

"Eh ... I must keep my wits about me, today of all days."

"Why today?"

"Ah ... no reason."

"That sounds like a contradiction in terms."

"Contra ... yes, everything is a contradiction and that's where the cock-up comes from. That's the one thing I've learned."

The man in the overcoat accepted one of the bitters and took a sip.

"Did Dilly leave the water running again?"

"Who are you?"

"All that matters is I know who you are."

"What do you want?"

"How about you tell me a story about code breaking. How about you start at the beginning."

The man in the shorts could not resist an impish wink at the barmaid. He raised his pint of bitter and took a long draught before returning his attention to his quarry. But the drink was fast acting. The eyelids of the man in the shorts fluttered and his head crashed down on the table. The barmaid rushed over to the table.

"Not to your liking, sir?"

Another man appeared beside her.

"I'm to take you back to Bletchley."

"What? But I've just fled Bletchley!"

"We've secured your unit. Orders are back to work."

"Secure? You nearly poisoned me!"

"He'll wake up with a headache. Then we'll ask him about his line."

"This makes no sense."

"Of course it does. I've read your notes. The contradiction is where the cock-up comes from."

A knock. Maddox opened the door to Lady Titchley.

"You're late."

"Only by a few minutes."

"And each an eternity."

Maddox began to unbutton his shirt. Lady Titchley wandered about the room, looking at the things upon his desk. She picked up a card with an illustration of two women on it. One woman was sucking a breast of the other woman, and sliding her hand between her thighs.

"I didn't know you could write in German."

"When the mood strikes me."

Lady Titchley picked up another card and averted her eyes from the image of one woman clasping the thighs of another woman and dipping her head between her legs.

"If you need money, Maddox, I could always ask Aloysius."

"Yes, and lose what modicum of honour I have left?"

"Forgive me. I wouldn't dream of interfering with your valiant picture business."

"Please don't trounce upon my war effort. Here, try this one."

Lady Titchley accepted the card he handed her. In the illustration, a naked official with an erection was giving a double salute to a picture of the Führer, standing over a woman face down on the bed.

"Ugh. Now cracks a noble heart."

"That's the job, of course. For both sides to break down the resolve of the poor fellows in the worst of it. The brave man on the front losing everything he believes he is fighting for."

Lady Titchley unclasped her crucifix and laid it on the dressing table. Maddox lifted the hem of her dress and brusquely applied his fingers.

"You don't believe in anything, then."

"What should I believe in? God?"

"I don't know."

Maddox pinned her down on the bed.

"What's it all about?"

"Whatever do you mean?"

"What is between you and the Jew?"

"Jew?"

"A man named Jacob Levy paid you a visit. Elaborate upon the nature of his visit."

"I ..."

"Answer very carefully."

"I heard about him. I was curious. I asked him to call."

"Why?"

"Aloysius had a file full of those leaflets and they were spread across his desk. It was like the first time he brought me one of your books. I was curious. I wondered if it was true about all those slappers in the drawings. Aloysius said in all probability Jacob Levy didn't exist. But he did!"

"Well, was he everything you expected?"

"No."

"You are lying. I can tell."

"Yes. It was amazing. He's a brilliant man. I want to leave Aloysius and help him in whatever way I can. I wish ... he were here."

"Marvellous! But first you're going to arrange a little meeting."

"It was really quite stupendous. I have never felt so alive ..."

Lady Titchley sat up and pointed at various cards upon his desk. "We did this. And this. And this. Mmm ... and that!"

Millicent surveyed the beautiful computers at work in their stiff crisp clothing with a look of satisfaction before passing through to Woolwett's impromptu office.

"Millie! How are you?"

"Well, I wouldn't sneeze at an orange."

"Stuff the lather, Millie. I heard about what happened. To your bloke, I mean."

"It's to be expected, Percy."

"Please, call me Woolly."

"Never you mind, Woolly. That's not what I've come about."

"Clever *and* pretty. Do tell."

"As you know, Operation Palimpsest is in full swing. Our bright boys have concealed experimental listening devices in cracking forgeries the enemy. may want more than a nibble of. So far it's getting on like a flat on fire. But there is a spot of bother."

"Go on. This is all terribly interesting."

"We were put in touch with a quite capable forger. The sticky bit is that even after meeting him, he doesn't seem to exist."

Woolwett spilt tea over his trousers.

"Blast! Computer! Tea-room tidy!"

The prettiest girl dashed in and knelt in front of Woolwett, grasping his haunches and dabbing him down with zeal.

"Sorry, Millie! You were just telling me about a chap that isn't."

"Thing is, he *was*. We think a number of these paintings are forgeries, only forgeries from the seventeenth century, which in a funny way makes them almost worth as much as the originals, maybe more so."

"That's a bit of a turn-up for the plus fours. But what does this have to do with nabbing Morse-tappers in the dot dot dot?"

"Someone claiming to be our seventeenth-century forger is actively selling paintings as we speak. There have been several sightings and reports of Vanderspeigle the Minor. Monkeys with our operations something awful. I was thinking a wonky limb of Special Branch, dangling in the breeze to see what catches."

Woolwett sighed, stroking the computer's fair hair.

"Shut the door, Millie."

She complied at once.

"Truth of the matter is, the whole painting story is just a marmalade mock-up to see what sticks. Flies with honey. Even this entire unit is a display window. The computers are not computers at all."

"Who are they?"

"Wayward wanton girls from island villages. Sorceresses, if you like. Don't frown so, Millie! They were about to be drawn and quartered when we picked them up. Stoned for witchery. We scrubbed them down and gave them a few bob. Thing is, they'll do anything for a biscuit."

"I *have* noticed."

"Don't be daft, Millie. The enemy is conducting supernatural manoeuvres the like of which we have never seen before. You didn't think we'd really get anywhere in the trenches, did you? This war will be won through oppositional magic. You needn't hold your fine nose over a few official witches if it achieves our primary objective."

"Of course not."

"Well, all this strategy has made me peckish. Blood sausages and a baby heart should suffice. An extended dinner hour is in order, I should think."

"As you wish."

"And while I'm at it, steer clear of Jacob Levy, both of you!"

The young woman sat completely still in the room. Her interlocutor closed the door behind him and sat opposite her. She was sitting there in her crisp white shirt and her checked skirt, the perfect weapon. Reminded him of a painting, come to think. The wife would know. She bit her lip, suppressing a smile, her eyes shining.

"Did I do all right?"

"Did you enjoy it?"

"Yes. It was very illuminating. But I am curious about what it means."

"You were told it was a work assessment test?"

"Yes."

"There is a Myers-Briggs personality-type indicator being used to assess which industrial jobs are suitable to women while the war is on."

She leaned forward, allowing the smile.

"So what am I suited for ... Mr. ...?"

"I'm generally known as Nippers. Now, I know you're going to tell me your name but please don't."

"I wasn't."

"Quite."

"What is your idea of a job for me?"

"We thought computer."

"Computer?"

"Only that's the cover. You see, we've tweaked the test to explore ... other possibilities. There is a great deal of contradiction in your test results."

"And that's undesirable?"

"Not at all. In fact, we were quite excited and wanted to meet you at once."

"Whatever for?"

"Let us say that the parametric bounds of your personality reveal a unique disposition, one that would be very useful in our line of work, and not purely for practical reasons, but for ones hitherto unexplored."

"What is your line of work?"

"Very special war work."

"But you won't tell me what it is?"

"If you want to work and at the same time to really help your country, I suggest you sign here."

She paused, and then accepted the pen. Nippers shivered. Already he could feel her shoving about the smallest bits of his mind and it gave him a headache. Feeling they were embracing in a cozy hotel room and he felt like a lion in the sun pouncing upon the squares of her checked skirt and no one would ever know, not ever. But Nippers shook himself out of this momentary slip of judgment. After all, that was how they got Reggie Rims.

"There. What's next?"

"You are to report to Bletchley Park as Miss Ellen Trust. But for all internal purposes you are strictly to answer to COCOA."

PLUMDUFF awoke groggily. His wrists and ankles were restrained on the cold, hard floor. The funhouse mirror revealed that he was also at the mercy of an American Indian headdress. But where? His best guess was not so far from Uckfield. He had been hot on the trail of a tidy forgery ring, most likely linked to a legendary munitions dealer, when he had come across some decidedly wicked trifle. The woman in crisp riding gear and prim quizzing glasses lifted his chin with the business end of her matching crop.

"Good afternoon."

"Wibble ..."

"We have a heady session of recolonization planned, followed by excellent tea."

"Yibble yibble ..."

"Don't strain yourself, savage! You know I cannot possibly fathom your gibberish."

"Whaaaa ..."

"We know who you are and what you are up to. Since ordinary methods are insufficient, we must first resort to a cracking game of British Museum. You are the naughty little savage and we have stolen all of your gods. But if you write ever so nicely we will hang your smashing letter ... guess where?"

"Mmmph ..."

"Yes, spot on. We will hang your darling letter directly next to your stolen gods! Just mind the little rotters crawling all over the Elgin Marbles! Where else but in the British Museum!"

"Brtshmmm ..."

"Yes, try not to fight back so adorably with your puny slings and spears! Because here comes the armada! The cannon!"

PLUMDUFF struggled to form gagged cries as the riding crop struck exposed buttock flesh.

"Then if you're a very good little colonial, we'll show you your tiny little gods, yes we will, yes we will!"

"Brtsh ... muuuuu ..."

PLUMDUFF felt the crop rubbing briskly between his legs.

"Then if you're a really, really noble savage we may even show you the display case where we intend to exhibit your precious little gonads!"

The woman lay lifeless. The gentleman was listening to a gramophone. Men waited at the window for him to make his next mistake. In a contradictory system, a big thick cock-up is bound to occur. BANQUO turned these thoughts over in his head, still not trusting his assigned binman on the other side of the liminal. The painting had spelled out everything perfectly, so perfectly that something contrary was nagging at him. Something like a picture of a big thick cock-up hanging unevenly on the wall. BANQUO figured they were about to make the perfect adjustment. Unless, of course, that was the fatal contradiction.

BLIMEY did not see the belt that wrapped around his throat or the crowbar that struck the back of his head. The surrounding men kicked him a few times for good measure before dragging him toward one of the barrels. Their agent, in the guise of a charwoman, assisted with the storage of the victim. They were all alert to the steps of an approaching witness in one of the adjacent squares. They signalled another agent and she gave a pair of children the victim's articles to bury under some loose tiling in front of their "front," where no one would even conceive of snooping.

The man gestured for the girl to switch on the gramophone, and the mounting undulations of *Das Rheingold* soon filled the room. The other woman ripped open the girl's crisp shirt and began to suck her pert nipples. After feeding her a few chocolate digestives, she slid her hand between the girl's thighs, reaching for her veritable seat of pleasure. The man smiled, keeping more than a stiff upper lip, taking his sweet time to adjust his eye patch before mutely ordering the swift removal of his soiled uniform.

"I am your Allfather, my tasty Rhinedaughters!"

"Heiajaheia! Heiajaheia! Wallalalalala leiajahei!"

"Our magic will be better than their magic."

"Ahhh … Percival!"

"Please … call me Woolly."

Two flagging members of the brain trust sat in tweed, sipping tea.

"Long day, Mumphries?"

"Indubitably."

"All going according to plan, I trust."

"Quite. Ah, there was one of those ... whatsits ... a mole!"

"A what?"

"Quite quite. Such is the mole of nature in them."

"Pray tell, what is the name of this mole?"

"Ellen something. The new girl."

"Blast me to bits, not Miss Ellen!"

"Ah, so it's that delicate a matter?"

"She brightened up the dampness is what I mean."

"Quite. Apparently she was filching facts for that swine COCOA."

"More spookish stuff. COCOA is one of ours."

"Not COCOA!"

"We are but chicken scratch in a child's paper-folding game. Thing is, no one really knows how many folds are involved."

"But the long and short of it is *goodbye, Miss Ellen.*"

"Ah well, that's the queer bit, if one can say drowned is queer."

"Drowned!"

"Dilly left the bath running again. Stupid devilish clever of him. I don't know the details but she somehow got herself locked in, poor stick."

"Then Operation Down Under was a roaring success, tragically."

"The question is, did COCOA know?"

"Not COCOA!"

"There'll be hell to pay, come hell and high water."

"Nonsense."

"Quite. Quite."

"Does Dilly know?"

"You know as well as I do Dilly's half past daffy with a good helping of taffy. Besides, he has his sums to focus on. Best not to disturb, I'd fancy."

"Egh. This tea's blasted cold."

"There's Brownian motion for you."

"Miss Ellen might have poured us fresh by now."

"We'll order another girl. From the PM if needs must. Just don't tell COCOA."

"Not COCOA!"

One of the innumerable operational Jeans moved into position. The factory responsible for those delectable bags of mystery was his assigned target. He paused over the gravy conveyor to consider his vulnerability. Jean had already died over a hundred times and had exposed himself even more. But this was sure to make his immediate masters happy, and if not, the enemy. Whether an all-out offensive or merely a sly gambit would suffice, he was no longer sure. But what did politics matter to a handsome mercenary? He planted the last of the charges and checked his timing clobber. Then a light shone in his eyes.

"A fox in the henhouse!"

The intervening party opened fire. One of the charges was hit. The smell of scorched meat and gravy lingered for quite some time.

Captain Frip accepted a hideous jacket and made his way through rows of dimly lit figures, taking care not to make the slightest peep. He located the Speaking Section at the very back and squeezed into a tiny soundproof room containing Lord Thanfrax and a bottle of Glenfiddich.

"Drink, Frip?"

"I don't dare reply."

"Thing about the Diogenes Club is, there's no talking. Strictly hush-hush, you understand."

"Yet here we are."

"Times are changing, Frip. They've been letting talkies in for ages."

"Even scruffs like me."

"Quite. Even hardbitten scruffs like you."

"What's it all about?"

Lord Thanfrax snapped his fingers and a waiter appeared, bearing a tray of photographs. He put down the tray and made his exit, closing the soundproof door behind him.

"This woman, Frip, has been wagging our tail for more than a fortnight. Funny bit is, we can't seem to track down her handlers."

"Could be one of ours, another ghostly prefect from Home Office."

"Or a foreign biscuit nearly ready for tea time."

"How about a domestic double googly?"

"Thing is, she doesn't play sweetly. Found Rimsy in a rundown council flat. Terrible business. Tawdry bit of mop-up. The rest are dropping like flies in swarms of casual slaughter."

"So you want her driven out of Portobello Road?"

"There is another option. We could recruit her and make her one of our phantom screws."

"Provided she hasn't been stroked and tamed and turned already."

"Then we're looking at a Yorkshire pudding. Terribly embarrassing to have that all over one's face!"

The waiter opened the door, entered, bowed, and closed it again.

"I don't want anything just now!"

"I believe you do."

The waiter pulled off a greying wig and oily moustache and revealed a handsome face and flowing golden hair.

"I say, they don't allow birds in here. Not even Jenny Wrens."

"Steady, Frip. She's the one doing the wagging, clearly."

"Aha!"

"We were just talking about some war work for you."

"I know."

"I say, this is all rather unorthodox!"

Lord Thanfrax poured a neat Scotch and handed it to the lovely agent known only as D MINOR.

"Join us in getting properly buggered?"

"I thought you'd never ask."

The illustrious Jacob Levy took a seat, taking great care to lift the knees of his Savile Row trousers. Lady Titchley poured two cups of tea.

"I'm surprised you came."

"I cannot resist the summons of such a beautiful lady."

"I'll get right to the point. A man named Maddox is itching to have you removed."

"Like a stain upon the old medieval tapestry, *hein?*"

"No. He wants you gone for personal reasons."

"Lover's spat, I presume. Quite the scandal, Lady Titchley. I expected better from you."

"Lord Titchley and I have an *understanding.*"

"I would hope you and I might reach an *understanding.*"

"You know, you're nothing like the propaganda they spread about you."

"Propaganda has its purpose. It suits my sang-froid to be known. I am feared up and down the House of Lords. I am not one to be ignored."

"But in person, I mean in the flesh, you are very impressive."

"Maddox has sent you as a decoy to betray me."

"Yes."

"But you won't betray me."

"No."

"I find that terribly amusing."

"What with me being C of E and the wife of Lord Tea Leaf, you mean! With a middling, penniless writer for a lover! And yet ..."

"You think of nothing else."

"I can forgive your history. The number of women or arms does not matter to me. I want the honour of being your head harridan smeared in grimy dealings!"

"That would boost the propaganda for certain."

"Of course, won't that beat off our brave chaps?"

"*C'est la guerre,* my darling. There are no more sides. Didn't Titchley tell you?"

"I love you!"

"Then lie back and think of Brighton."

FALSTAFF ran through the copse as fast as he could, seeing nothing and hearing bullets whizzing past his ear. Reports continued to follow his jouncing frame. The Coriolanus scenario had come about. He suspected as much anyhow. Unless the enemy was actually hot on his tail. It was all so very contrary. Like the way the wood moved and trees sprang up and the way the heart stopped.

UMLAUT listened carefully. He had bet his last quid she would not bottle it. And SPARROW had turned up, a bird in the hand. He listened to the soft unbelting of her overcoat and then the sounds of exhilaration that mingled with those of WOODPECKER. Two in the bush, sunshine. UMLAUT finished his sticky bun and licked his fingers, concentrating upon the squealing and slurping and squinching sounds. Often, when he drew lovers together for surveillance purposes, he felt he could hear the music of the spheres. As he shut his eyes, a perfect octagon appeared before him, squinching into the most comely flutings of a muqarna. For a second, he believed the swift force of their love could support a massive dome, if not the entire world. He scraped at two pages of a slim volume of Keats that would not separate with a butter knife. Sticky bit of business. But we all know elevenses must come to an end. UMLAUT shifted in his chair, hearing screams that became shrieks.

The sedge is withered from the lake, you misguided mare. And no birds sing. And not a stick of rock between you.

Rachel Birnbaum flaunted her indifference as her "new felluh" downed the last of his glass. Slim pickings, but leave it to her to find this broken-down waterspout. Joe, the oddjobsman and general dogsbody. The sort to nod off with his fingers in your knickers. Joe belched and laughed as if he had made a gem of a joke. Rachel smiled murder at him, letting him put his arm around her waist and lead her down the lane.

"Ere, give us a trial, love."

"It don't work that way, Joe Cock-up."

"Then 'ow's it work?"

"Tell my flaming father your intentions first! The gentleman wants to know 'ow's it work."

"S'only a spot of war work, love."

"And what do you know of war, sunshine?"

"I was sent back on account of my injury."

"What a bore, living without your bait and tackle!"

"We better settle up on that score right now, love."

"Not till I see the dosh, Minister of War."

Joe pushed her against the wall.

"You'll do what I tells ya."

"I'll scream for the beagle."

At that moment, Rachel heard a great swishing sound. Joe convulsed as if he were being stung by giant insects in several places. Next thing she knew, he lay motionless in the middle of the lane. She observed the initials on the walking stick that had come to rest. In the mouth of a roaring lion, she could make out the letters.

"J.L."

"At your service, young lady. I hope you are in perfect health."

His voice was slightly foreign, though polished. Otherwise, he was topped up to the nines, a real gentleman.

"I said I'd cry for the beagle, not ring the bleedin' war minister."

"It's a busy night for everyone, though you're not far off, my dear."

"Fancy a cuppa, 'ooever you are?"

"If that is your pretext for our reaching a more delectable arrangement, then by all means. Would you be so kind as to lead the way?"

Rachel took his arm and kept time with his brisk stride and the clip of his walking stick.

"Nuffing in 'aff measures, governor!"

BLOOMERS had anticipated the need of a ladder. He was quiet, of course. Rung after rung, he made it to the windowsill. He was careful not to pop his head up. Training had prepared him to take an eyeful and absorb but not to become absorbed. It was the usual stuff, although not yet part of Operation Peekaboo. As he was watching the Jew unbutton his coat, the ladder started shaking. He looked down and that was the last thing he ever did of his own accord.

Maddox had not received the signal as agreed upon. He bit his fingernails and tore at his hair until he could wait no longer. He raced into The Wiggle & Snitch and bounded up the stairs. Music from a gramophone was audible. He braced himself to break down the door.

"Hang about, Maddox."

It was the most beautiful woman he had ever seen.

"You, you're one of them."

"Steady on. You're sniffing up the wrong elm, old chap."

"I know she's in there! With *him*."

"He's in there ... with a *lady*."

"I'll kill him!"

"That is not for you to decide. Nor when."

"Try and stop me."

"Be a sport. I could show you things you've only dreamed of."

"Surely you know the only thing I dream of."

"Stubborn *and* stupid."

"Now, would you be so good as to step away from that door?"

"Your books are rubbish, you know."

"What?!?"

D MINOR lifted her umbrella and prodded Maddox a few times in the ribs. He moved backward in surprise and suddenly found himself falling head over heels from the upstairs railing. It was neither the first assassination she had stopped, nor the first murder she had committed, although either way, it was her favourite.

Horace nursed his stout. He had missed the departure of the other two punters adjacent. Funny lot, anyway. Nancy boys, three out of a fiver. He snatched up the soggy beer-soaked picture and placed it on the bar where he could keep an eye on it. *The Girl You Left Behind*. In the illustration, Jacob Levy had a pretty girl on his arm whom he was studying lasciviously. Behind them, a man with a black eye lay slumped against a wall, while a soldier in an overcoat was on crutches, trying to call back his best girl and prevent the inevitable from happening.

Everyone is hurting. Whether he is too injured to serve or one of the wounded, Edgar cannot catch up with the subtle chicanery of a character like Jacob Levy. He calls out to Rachel, but she can barely recognize him or remember his name, now that Jacob Levy is buying her jewellery and furs. Edgar had better face facts. While giving his all at the front, he is losing the war at home. Even Joe Cock-up tried it on with her at his local but he's no match for the machinations of this war profiteer. Have you seen the other pictures of "The Girl You Left Behind?"

X

Thus concluded the most sumptuous adventures of your fair Dim. Now, do not think I am unaware, delicious reader, that some stuffed shirt of a prude shall conclude that I slept my way through history and did more than my share of two-timing to achieve my own ends, although I suspect it would take more than priggish brains to reach this conclusion, based on the rather scatty presentment of evidence. Truth be told, there were incidents at Ecole Jeune Colibri that rivalled those in the brutal fleshpots of Tiberius and the orgiastic atmosphere of Lupercalia. It was widely known that mountain men and village boys in the Kanadas often went missing, but fortunately it would have been a violation of our religious freedoms to investigate any further. Being merely a sprout in her salad days, I was hardly responsible for the procuring of bemused innocents, although I confess to complete culpability in sharing the thrill in watching them being pressed to their utter extremity by our headmistresses, since we had one for every specialized talent brought to our outstanding institution. Madame Tripotage was rarely observed without her immaculate riding gear or her long raven hair tied back. She had an impassive mannish air that could only be disrupted by a flash of devilish mirth, which charmed and disarmed even her victims at the height of their suffering.

La Société Hirondelle was by no means for our alumni, since this is an organization far thicker and pithier than my own tenuous association with it might penetrate. But it is often said that those girls first fledged at Ecole Jeune Colibri achieved more than stupendous flight at Hirondelle. I cannot argue with this statement, although after my adventures, I was hardly in a mood to beat my brains about social caste systems. The matron removed my clothes and helped me on with the velvety robe bearing the stitched pattern of a swallow over my heart. Then, after examining me in the mirror over my shoulder, she flung me inside with a cheeky slap to my posterior. I hurried past the room for initiates and entered the second circle of this select branch of this society, which practised a form of entertainment known as seed dating. At once I found a place upon a divan beside a marchioness well known for her piety and good deeds. An excellent cocktail was served to me and I toasted her health. Then she put her hand on my knee and began to speak.

"Drink that mulish stuff if it gives you a thrill, my dear. But do not look at me as if I have not known love. I have known it too well. Even the proportions of your illustrious father are no longer a mystery to me, and what is more seem like a faint memory. But since it's just us girls, what I wish to speak of is a boy from my youth."

The Marchioness Y. clutched her walking stick tighter, her eyes far away. I was mesmerized by its silver wildcat that appeared ready to pounce the instant she gave the signal. I lay down in a classic pose, imploring her to continue.

"You must have some idea how much I contribute per annum to Ecole Jeune Colibri. The reason is that my girlhood was not the happiest. As in most French tales, the parents were either dead or among the missing. I was a very pretty child and was welcomed into the home of a rather eccentric marquis. There is much to be said of him, although I would lose the thread of my tale to do so. In any case, he was often away and I was left in the charge of a miserable old maid who did not care for me, particularly because I was not of the illustrious family M——. There were endless chores and beatings and little food. The old woman had convinced me that if I spoke up of my treatment, the marquis would give me a punishment a hundred times worse. It was not until my little hero caught my eye that I could scrape up any feasible way out of this situation. I must have been a few months shy of thirteen at the time. I was untying my hair in the window of my room when I noticed a boy from the village staring up at me, his mouth agape."

The Marchioness Y. sipped from her glass and stroked my hair, smiling.

"That was the first taste of it, what I hope they taught you and other girls at that school in the mountains. The first taste of it for that boy, too, I gather. He returned every day, and every day I showed him a little more at the window. We began to exchange notes through a hole in the garden wall. Little by little, using all the literature I could sneak out of the marquis's locked library to soften the blow, I was able to press home my main theme with him. For each protestation, I punished him, either through deprivation of my heavenly vision or through my insistence that a stronger boy would do the right thing and not be nearly so feeble. Within less than a month, he knew the arrangement and was entirely prepared. Now, I happened to learn from the marquis's diary that he kept a decent amount of arsenic in one of his cabinets. It was not for me to assume what he used it for. It was the fashion to have some around in the best families, naturally. It was very easy for me to bottle some and leave some by the garden wall for my anxious paramour. It so happened that the old woman would pass by his house on her way to purchase supplies for the marquis. As per my instructions, the boy had already gained her trust by the time he offered her a free draught of refreshment. It did not take much and the arsenic quickly took effect. I met him as promised and helped to drag her across the field to some nearby cliffs. This was all rather convenient, as in a gothic tale, but I assure you it was easier to achieve than one might imagine. Once her body had fallen from the bluff into the sea below, he did not mourn or waste any time, although his eyes were full of tears, on account of my making him wait so long before he could have his own way. And I fell back like a maiden in a fable and helped him reach his first and last conclusion. What has amused me to this day is that like some green girl, I had wanted to save some token of that stormy morning. Of all things, I urged the boy to give it everything he had, to let loose in the empty flagon until he was as dry as a day-old wishbone.

The deed done, he lost his footing. In fact, I can still see the expression on his face as he fell backward from the bluff. As you must realize, this was also quite convenient for me. I returned to the chateau with my flagon in hand, taking great care to transfer the contents to a small bottle. Then I informed the servants that I had seen the boy riding off with the old woman. No one asked any questions, although perhaps the boy's parents missed him. Perhaps not. The servants assumed something nefarious and suggested to the marquis that perhaps it would be best if he found a reliable tutor for me."

I sighed and took a moment to consider everything she had told me.

"Then what happened?"

"What happened? I married the marquis, of course. That is, once I was old enough. There is no need to speculate upon our relationship before that fact. Let us say, we knew one another well enough. Of course, he came to a bad end as well. Ah, my dear, you see how easily I digress. I was still talking about the boy, wasn't I? What matters is that the world's most acclaimed sommeliers have bored me stiff with their ravings about this wine or that ... why, I could give them something astonishing to spit about ..."

The Marchioness Y. raised her glass and held it under my nose.

"Want to give it a whirl?"

"That is very generous, but no thank you."

"Already have your own supply. I see."

"I would like to abide by the rules of our little club."

"But what has aged better than this, a memory of a fatal day by the seaside? Surely this is the most desire the boy was ever to feel, and I fancy I can even taste the salt of the sea and the tumult in the air, along with a drop or two of arsenic that never managed to escape. Not that I mind at my age. And what am I to worry about? As the poet says, morality is a softness in the brain. So what if raddled flesh and shrunken bone want a bit of enlivening now and then, right, dearie?"

She gave me a long lingering kiss and I swore I could taste the arsenic of her imagination upon her tongue, mingling with the last hurrah of a lad departed long ago. It was an excellent year, I might add. We were deep in our reveries when we were joined by a tall vamp in an edible lime pantsuit. She spared us any formal introduction and at once began telling her own tale, as was the custom in this club, particularly as the night wore on.

"I run my offices with an iron fist. Also, I have earned my reputation, never confusing business decisions with personal ones, never mixing up pleasure with profit. Until I clapped eyes on Titus, one of the temporary staff in one of my departments. I could have accused him of being ordinary, even incompetent, if not for his brilliant backside. At last, here was an ass I could deign to kiss – here was a rump that I could respect. Such was the singular talent of Titus, never failing to keep his sole asset beautifully encased. Ladies, I do declare, the thing was alive!"

The Marchioness Y. burst into laughter at this remark, which ended in a violent coughing fit.

"So when his performance reports were brought to me, I had no choice but to shred them. Over the years, had I not won the privilege of this one guilty pleasure? It would have been too obvious to make him my personal assistant. Instead, I transferred him to one of our warehouses. It took very little effort to ensure this location was continually kept at a high temperature, or to explain to Titus that the delicate materials within must not become too cold. I gave him light physical tasks to do, and found myself spending more and more time supervising his efforts. Due to the heat, we were often in a state of semi-undress, and I even went to the trouble of inventing a complicated system of punishments and rewards in order to gain increasing influence over his behaviour. Soon, he began to fear my disapproval and yearned for any display of encouragement."

The Marchioness Y. clapped her hands together.

"Don't spare the rod and soil the child?"

"Needless to say, I was never far from the temptation to strap on my industrial automatic and teach the lad a thing or three. However, I was keenly aware that any kind of inter-office hokey-pokey could be misconstrued and open the floodgates to the wrong kind of action. Instead, I invited Titus to join me in my box ... at the opera, of course. When the lights went out, I calmed his bemusement with my whispers. He didn't grasp one whit of it, and I explained to him how Princess Turandot was merciless toward all men because she was possessed by the spirit of her Chinese ancestress. One by one, suitors vied for her love. Failing to solve her riddles, they were promptly put to death. I was eager to hear my favourite part of the opera, where even after the prince's besotted servant girl has sacrificed her own life to save his neck, the pigheaded hero still wants to smooth things over and have his way with Princess Turandot. Let that be a lesson to you that no matter what, life moves on!

Il principe

> (*la bacia con ardore*)
> *Mio fiore!*
> *O! Mio fiore mattutino! Mio fiore, ti respiro!*
> *I seni tuoi di giglio,*
> *ah! treman sul mio petto!*

Voci femminili

> (*interne*)
> *Ah!* ...

Il principe

> *Già ti sento*
> *mancare di dolcezza, tutta bianca*
> *nel tuo manto d'argento!*

"After the intermission and another glass of wine, when the lights went down, the only thing Titus did understand was the pale-pink glove that suddenly launched into his lap. No, there were no surtitles necessary for what that soft glove wanted, and he was positively gasping for it. The opera box was too dark for either of us to see very much, and you will forgive me if I suggest it required no small amount of expertise on the part of the glove, not only to give pleasure, but to time his excitation to reach its peak just as the tenor was to sing the final high C in 'Nessun Dorma'. Then, during the appreciative applause, I behaved as a girl who will neither part with soiled sheets nor articles from her first lover. Within seconds, a sweaty, panting Titus had been carefully *milked* into this small bottle."

She produced the bottle from her pantsuit and held it up for our approval. The Marchioness Y. smiled, almost wistfully.

"Yes, by all means, milk away. Just don't buy the cow!"

We all laughed and made lewd gestures, but our storyteller shook her head.

"Ah no, it ended abruptly. You know Puccini died before he finished *Turandot*, hmm? Well, it's always been a cursed thing, I suppose. Not to mention the soprano careers it has killed. As for Titus, he was even more eager than I was to leave. We ended up taking a side exit that led into the alley. I wanted to call a cab to speed us home at once, but poor Titus had caught my exhibitionist bug. Before going anywhere, he wanted something to happen in the cool night air. I took his hint, guessing what would best follow our prelude. We were right in the middle of our quasi-private quickie when we heard yelling. A number of drunken ruffians were coming down the lane toward us. To be on the safe side, Titus insisted that I hurry home, or even around the corner to a nearby shop. I did as he asked, finding his show of chivalry touching, and thinking we would find it very funny in the morning at work. I went into a pub, had another drink, and waited for my cab. It wasn't until two days later, when a tall and handsome policeman paid me a visit, that I knew how that night had ended. Apparently, a man of the same description as one of my employees had been found, stabbed to death, twice. It's just one of those things. The policeman seemed unable to keep from telling me that the man had died with a smile on his face. In any case, the aftermath held no interest for me. Could I have asked for more than his last gasp of pleasure, tidily saved in this bottle? I turned the entire matter over to one of my underlings, in the hope of finding someone who had known the man well. The policeman and I went out for coffee, before starting a short and tedious liaison. But that is another story entirely ..."

After such a tale of ecstasy and woe, my own seemed to swish about my mouth, until my lips were moist with it. The other ladies could feel this, and looked at me expectantly. Thus, I was not in any position to let them down gently. I laughed at first, and then at length began to recount many of the wondrous adventures you have heard already, and a great deal more I would not dare put on record. At this point, a cheeky peach of a debutante reached under my robe, finding what she sought on her first try, and stuffed all of her remaining determination into a baleful look.

"Tell us more ... about this thing you call ... *history*."

"Yes, tell us the rest. I trust you got what was coming to you."

"Really? Came to a bad end, I expect. All our stories seem to."

Thus, as I felt compelled then, I feel compelled now to tell you the rest of what I remember about this thing I call *history*.

Things were never quite the same after the war. I do not know why it took me this long for the futility of everything to sink in. It was something of a downer to realize the dedication of energy being put toward arbitrary destruction when it could be put to use in other ways. That is to say, it was not even concentrated, efficient destruction. This was destruction without a thrill to be had. Perhaps it was simply my paternal heritage to feel that bloodshed should never occur without direct emotional involvement, or at the very least, without charging admission. Therefore, sheerly on principle alone, the thought of this abstract battlefield of anonymous warriors randomly dropping bombs put me not a little in the dumps. Upon my return, the spectacle of Fuddlemuck and Gimmick waging their own assault on some brainless good-time-boys-and-girls did not charm me as it formerly had. Anticipation of fulfilling my duties as inheritrix and becoming the lady of the estate worked its magic over me. I realized my error in having become too familiar with Gimmick, and what is more, in encouraging the outrageously expensive Fuddlemuck to take liberties, all on account of my naiveté.

"Gimmick!"

The manservant jumped, unhanding a boy who clearly, like the other boys and girls, was exactly eighteen years old. Then he regained his composure and grinned.

"Mistress! This *is* what it looks like."

"Mr. Gimmick, I think it is high time we had a quiet word."

"Of course, mistress."

With no more than a few graceful gestures, he had straightened out his livery and had closed a pair of doors, leaving a gaggle of groans and screams behind it.

"Let me start off by saying I hope for us to be fast friends."

"It was my understanding we had already become *more than friends*, Mar'm."

"Too true, Mr. Gimmick. But that was my error, as I was unaccustomed to my sudden turn of good fortune, and what is more, to having all of these lascivious trappings at my beck. From this time forward, in deference to the legacy grafting together our two great families, I should like to exercise a modicum of decorum in your presence, and have you do likewise."

"Your wish is my domination, mistress. But in the eventuality you get lonely in the night?"

"That is a bridge, Mr. Gimmick, we have not yet burned. However, if there is a fire to put out, I promise that you shall be the first to hear of it, should the situation arise."

"How very kind of you to consider me!"

"As for Master Fuddlemuck, I would appreciate it if we could limit his visits, lest he bleed us dry before we receive the necessary financial transfusion. Also, I fear he may have a less than beneficial influence on you."

"He certainly has imagination, mistress. I would not have thought to conjure up a retinue of sexually deprived villagers on my lonesome."

"Yes, well, everything comes to an end, Timothy. At some point we must put away our childish playthings."

"Must we, mistress? I suppose you are right."

Truth be told, I was quite content to be on my own again. One unfortunate side effect of all the NGFs I had taken, if not merely time-lag, was a series of temporal flashbacks that happened at the most inconvenient instances. I sat down on an M-shaped divan and tapped my temples. It was the visceral sensation of hopping like a flea from moment to moment across linear history. But they were too vivid to be memories. I poured myself an Absurde and popped another NGF to settle my nerves. To be fair, this NGF related to my new instructions, which I hoped would clarify everything with regard to winning my inheritance.

At once, I knew where to uncover a giant crate made out of a mysterious substance I had never encountered before. I dragged it back into the safe-room and began unloading the beautiful *objets d'art* I had managed to collect. In went the painting of me by Parrhasius that I had stolen from the de facto emperor's bedroom. In went the brooch poor Loki had lost his life over. In went Botticelli's sketches of the hanging conspirators. In went the play from the time of the Sun King. In went the preliminary plans of Ada Lovelace that I had absconded with. In went the painting allegedly by Vanderspeigle the Minor, which more or less remained a mystery, even to me. It was not lost on me that many people had died for this art, which in turn had been stolen by yours truly. However, the Absurde was having a more stimulating than depressing effect upon my nervous system, and there seemed to be no point in becoming maudlin over the matter. The course of history never did run smooth.

I suppose I should have marvelled at making contact with creatures from a world other than my own, but my wild adventures in combination with the NGFs had dulled my ability to be very much surprised at anything that happened. I was no longer the same girl in a room doing things with butter for countless strangers. Nor could I go back to thinking in linear fashion about my life or the lives of anyone else. It made sense that I was not alone in the universe. It made sense that there were many things beyond my comprehension, and other questions that could be answered in another place across space and time. My rightful reward within reach, I now understood what my real inheritance had been. To merely be given a great deal of money would not have accomplished my father's wishes for me. He wanted me to fend for myself, to put my mind and energy and wiles to use, in other words to prove myself as a Minor. For all the times I might have cursed his name, I now praised him in my heart, fully realizing the poignancy of everything I had experienced and accomplished.

The Pedantians were scarcely different from myself. They were shorter and somewhat nearsighted. I knew all about them from the information I had popped, but there was hardly anything worth mentioning. Their one quirk was a weakness for following the history of our planet, a place they called Terra Dulkis. I have no idea why, but they were very interested in me and asked a lot of questions about my many trips to various time periods. This grilling was entirely tedious for me but thrilling for them. I even let them put me in their molecular debriefer so they could collect as much data about my journeys as possible.

Once they were appeased, I asked to see their largest matterpult. It was my understanding that I needed this device to complete my final task. I was escorted by one of the smallest Pedantians, named Churchill, who could not hide his glee at being given the honour of leading me to their mysterious machine. Although it was not perfect, my amulet did an excellent job of translating their alien tongue into my own language. He did not redden like anyone I knew, but he oranged slightly, which appeared to be pretty much the same thing.

"I've seen all your adventures. I'm your ... biggest fan."

"Well, eff me in the eh-hoo! Thank you."

"You are so wonderful and charming."

"Good of you to say."

"No, good to meet you, *the* Diminuenda, in the flesh ..."

"Yes, that is me ..."

"In particular, I think I loved your foursome with the medieval polyphony singers ..."

"Ah yes, there is nothing quite like making out to plainchant ..."

"I've watched that one over and over again. I'm not supposed to be a quarkhog but I won't let anyone borrow that intradot ..."

"Umm ... how sweet."

"Zowpow ... you seemed so real and alive to me, and now here you are in the flesh. So close I can almost taste you ... whoa ho ho ..."

"Are we getting any closer to that matterpult?"

"Of course. But first I must tell you something."

"Yes."

"I ... have never known ... what you dulklings call ... love."

"Well, you know what I think, Churchill?"

"What?"

"You never will."

I knew from the NGF that Pedantians had no tear ducts, but I noticed that Churchill had become rather moody and from that point on looked as if someone had deflated his balloon. He talked me through the controls for the matterpult in a tone of utter disinterest. When I tried to engage him with more scraps of history, he told me that it was fine for me to play those kinds of games, since history was probably not all it was cracked up to be. In my old life, this might have been a cue to start up a hot interspecies scene, but I was far too focused on my goal to be distracted now, even by the promise of some submissive Pedantian action, which I would have promptly filed under *L*, along with other librarian fantasies I had fulfilled in the ancient world. But the NGF was wearing off and I needed additional instruction.

"So now what?"

"You're the time-hopping trampramp. You figure it out."

Churchill might have called me worse in his native tongue. I watched him storm off and then peered into what looked like the crosshairs of a sight. What I saw filled me not a little with alarm. The device, which I took to be a weapon, was aimed at the only planet I could instantly recognize. In spite of everything I had seen and heard that had left me unmoved, here was an action that seemed to do worse than bend some moral code of conduct. To destroy one's homeworld? Why, it simply wasn't done! But at the time when I was most dubious, I felt a voice and hands guiding me. The voice told me what to do, how to correctly preprogram the matterpult and then find the trigger. The hands rested upon my hips and helped me to relax my body.

"Easy now. Don't tense up ..."

"But why? This feels so wrong ..."

"But it also feels sooooo right ..."

I yanked the trigger with all my might. At first, I thought I was suffering another side effect from the NGF. The walls opened up and suddenly I found myself in a sort of stadium in the middle of what appeared to be endless rows of screaming people. A grinning man with a crooked toupee and a sparkling blazer ran up to me and took my hand.

"Diminuenda ... Diminuenda ... do you know where you are?"

"What? No."

"Can we give her a clue? Audience, where is the lovely Diminuenda?"

"WHENEVER!!!"

"That is absolutely right, ladies and gentlemen. You are only this season's winner on the most popular show in the universe, *Whenever* ..."

Somewhere a gong was struck. Random cries went out as members of the studio audience relieved themselves and/or exploded. It was a phenomenal thing to be a part of. Or even parts of.

"You know what, Diminuenda ... why, I can't even say it ... we have outdone ourselves. But first, let's take a little trip through time ..."

A lone fiddler began fiddling, joined promptly by a cellist and then a vast orchestra and then a chorus of at least a few thousand. Their fiddling and murmuring was followed by a fainting epidemic as the lead singer of Lunarphobe appeared. As the audience received an invasive frontage feed of various scenes from my adventures, he performed his new song dedicated to me:

> After the other night
> I tried to prioritize ...
> Not gonna sink tha temporally challenged
> Not gonna ostrich yer bush
> Or give ya tha final push, babeeee
> You will always be my time-laideeeee ...

Most everybody took the phrase "ostrich yer bush" as a cue to begin pleasuring themselves, including the host, who was so into it he nearly lost his hairpiece. I did my level best to hide my irritation. When the song was over, the host wiped his hands on a steaming Whenever towel before taking my arm. His eyes were glistening.

"So many memories ... it's sad that such a wild ride like this has to come to an end. But you, Diminuenda, you faced every challenge, no matter how difficult or greasy, with the same attitude. Well honey, you ... got ... things ... done."

"One question."

"Hell yeah, dollbush!"

"What did I win?"

"That is insane. You just checked into the asylum, baby! No, not really. You hear that, everybody? The lady wants to know ... what ... she ... has ... won. Well, Diminuenda, do we have a surprise for you ..."

Truth be told, a very uninteresting year passed before I could know exactly what the outcome of all my efforts would be. I was mobbed everywhere by everyone from media speculators to speculum enthusiasts, with all of them wanting a piece of me. Also, I was more than a little vexed to learn that the reality game show I had won was produced by the Pedantians, and I had to remain in their clutches until the lethally injected special tubecast of *Whenever*, lest I forfeit my prize. In spite of everything I had overcome, this was the hardest test of my willpower, to not let myself be eaten up by curiosity and impatience. Since I was a historical celebrity (or a celebrated historinatic) with nothing but time on my hands, I ended up initiating many of the Pedantians in the extraordinarily diverse ways of what we dulklings call love – except for Churchill, because it was a constant source of amusement to leave him wanting, and there was really so little to do in the interim.

At last I was taken to the largest, most luxurious Notel Hotel, generally known in this nebula as the Imperatore. Even Griselda Notel, the matriarch of that illustrious family, was there to welcome me. I gathered that the streaming bloodcast of this occasion was giving their chain of somewhat stayables a whack of unparalleled publicity. I waved aside pleasantries, anxious to know how this would all pan out. I swear, if this were a real book and not a bastardized autoerotography, I would flip right to the end and head straight for the climax. Ms. Notel, with an elegant smile, having freshly buried number fifteen, neuralated the access code for Room 1003, otherwise known as the Smyrna Suite, at least since the latest renovation.

I stood for a moment. I blinked. The door opened. The room was dark and I could only make out a shadow that was seated. I nodded, and a lamprey sprang to life. It was an old man with greasy hair and a thick beard. His clothing was muddy and ripped in many places. This was not what I had expected, and yet something about him seemed very familiar to me. As he grunted a greeting, I laughed heartily. Once my *suitors* had left my room (my public domain) and Luther had given me my takings, I would always run into this beggar fellow, and reward handsomely for croaking out some disheartening little ditty that began like so:

> I've got a broken soul
> like a cleft in the road ...

He took off his bowler and grinned warmly albeit foully at me. I remembered that Luther had wanted to involve him in some kind of extreme indigent fantasy, although even for me, that was going too far. I have always had a weakness for oddity, and this bedraggled man with his sad and filthy songs triggered something akin to a sense of charity within me. And suddenly, finding us in the same room together, I had no idea how to react. It was neither the time nor the place for it, but my darling beggar had other ideas.

"Bathos."

"Indeed."

"Bathos!"

It took me a long time to figure out what he was getting at. Fortunately, I was not left in the lurch by the omnipresent host of *Whenever*, nor the hidden studio audience, who begged, nay, commanded me to give this beggar a proper soak. I led him toward the rotating tub and activated the cleansing jets. Then I helped him out of his clothes. Even as I turned up my nose at his raunchy odour, I could not help but observe that his body appeared firmer and stronger than I would have guessed. As I began to scrub him all over with a Get-Away Sponge, knowing full well that the promotional aid would benefit a subsidiary of companies I was heir apparent to, I noticed an irregularity upon his left inner thigh. Then, as I leaned in for a closer look, he suddenly leapt up with a great *plash*, causing the studio audience to whistle and whoop at the sight of his naked body and my sopping strapless, provided courtesy of *Whenever*. I was shocked. He appeared years younger and his body was aglow beyond even the spiffing powers of the Get-Away Sponge, while supplies last. I recognized something familiar yet almost unfathomable in his deliciously ignoble mien, although I could not entirely look away from his netherhalf either. Instead, I pointed dumbly at the scar upon his inner thigh like a green girl.

"I ... know ... that ... scar ..."

"That happened a long time ago at the Cuckold Club. You know who I am, Diminuenda. You have always known."

"No. This is impossible."

"Relax. Soon the letdown reflex will kick in."

"_?"

"There are copious amounts of oxytocin in this room. This is perfectly natural, and occurs whenever most bipeds experience a mode of regression that has manifested itself in reality. This is the thrilling rush of mythopoeic concepts infringing themselves upon our lives. I trust we can act accordingly, like responsible and unattached adults ..."

"But this is madness! There's not even a blindfold."

"Resistance is futile. Keep in mind that the entire script for your reality experience on *Whenever* is based on your biopsychical imprint. This is a classical abandonment scenario, bordering on an Electra complex. This is what you wanted, deep down."

"This is not what *you* wanted?"

"Well, maybe a little. I do have interests in absolutely everything ..."

"Then ... you are alive."

Delicacy prevents me from saying much more about the mysterious man in Room 1003. Truth be told, my neural transmitters were firing something awful and much of what happened was such a blur, although I will leave it to your imagination, now in syndication everywhere. The most I can freely admit is that my father's dog Dotty was present in the company of the other dalmation, Cicero, who had helped me out of many jams, and that one of them was behaving like a real bitch.

However, I did learn that my father had created some type of rent in the space-time carpet, and had been popping in and out of various times and universes, which was explained to me in a lengthy and comprehensive demonstration of temporal glory-hole theory, otherwise known in layman's terms as the Lucky Loo Theory of Randomness. It had all been going like gangbangers until he had been red-flagged by the Time and Energy Management Policy Interpreters (TEMPI). And in times of crisis, my father has always resorted to the closest publicity stunt at hand, in this case faking his very own death and lying low until he could find alternative means to plead his case. In the end, the legislators were willing to overlook his infractions in exchange for a new historical awareness project that would enrich the universe as a whole and make a lot of people at TEMPI into thrillionaires. Happily, this agreement resulted in the realization of the *Whenever* show, originally the abandoned brainchild of one Linus Schlock. I was pressed to understand that all of my adventures had been part of a Minor scheme to raise the value of the historical objects in question and to auction each of them off to the highest bidder, thus securing his arrangement with TEMPI and freeing himself from any threat of lethal gastrobation.

The one thing that threw me was the matterpult. Do forgive me, but at this point, it was rather an afterthought whether or not I had annihilated my home planet. It turned out that when the *Whenever* show in its inception was facing financial collapse based upon various interstellar derivatives, my father had to arrange for a few events to take place that would put him on the right side of a bet here and there. I learned that the inveterate gambler had even bet upon the course of human history. Well, in this case, it was betting upon the end of the Cretaceous. I was stymied for a long time, until at last I grasped that I had fired an object at the earth when the environmental conditions were such as to lessen the chances for clade Dinosauria to survive. Something very like an asteroid or comet striking my home planet, in addition to the effects of the volcanic activity and continental drift, would be enough in a darkening world to give small, nocturnal, warm-blooded creatures the advantage. I had inadvertently wiped out the dinosaurs to help my father win a bet. For once, he had bet on mammals.

The Marchioness Y. raised her silver wildcat stick and pointed at me.

"Well?"

"Well?"

"We all know the rest. You are the daughter of that munificent multipotent man. And surely you are not hard done by. We all know the style you have become accustomed to, and the sorts of japes you get up to."

"I apologize if I am putting you to sleep, marchioness. There is a great deal more to tell."

"Not at all. But it is getting late and you know the rules of La Société Hirondelle."

"Don't hold back. Say what is on your mind."

"Spunk, woman. Spunk."

The other ladies who had gathered like flies upon a honeyed joystick to hear my tale all began to chant in unison, echoing the hoarse croak of the Marchioness Y.

"Spunk ... spunk ... spunk ..."

I could not help but burst into laughter as I produced a comely bottle and without warning uncorked the latest personal advert. Then they rolled their eyes and pretended not to inhale ...

A nose neither roman nor aquiline. The luxuriousness of a full belly. Clomp clomp clip. The echo of heels in the street that snap of a woman stretching her new boots outside a yawning house of pleasure. The rain loses its monotonous tone and increases its sense of urgency. An antelope flees through the green out into the savannah of moist macadam. There is no umbrella to speak of. Gull moans and glaucous eyes. A dusty page-burner, used. The most obvious of hats and a fantasy of being followed. A cerulean snuff box full of potencies. An inscription upon the bottom in vulgar old tongues. To look at them is to taste them upon your own tongue.

"I have learned the art of invisibility."

"You're hilarious."

The lock jimmied, the box knocked open. Nails the key. Warning font melting beneath cool prints. A swirling Ferris wheel on fire. A whiff of immemorial time. A line of questioning. The nature of that fateful afternoon. She moves awkwardly, conscious of being shadowed. She adjusts nimbus accordingly, pulls it tighter, then lets it dangle provocatively. A man in an undershirt leans out of a single-occupancy room upstairs. He can make out the cut of her dress and the vacuity of her flesh beneath purpling nimbus. Manna. He returns his attention to the cracked mirror and resumes watching the rapid movement of his hand until he can fill the throat of the sink. The cerulean box snaps shut like a guilty thing.

à trois ~ the fragrance for Them
because 3 is never a crowd

Dark early. He feels under flap of coat for the box. Her nimbus growls softly with animal heat. Her heels clip faster ahead. The concrete melts, becomes mud then toffee then stiffens again. Hips wade through this sidewalk swamp. She is on to him. Trying to throw off the scent.
"You smell."
"Smell like?"
There is no kiss. He tears her nimbus and sinks teeth into pale shoulder. The alcove around them chortles at this concealment. Her eyes shut and start to flutter very fast. The scented nimbus rises and clouds her eyelids. She aches for the innards of that box. She wants to open it and then shut it very quickly. But he grips her wrist and tries to guide it. She stares up in wonder at the leering flyboy skywriting in sailor's delight over the overcast sky. They exchange a meaningful glance with a hint of bladder commercial romance. Then she howls up at yawning eclipse . . .

à trois ~ the fragrance for Him
because friends let friends ...

Sober grey afternoon. Limbs of maples aching upward. That chase. Poppy lost to gutter. A faux flower, to remember. He swaggers through smoke and mirrors, bolstered by the contents of his goblet. She stirs in tarnished armour, asleep beside informative cairn. He pries at her well-thwacked greaves and her stubborn visor with both hands. Underneath, her eyes are fixed like a promissory note. He is visibly flummoxed. He remembers nothing of his origin. A foghorn sounds. Mournful as goldeneyes. He is wearing a great chain letter. She fingers a few of those perforated prophecies . . .
The morning after, she sits up and reaches for a lint brush. She has no face on to mask her aurora borealis. Her breath is suspect. He slashes the Indubitable-Tape that held together the breasts she hardly bothered about. Then she makes good with the multitasking teats of a matri-archal goddess. He offers his lips. This suckling has the making of an excellent reproduction of a number of masterworks.

A bottle materializes. At the aureole of his pinnacle, she remembers. Their minds crawl back through a door alarmed for pet collars. She is miffed at every act of sacrilege. But it is too late. She has become the omphalocentress, the everywoman to everyone for everything. She washes words she loves most out of his beautiful mouth. He bawls and shrieks. As it happens, every night.

à trois ~ the fragrance for Her
because you brought her home

Cadenza

Diminuenda raised her arms and yawned. The moments directly after seriously intense anagnorisis were bound to be awkward. She turned onto her side, making herself more comfortable on the loveslab, and lifted her eyes to face that unidentified man in Room 1003, who was sitting porn-Indian-style (with respect to the once proud indigenous pornography of the former colonies) and rummaging through a heap of tchotchkes. He selected one particular lagniappe, a large shiny disc, and touched it with his quivering digimitter.

"Mmm ... I hear trumpets."

"This is for a gramophone. It's an old-timey musical record."

"Yes, I know. They were instrumental in wartime Britain."

"Darling, it completely slipped my mind you were there."

"Where haven't I been, love?"

"That's a clarino trumpet you hear. After Bach, this playing technique was lost for centuries, and then reinvented, so to speak. This concerto was sent out into space, before you were born."

"What about this piece, now?"

"Stravinsky's *Rite of Spring*. Drums pounding, the sacrifice of a dancing virgin ..."

"What about this etching?"

"That is from a different probe. Drawn by a man named Carl Sagan and approved by committee."

"Pardon me, but she doesn't have a hoo-hoo."

"Caused quite the foul-up too. But that's another story ..."

"Then tell me about that little knock-off, the one by Vanderspeigle the Minor."

"What about it?"

"For a start, it *is* by Vanderspeigle the Minor, yes?"

"It would appear so, my darling."

"Then I am the model. What is she called again?"

"Clio. The Muse of History."

"I was wondering if it was possible that I posed for the real painting as well as the later forgery."

"Nothing would surprise me, truly. If the real painting has been mistaken for a knock-off that has received new valuation due to incidental circumstance, then the real painting is now the knock-off. The Third Reich's finest stashed something in a salt mine and that is what we have left. If the forgery has indeed *become* real – well – some would think that poetic."

"It's hard to keep straight. Everyone was painting in the new Dutch Republic just then and I posed for a lot of things. Then I posed in other times for other paintings and also for other forgeries."

"That would involve taking other lovers, I imagine."

Brutal silence. Our couple had finally exhausted, however, the study of these annals, and Diminuenda was to take up a different matter, or one at least with which the immediate connexion was not at first apparent.

"Were you amused at me just now – when I wondered about the hoo-hoo? Did you think me, well, fatuous?"

"Fatuous?"

"I mean sublime in *our* happiness, if one is to warmly and generously include the hoo-hoo in a conversation about happiness – as if looking down on others through a pulsating window. Or, rather, sublime in our general position – that's what I mean, as I have no wish to be blinded, or made 'sniffy,' by any sense of a social situation."

The man in Room 1003 listened to this declaration as if the precautions of her general mercy could still, as they betrayed themselves, have surprises for him – to say nothing of a charm of delicacy and beauty; he might have been wishing to see how far she could go and where she would, all touchingly to him, arrive. But she waited a little – as if made nervous, precisely, by feeling him depend too much on what she said. They were avoiding the serious, standing off, anxiously, from the real, and they fell, again and again, as if to disguise their precaution itself, into the tone of the time that came back to them from their other talk, when they had shared together this same refuge.

"Don't you remember how, when we first returned to this room, I broke it to you that I wasn't so very sure we, ourselves, had the thing itself?"

"A religion or a social situation, if not infinitely expanding industry?"

"All of the above. At the rate we were going, we should never have one."

Diminuenda descended into another brutal silence, in fact, the very kind depicted in once proud indigenous pornography of the former colonies, taking it from him that he now could both affirm and admit without wincing that they had been, at their critical moment, of one mind about the thing itself, and the thing to be done in terms of the thing waggling itself in front of them, just out of reach. It was as if this recognition had been threshed out between them as fundamental to the honest view of their success.

"Well, those were the feelings we used to have."

"Yes. I remember the feelings we used to have."

"And now, and now—"

"And now they see, still more, that we can have got everything, and kept everything, and yet not be proud."

"No, we're not proud. I'm not sure that we're quite proud enough."

Yet in the next instant she changed that subject, too. She could only do so, however, by harking back – as if it had been a fascination. She might have been wishing, under this renewed, this still more suggestive visitation, to keep him with her, for remounting the stream of time and dipping again, for the softness of the water, into the contracted basin of the past. Yet, she persisted, with the nightingales of her hands and with her trembling flower of a mouth, as in the background a tender cavatina set the scene.

"We talked about it – we talked about it; you don't remember so well as I. You too didn't know – and it was beautiful of you; you too thought we had a position, and were surprised when I thought we ought to admit we weren't doing what might be supposed of us as we are. In fact, we're not doing it now. We're not, you see, really introducing ourselves. I mean, not to the people we most want."

"Then what do you call the people watching us?"

"That's just what you asked me the other time – one of the days there was somebody. And I told you I didn't call anybody anything."

"I remember – that such people, the people we made so welcome, didn't *count*."

She had awakened, his daughter, the echo; and on the interior swing there, as before, he nodded his head amusedly and kept nervously shaking his foot.

"Yes, they were only good enough – the people who came – for *us*. I remember, that was the way it all happened."

"That was the way – that was the way. You asked me if I didn't think we ought to tell them right then and there. Of entertaining others under false pretences."

"Precisely – but you said they wouldn't have understood."

"To which you replied that in that case you were like them. *You* didn't understand."

"No, no – but I remember how, about our having, in our reunited innocence, no position, you quite crushed me with your explanation."

"Well then, I'll crush you again. I told you that you by yourself had one – there was no doubt of that. You were different from me – you had the same one you always had."

"*Then* I asked you why in that case you hadn't the same."

"Then indeed you did."

He had brought her face round to him before, and this held it, covering him with its kindled brightness, the result of the attested truth of their being able thus, in talk, to co-exist without inordinate displays of surrender or recrimination.

"You know I loved her – that is to say, I love her. For all of time—"

"She is not here presently."

"No, she is not."

"What I *don't* mean, is that I'm jealous of her. Or jealous of anyone, really."

"You *could* be – otherwise?"

"How can we talk of otherwise? It *isn't*, luckily for us, otherwise. If everything were different of course everything *would* be. My idea is this, that when you only love a little, for the greater part of one's life *in absentia*, as it were, you're naturally not jealous – or are only jealous a little, so that it doesn't matter. But when you love in a deeper and more intense way, then you are, in the same proportion, jealous; your jealousy has intensity and, no doubt, ferocity. When, however, you love in the most abysmal and unutterable way of all – why, then you're beyond everything, and nothing can pull you down."

"Then that's the way *you* love?"

"Not to talk about that. I do *feel*, however, beyond everything – and as a consequence of that, I dare say, seem often not to know quite *where* I am."

"I've never been jealous."

"Ah yes, but it's you, who are what I call beyond everything. Nothing can pull *you* down."

"Well then, we make a pair. We're all right."

"You say we're all right!"

"Well then—?"

She spoke as for the end and for other matters – for anything, everything, else there might be. Whether it be sequel or prequel, they would never return to it. Unless that was to say, they would always return to it, and that each parting would divide them and promptly restore them in renewed greeting. The prelude in C had come to its close. The fugue was about to begin, for any who could claim to fathom its exquisite intricacies.

"Well then—!"

His hands came out, and while her own took them and impulsively pressed them to her lips, he drew her in totality to his own familiar sense of impetuousness and held her. He held her hard and kept her long, and she let herself go; but it was an embrace that, august and almost stern, produced, for all its intimacy, no revulsion and broke into no inconsequence of tears.

On the contrary. The unimaginable damage to Room 1003 knew no precedent.

Acknowledgements

For everyone at Talonbooks, in particular Gregory Gibson, Leslie Thomas Smith, and Chloë Filson, whose energetic efforts and thoughtful design suggestions helped to bring this book into being.

Special thanks to Lynn Schellenberg, whose total immersion and vital input definitely qualify her as a "time mechanic."

Also, a shoutout to Coby Stephenson, Dina Del Bucchia, Mariner Janes, Marion Farrant, Martine Desjardins, Melanie Schnell, Sandra Kasturi, Sharon Thesen, Sonia Di Placido, Stasja Voluti, and Tracy Hamon, whose continual brilliancies and kindnesses keep me going in a world afloat.

Thank you, Michael Barnholden, Jonathan Ball, Nicholas Hauck, Carmen Papalia, Aubyn Rader, Missy Clarkson, Amanda Joy Ivings, Thor Polukoshko, Elliot Lummin, and Brook Houglum for having the foresight and futuristic gumption to publish unexpurgated splices of The Chaos! Quincunx series. Kudos to *West Coast Line*, *dANDelion Magazine*, *Memewar*, *The Maynard*, and *The Capilano Review*.

And thank you, in some Hegelian notion of eternal due process, Karl Siegler, for your stalwart support of my experimental fiction and for having more than minor expectations of me ...

Collect all three books in The Chaos! Quincunx series

The Chaos! Quincunx series includes five "nodal" novels that parody various writing styles and literary genres, including surrealist prose, speculative fiction, environmental dystopia, historical narrative, and the most prurient bodice-rippers.

"Of contemporary surrealist writers, Garry Thomas Morse is the most uncompromising. He courageously severs the umbilical cord with so-called reality and ventures into an invented world paradoxically more real than our own."
– Barry Webster, author of *The Lava in My Bones*

"Like a beguiling house of mirrors, *Minor Episodes* bends, twists, fractures, and deforms reality through phantasmagoric visions, orgiastic inventions, and a mischievous use of language."
– Martine Desjardins, author of *Maleficium*

"*Minor Episodes / Major Ruckus*, with its themes of sex, money, and intrigue, and with its over-current of hilarity running amok, explodes from the page. To say this novel is on steroids is to downplay things."
– M.A.C. Farrant, author of *The Strange Truth About Us*

"An outrageous romp – wickedly inventive, clever as well as wise, deliciously satirical and steamier than sex and vegetables."
– Des Kennedy, author of *Climbing Patrick's Mountain*

"Surreal, complex, and hilarious ... *Rogue Cells / Carbon Harbour* is best savored slowly ... Reading it is like reading poetry, a synaesthetic experience where technology and terrorism are as intimate and tangible as the smell of food or the texture of mud. Infused with Morse's irrepressible humor, the books [in The Chaos! Quincunx] satisfy all the senses."
– *Rain Taxi*